Praise for Samantha Sommersby's *Forbidden: The Sacrifice*

"Forbidden: The Sacrifice is a beautifully written paranormal romance that will astound you and leave you wanting more...fast-paced, unique, and captivating."

~ *Night Owl Romance*

"Forbidden: The Sacrifice by Samantha Sommersby was action-packed, emotionally charged, and sexy as hell."

~ *Bitten by Books*

"The combination of romance and horror is exquisite and positively enrapturing...a shining example of how a horror romance novel should be."

~ *eCataromance*

"Forbidden: The Sacrifice is a fantastic book... Samantha Sommersby has created deeply sympathetic characters"

~ *Whipped Cream Reviews*

Look for these titles by

Samantha Sommersby

Now Available:

The Forbidden Series

Forbidden: The Sacrifice (Book 1)

Forbidden: The Ascension (Book 2)

Forbidden: The Revolution (Book 3)

Forbidden: The Temptation (Book 4)

Shelter from the Storm

Forbidden: The Sacrifice

Samantha Sommersby

A Samhain Publishing, Ltd. publication.

Samhain Publishing, Ltd.
577 Mulberry Street, Suite 1520
Macon, GA 31201
www.samhainpublishing.com

Forbidden: The Sacrifice

Print ISBN: 978-1-60504-771-3
Digital ISBN: 978-1-60504-758-4

Editing by Tera Kleinfelter
Cover by Natalie Winters

This book has been previously published and has been revised and expanded from its original release.

First Samhain Publishing, Ltd. electronic publication: September 2009
First Samhain Publishing, Ltd. print publication: July 2010

Dedication

For my mother. You've been there for me every minute of my life. Always encouraging. Always believing. I love you. Always.

Chapter One

I felt myself flying backward. It happened in the blink of an eye. One second I was on top of the world, the next plunged into darkness, surrounded by the sounds of metal scraping against metal, shattering glass and terrified screams—one of them my own.

The railway car I was on had jumped the tracks. It was skidding sideways, momentum causing it to careen out of control. In the dim tunnel light I caught a glimpse of the rapidly approaching wall. The car crashing into it sounded like an explosion.

Then, just as suddenly as it had started, it ended. For a moment it seemed the earth stood still. Silent. I was wedged on the floor between two seats, my left arm and shoulder throbbing in pain. Using only my right arm, I reached for the seat in front of me and pulled myself up to a standing position. Without a moment's hesitation, I reached into my pocket for my lighter and struck a flame.

The air was thick with dust and debris that stung my eyes and filled my nose. I waved my hand in front of my face in an attempt to clear it. Squinting into the darkness, I called out for the woman who'd been in my arms just seconds earlier.

"Katherine?"

I spied her lying on the floor; she appeared unconscious. On impact she'd been thrown clear across the aisle.

"Katherine!"

She didn't respond. I fell to my knees alongside her. Reaching out with a shaky hand, I offered up a silent prayer before checking for a pulse. Thankfully, she still had one and it was strong, steady.

I guided the light over Katherine's body, assessing her injuries. The butane burned and as seconds ticked away, the outer casing of the silver lighter became increasingly hot. Just as I noticed a tiny rivulet of blood seeping from her left ear, I dropped it.

"Bugger!"

The blood concerned me. The fact that she was unconscious concerned me even more. I pushed down the rising feeling of panic, then methodically began to search the area in front of me for the lighter. Within a few seconds I'd found it and was able to illuminate her face.

"Katherine, love, open your eyes."

Still no response.

"Henry? Where are you?"

It was the elderly woman Katherine and I had been sitting across from just minutes ago. It had been after midnight when we'd pulled out of the Mornington Crescent Tube station. There were only five of us in the car, Katherine and I, the elderly woman and her husband and a young man.

I stood and held the light out behind me, in the direction where the young man had been. I heard a cough and seconds later he emerged, stumbling down the aisle through the rubble and awkwardly stepping over a section of twisted metal frame.

"Is she okay?"

I remembered seeing the young man nursing a bottle in a paper bag as he boarded. He was obviously pissed, unsteady on his feet.

"I'm trying to find out. I need your help. Are you hurt?"

"No, I don't think so."

"I'm Wes. What's your name?"

"Mark."

"Mark, I need you to help me. I've been injured." I was suddenly acutely aware of the pain in my left shoulder. "I need for you to do as I say. Do you have a set of keys?"

"Yeah."

I handed him the lighter, then leaned over and opened one of Katherine's eyelids. "I'm a doctor," I explained. "Move the light up here, in front of her eyes."

With some relief I saw that Katherine's pupils were dilated, and although they were non-focal, they were still reactive to light.

I ran my hand over her hair. "Stay with me now. We'll get you out of here," I assured her before turning back to Mark.

"Remove her shoes. We need to check her motor response. That's it. Now, firmly run the key up the length of her foot."

For a second I held my breath.

"Like this?"

Katherine's foot retracted.

"Thank God!" I whispered. She'd clearly felt it.

"So she's okay?"

"Not by a long shot. But it could be worse. Much worse."

"What's wrong with her?"

"Head injury. She's had a bleed, I think. We've got to get her to a hospital."

"Somebody help me. Henry?" It was the elderly woman again and she sounded short of breath.

I leaned down, placed a gentle kiss on Katherine's forehead, then whispered, "Wait for me, love. I'll be right back."

My coat was crumpled under one of the nearby orange seats and I reached for it.

"Help me get this over her."

"What's wrong with your arm?"

"It's nothing." I climbed to my feet.

"Do you have a signal?" I asked, pulling my own mobile out of my pocket.

"No. You?"

"No. Let's check on the others."

Mark went first, holding the lighter out in front to show the way. First we reached Henry. He'd also been thrown across the carriage on impact, only his head had struck the window and shattered the glass. The scene was gruesome. The lighter went out, once again plunging us into darkness. I was almost grateful.

"Sorry," Mark apologized. He relit the flame, now holding the outside of the lighter with a bandanna he'd retrieved from his pocket. "The casing's hot."

Mark turned his head away from the dormant body. I couldn't blame him. The man's face was covered with blood; his neck had been partially severed by a section of glass. He was gone.

"Is he dead?"

"Dead?" The woman began to franticly call out for her husband. "Henry? Henry!"

I quickly crossed the aisle and crouched down next to her. "What's your name, love?"

"Margaret." She was struggling for breath. "Where's Henry?"

"Margaret, I'm a doctor. I'm going to try to help you. Are you hurt?"

"My arm. And my chest. It feels like something might have

fallen on top of me. Where's Henry?" Her breaths were becoming more labored. "Henry!"

There was nothing on top of her chest. I checked her pulse. "I want you to calm down for me now. You're heart's beating like a humming bird. Do you have a heart condition? Do you take any medicines?"

"He's dead, isn't he?" Margaret looked me right in the eye. "Tell me!"

Before I could respond, the old woman gasped in pain and clutched her chest.

"What's going on?" Mark sounded panicked. "Is she dead, too?"

Things were going downhill fast. If we didn't act quickly, we were going to lose her. I bent over and placed my face next to Margaret's.

"She's not breathing and I've lost her pulse."

"Fuck!"

"Could be just a heart attack, but she was struggling for breath earlier. Could be an injury to the chest wall, or a collapsed lung, maybe an embolism. I'm a psychiatrist, for Christ's sake. It's been years since I've done this sort of thing and my left arm is useless! You're gonna have to help."

"Help do what?"

"Save her. Come over and sit by me. Give me your hand. I'll guide the chest compressions."

Mark dropped the lighter on the floor. "Damn it!"

"Leave it! Look, we don't have a lot of bloody time here. We need to open her airway. I want you to place your hand under her neck to tilt her head back and then pinch her nose, move her chin forward, and give her two breaths. Got it?"

There were a few scattered lights lining the left wall of the tunnel. My eyes had begun to adjust to the darkness and I could now see the outline of the woman.

"What if I do it wrong?"

"Do it!"

He did, then I leaned over the woman again to assess her breathing. Nothing. I reached for Mark's hand and placed it beneath mine on her chest.

"We're going to do chest compressions. Not too much force. Fifteen times. Ready? One, two, three, four," I counted. There was an audible crack. I felt Mark begin to pull back.

"I can't do this." He sounded as if he were about to cry.

"It's just a rib. Not so much force. Keep going all the way to fifteen. That's it. Now, breathe twice!"

We continued the cycle six times with no response.

"It's not working!"

He was right. For the first time in ages I felt incompetent. I'd been of no more use to Margaret than the pissed boy had been. I reached up and wiped the sweat from my brow.

"No, it's not working," I admitted, realizing that I had to accept defeat and move on. Katherine was still alive and she needed me, was depending on me.

"Now what?"

"Now we check on my girl. We've got to get her out of here."

I stood and made my way back to Katherine, Mark following closely behind.

"Maybe we should wait? Don't the Tube rails have electrical current flowing through them?"

"We'll be careful. I made a promise to the lady. I intend to keep it."

"Take a chance, Katherine. You know I'm right. You know it. You can feel it, can't you? You won't regret it, not for one bloody second," I'd promised her, leaning down to steal one more kiss,

enticing her into wanting, into forgetting, into surrendering.

"We have no lights. What if they send through another car and they don't see us?" I asked him, before crouching down to examine Katherine again. "Ow! Bugger it!"

Pain shot through my arm and shoulder as my left elbow grazed a nearby seat. I rolled up my tie, placed it in my mouth, and bit down. Then I straightened my back, closed my eyes and tried to push the dislocated ball joint back into place. I couldn't manage it.

"Dammit!" I yelled, spitting the fabric out of my mouth, gritting my teeth against the pain.

"Christ, I could use a drink."

"Me too, Mark." I managed a small smile. "My shoulder's dislocated. You help me fix it and I'll buy you a bottle when we're out of here. Deal?"

"No. No way. What if it goes to pot? I didn't do so well with Margaret."

"You did fine. You'll do fine. This works ninety percent of the time like a charm."

"What do I need to do?"

"First you need to pull on my wrist with one hand and brace against my upper chest with the other. Pull gently, increasing the pressure until I tell you to stop. Then you'll hold that position, keeping the pressure steady for a bit."

"How long is a bit?" Positioning himself as instructed, Mark began to pull.

"Until it relaxes," I ground out.

"Relaxed yet?"

"Stop! Hold steady, now." I tried to breathe through the pain. My eyes were watering. "All right! Now, I need for you to rotate the joint back into place. Like this." I did my best to demonstrate. "Only at the same time."

"I don't know," Mark said hesitantly.

"Stop being a nancy! We're wasting time. Just bloody do it."

Mark closed his eyes, then took a deep breath. I took a breath too and steeled myself for what was coming. With a swiftness I was grateful for, Mark twisted the joints. The pain was excruciating, almost dizzying. I cried out in anguish as the bone clicked audibly back in place.

"All right?" asked Mark wrapping his arm around my waist. "You're not going to pass out on me, are you? I sure as fuck can't carry both of you out of here."

"No." I swallowed down the bile that had risen in my throat. "No, I'm not going to pass out."

The pain was subsiding. Gingerly, I tried to move my arm.

"Good job. It feels better. I have a bit more mobility."

"So I did okay?"

"You did great. I won't be able to carry Katherine out, though. I'm gonna have to ask you to do it. Can you do that, Mark?"

Before he could answer, the bright beam of a flashlight shined through the window of the carriage. Help was on the way.

Chapter Two

I rode in the back of the ambulance with Katherine and one of the paramedics. As soon as we pulled into the bay I opened the rear door and jumped to the ground. Laura Stanton, trauma surgeon, burst through the double doors leading to Accident and Emergency. Eric Riley, the hospital's top neurosurgeon and a friend since medical school, was close in tow.

"Any change since the last radio report?" Laura asked.

"No." I was trying my damndest to not think the worst. "Laura, she's been out for nearly thirty minutes."

"What's her GCS?"

"Eight, I think. I'm not sure. It's been a long time since I've assessed—"

"Don't worry, you've done well. Let's get the patient intubated and into CT."

"Her name's Katherine."

"Katherine. Okay, then. You can come, Wes. But stay back and let us do our jobs. We're good at what we do. You know that. Right?"

She gave me an encouraging smile. I was glad she was there. Laura was extremely competent. She had a quiet confidence about her, but not a shred of ego. More important than that? I trusted her.

"Right."

“Then let’s get cracking.”

I followed the trolley down the hall toward the trauma room. I made rounds at this hospital almost every day, but I’d never been in the trauma center, not once. I felt helpless, out of sorts. Six, maybe seven people crowded into the room. I stepped back and anxiously watched as the team of professionals quickly and efficiently went about their various tasks. Within minutes Katherine was stripped of her clothes and intubated, a ventilator breathing for her. Someone handed me a bag with her clothes in it. I set it on a nearby counter.

Eric ordered a CT with and without contrast, type and screen/cross. “I’ll meet you in radiology,” he said before walking out of the room.

Laura turned to the lab technician. “Did you get that?”

“Yeah.”

“Run a CBC, Coag profile and lytes as well.”

“Got it covered.” The petite Asian woman began to search for a vein.

They were going to operate. I ducked out into the hall, my stomach in knots. “Eric!”

He paused and turned back to face me. “She important to you?”

I nodded.

“She’ll be okay, Wes. Have I ever let you down?”

The question made me chuckle. “Too many times to count.” I looked him in the eye. “But never when it really mattered.”

“Don’t worry. I’ll take good care of her.”

The elevator arrived and Eric ran to catch it, leaving me alone in the long, sterile hall with blood on my hands and remorse in my heart. It was my cock-up, my fault that Katherine was in that carriage, my fault she was here. It was *all* my fault.

“Wes? I thought you might want to hold onto this.” Laura placed Katherine’s engagement ring in the palm of my hand. “We’re taking her up to CT. We’ve got to get her registered. Is there family to notify?”

“Family? Yes. In the States. I’ll take care of it.” They wheeled her past me on a gurney. There were lines and tubes everywhere. It seemed surreal.

“Wes?” Laura was frowning. “Are you all right?”

“Me? Yeah. I’m fine. Go.”

Laura started after the trolley. “Do me a favor. Go to A & E and get checked out, just to make sure?” she shouted back over her shoulder.

I agreed.

“Doctor?” The paramedic was standing just inside the entrance. He was holding Katherine’s purse and my coat. “The belongings?”

“I’ll take them.” I reached into my pocket and pulled out my cigarettes. My hands were shaking, but I managed to get one out of the pack.

“Need a light?” he asked as we stepped outside into the cool night air.

“Thanks, I’ve got one.” I sat on a nearby bench and began to search though my jacket pockets. Then I remembered I no longer had my lighter. Mark had dropped it and I never picked it back up. I checked my watch. Had it really been just a few hours since I’d committed to abstain from the fags for the night?

“You smoke?” Katherine asked, surprise evident in her voice.

“Yeah.” I placed the cig between my lips and flipped open the cover of my lighter.

“Didn’t anyone ever tell you that’s bad for you?”

"A man needs some vices." I shrugged.

"How come I didn't smell it on you earlier?"

"I showered? Hell, I don't know. Maybe you haven't gotten close enough." I stepped closer.

"Whoa there, cowboy! I agreed to a perfectly platonic dinner. Just two people eating food and watching a play." She pulled the cigarette out of my mouth and placed her hand on my chest.

"Together, like a date." Clearly I wasn't going to have time for a smoke.

"Date? This isn't a date!"

"It isn't?"

"No!"

"You sure?"

"Yes!" she said, getting increasingly flustered. "I told you, I'm engaged."

"I, for one, thought this was a date." I couldn't help but smile.

She changed the subject. "Why don't you quit smoking?"

"I guess I just haven't found the proper motivation. Tell you what, kiss me and I'll abstain, from the fags that is, for the rest of the night."

"What about tomorrow, or the next day?"

"That depends," I told her as I leaned forward and lowered my lips to hers.

"On what?"

"On how well you kiss."

"What on earth are you doing here at this time of night? I thought you psychiatrists all kept normal business hours?"

Pulled back to the present, I noticed one of the critical care nurses coming toward me from the parking lot.

"Hey." I tossed the pack of cigarettes into the dustbin beside the bench.

"Jesus, what happened to you?"

I glanced down at my shirt. It was spattered with blood. When I looked back up, the nurse was staring at Katherine's bag. I'd almost forgotten it was there.

I picked it up and started to search through the contents. There was a gold compact, a tube of lipstick, a wallet and a mobile phone. I pulled the phone from the bag, opened it up, glanced at the display, then snapped it closed.

"Dr. Atherton?"

"Hm?"

She had taken a seat next to me, concern etched on her face. "What happened?"

My eyes burned. My head was pounding. I didn't know where to start.

"There was an accident, in the Tube," I finally managed to choke out. "My date, Katherine, she uh...she..."

"She got hurt?"

I nodded. "It looks like she has a subdural. She's in CT now. I think Eric's going to do a crainy. I've got to call her mum."

"Can I help?"

"No. Thanks. I can handle it. I'll see you up on the ward in a bit. Katherine will be coming your way, no doubt."

The nurse nodded. "She's in good hands with Mr. Riley."

"I know. Go on. You're going to be late for your shift."

"I'll have a fresh pot of coffee waiting," she promised before walking away.

I took a deep, steadying breath, opened the mobile once again and started to scroll through the recently dialed numbers.

George. Damien. Mom work. Home. I dialed home.

"Hello?"

"Hello, Mrs. Lawson? My name is Wesley Atherton. I'm calling from London. I'm a friend of Katherine's—"

"Has something happened to Kate?"

I took a fortifying breath and then tried to calmly explain.

"I was out with your daughter tonight. We had dinner and went to the theater. We took the Tube and on the way back... Well, there was an accident. The carriage we were in derailed. I'm afraid Katherine was injured."

"Can I talk to her?"

"She's being evaluated. They're doing a CT now. She's unconscious. She may need surgery."

"What kind of surgery?"

"Neurosurgery."

"Dear God," Katherine's mother gasped.

"We'll know more shortly. I'll call you back when there's news. I'll have her mobile if you want to reach me."

"Let me get a pen. What was your name again?"

"Wesley Atherton. Dr. Wesley Atherton. She's in good hands, I assure you."

"You're a medical doctor?"

"I'm a psychiatrist."

"Where is she? What hospital?"

"We're at Saint Catherine's, in Camden Town."

I walked back into the hospital and headed for the radiology department.

"Dr. Atherton?"

"Wes," I said. "Call me Wes. And you are?"

"Julia. Don't lie to me, Wes. It's bad, isn't it?"

"It could be. The truth is, we don't have enough information yet."

"I'll be on the next flight. If Kate wakes up, tell her I'm on my way."

"Will do."

I pushed through the swinging double doors. The receptionist behind the counter pointed me to room three.

"I'm counting on you to take care of her," Julia said.

"You have my word," I assured her before ringing off. "What's the verdict?" Eric and Laura were standing in front of a series of images.

"See this?" Eric pointed to the film. "The hyperdense crescentic mass—"

"Subdural hematoma?"

"Exactly. I'll make a couple burr holes, to relieve the pressure. I say we continue conservatively for now, a corticosteroid, to reduce the inflammation and swelling, and an anticonvulsant to control her seizures."

"She had a seizure?"

"A mild one. It didn't last long. Let's scrub," Eric said. "The sooner we get her in, the better."

"You haven't had your shoulder looked at yet, have you?" Laura asked as she backed out the door.

"I'm heading over to the A & E now. Anything happens..."

"I'll page you," she assured me.

"Jesus, Wes, I heard what happened. Sorry to keep you waiting. It's been a crazy night," said the resident.

"No worries. I've already had the x-ray."

"I saw it. Did you really get some kid to pop your shoulder

back in?"

"Where did you hear that?"

"The paramedics that brought you in. Is it true?"

"Yeah. How's the x-ray look?"

"Kid did a great job. You'll need to keep it immobilized for a week or so. You should see an orthopedist though."

He wrote out a prescription, then handed me the slip of paper. As soon as I read it, I tried to give it back.

"I don't need that. Just give me a couple ibuprofen."

"You say that now. Fill the prescription that way if you need it, you'll have it."

As he left the examination room I heard him call out to one of the nurses. "Some ibuprofen and a sling for Dr. Atherton here. We need to immobilize his shoulder."

I leaned back against the wall. The evening had started off so well. I closed my eyes and a series of images washed over me.

The wind blowing Katherine's hair in her face as we walked to the restaurant. The sideways glance she threw my direction during dinner when she thought I wasn't looking. I lifted the collar of my shirt and inhaled. I could still smell traces of her on it, where she'd comfortably rested her head during much of the play.

I remembered the way she'd laughed as we ran from the theater to a taxi in the pouring rain. How her breath hitched when I'd pulled her close in the back of the cab. How she'd gasped, opening her luscious mouth to invite me in when I crushed my lips to hers.

Even now, I could almost feel the curve of her breast beneath my hand. The way her nipple had hardened through her bra and silk blouse when I'd brushed my thumb across it. The warmth of her breath. Those deliciously intoxicating panting sounds she'd made as I kissed down the long column of her neck and across her collarbone. Her lustful moan as I slipped my hand up her leg, under her skirt. And the exquisite realization that her legs were willingly parting for me, in encouragement, in need.

"Wes," she moaned. "Don't. Stop."

"I won't," I assured her. "I'll never stop."

"No. I mean, stop. He's...he's watching us," Katherine whispered. "What am I doing? This isn't me." She was gasping for air, her chest rising and falling rapidly in the heat of passion.

"Let him," I growled, crushing my mouth to hers in another demanding kiss as my hand continued the forbidden journey under her skirt and up her leg.

I was getting hard again, just from the mere thought of her.

"So, do you need some help with that?"

My eyes flew open. I hadn't heard the nurse come in.

"The ibuprofen." She nodded toward the sealed packet and cup of water on the bedside table.

"No, thanks. I've got it." I picked the packet up with my good hand, tore it open with my teeth, and poured the two tabs out onto my waiting tongue. I dropped the empty packet back onto the tray, then washed the pills down with a swig of water.

"Dr. Atherton to recovery. Wesley Atherton to recovery," came the overhead page.

"I've got to go."

"Let's get this sling on first."

She worked quickly, then sent me on my way. The elevator took too long, so I opted for the stairs.

Eric was waiting for me in the hallway outside of recovery to escort me to Katherine's bedside.

"She came through the surgery just fine," he said as we walked. "Her vitals are stable. We'll keep her here for a while longer, just to make sure, then she'll go up to ICU."

"Okay."

The recovery room was cold. Katherine looked small and pale against the stark white sheets.

"Sprain?" He nodded toward my sling.

"Dislocated shoulder. I'll be fine."

Eric looked like he had something to say. Normally he wasn't one to hold back.

"Out with it."

"Laura seems to think that the two of you are engaged."

I slid my free hand into the pocket of my trousers and fingered Katherine's ring.

"Well, she's half right," I admitted, remembering the moment we first met.

"Here, take my seat." I offered my seat to the elderly woman who'd boarded at Moorgate Station.

"That was nice of you."

I shrugged off the compliment. "Yeah? Well, don't tell anyone. I've got a reputation to uphold."

I turned around and looked into the most beautiful pair of green eyes I'd ever seen.

"What? I have spinach in my teeth, don't I? I knew I should have chosen the pasta salad for lunch."

I grabbed hold of the bar she'd been holding on to so that my hand was positioned adjacent to hers. "No. It's your eyes. They're stunning."

"Are you sure there's no spinach?" she asked, grinning widely, showing me her teeth.

"No spinach," I confirmed. "You're American?"

"Yup! Guilty as charged."

"Visiting?"

"Here for a few months, finishing my masters."

As we pulled into the next stop I glanced down and noticed the ring. The car lurched, throwing the American off balance and she bumped into me. Without thought I reached out and wrapped my arm around her waist. As soon as I was able to steady myself I apologized and let go.

"Sorry."

"It's okay." She looked away shyly.

"Really?" I slipped my arm back around her waist. "Have dinner with me."

"What? No! What are you doing?" She pushed my arm away.

"You said it was okay."

"Because it was an accident. I'm engaged." She held up her hand and wiggled the finger that held her engagement ring.

"That is not an engagement ring."

"What do you mean?" She pulled her hand back and looked at the classically simple solitaire. "Of course it's an engagement ring."

"You're not going to marry him. He's all wrong for you."

"You don't even know him. You don't even know me. I take it back. You're not nice after all." She turned around.

I leaned down and whispered in her ear, "So have dinner with me. Convince me that the two of you are perfect for one another and I'll apologize."

She turned her head slightly. "No."

"Please? Look, I'd rather not beg, but I'm not above it. Agree or I'm going to have to fall onto my knees in supplication. It's

likely to be embarrassing for you and a bit humiliating for me but what the hell? You're worth it." I hitched up one leg of my trousers, preparing to kneel down.

"You don't have to do that." She reached for my elbow, preventing me from fully kneeling in front of her.

"Fantastic! So, how does Italian sound?"

"I'm not having dinner with you."

"You agreed," I pointed out. Looking around, I asked our fellow passengers, "Didn't she consent?"

Four or five of them nodded.

"See?"

"Do you always get your way?"

I shrugged. "Pretty much."

"Well, not tonight," she declared as we pulled into her stop. "Mr.—"

"The name's Wes."

She moved to walk away. I reached out, just barely grazing the back of her hand with my fingertips. "And you are?"

"Katherine." She turned to go, not looking back. Not until she got off, that is. Just as we pulled out she spun around. For the briefest of moments our eyes locked, then she was gone.

"Christ, you know how to pick them," Eric said. "First Reese, now you're dating a woman that's engaged to someone else?"

"Katherine wouldn't say we're dating."

"You were out together."

"We had dinner and went to the theater."

"And you were heading back to your place?"

"You make it sound sordid. It wasn't like that. It isn't like that. It's complicated."

"I can imagine having a girlfriend with a fiancé can get pretty complicated."

I ignored his jibe and pressed on. "After that first day we kept bumping into one another on the Tube. She'd board at the same stop, like clockwork. We'd chitchat, that's all."

"Until?"

"The fourth day. It was raining outside and Katherine had forgotten her umbrella. She was drenched when she boarded. I tried to get her to take my mine so she wouldn't catch her death, but the silly bint wouldn't listen. I almost let her get away with it too. But just before the door closed, I ran out."

"You walked her home."

"We stopped for a cuppa just down the street from the flat where she's staying. We were in the café for hours. Just as we were about leave, I got an emergency call, an admission. I left her with my brolly."

"In exchange for her number?"

I shook my head. "No. Didn't even ask as a matter of fact."

"Wesley, wait!"

It was pouring rain. I'd walked only a few meters, and already I was soaked. I turned back. Katherine was standing under the awning of the shop, umbrella open. She was holding it out to me.

"You forgot your umbrella!"

"You can give it back to me tomorrow."

"What if I don't see you tomorrow?"

The thought hadn't occurred to me. I returned to the shelter of the awning, pulled out a business card, and handed it to her.

"Call me," I said, then I dashed off.

"And she called you?" asked Eric.

"Later that night, to thank me. Seemed like we talked forever, about everything and nothing. We really connected. You know?"

"Wes, you're a shrink. You're a professional listener. You connect with everyone."

"Not like this. As we were about to hang up I noticed a pair of theater tickets sitting on my desk. I've yet to cancel my father's box. I keep meaning to, just haven't gotten 'round to it."

"So you asked and she accepted."

"Yeah. I'm telling you, Eric, the second I laid eyes on her I—"

"Does he know?"

"Does who know what?"

"Her fiancé. Has anyone called him about the accident?"

"Bollocks!"

"I take that as a no?"

"I called her mum. Maybe she called Damien?"

"That's the fiancé?"

"Yeah." I checked my watch. "It's been a while since we spoke. Surely she's called him by now."

"One way to find out," Eric replied. "Can I get you anything? I'm going to grab some coffee."

"No thanks." I pulled out Katherine's mobile and rang Julia. There was no answer. Not at home and not on her mobile. So, I tried Damien.

He picked up on the third ring. "Hello?"

"Hello, is this Damien?"

"Who's calling?"

"This is Dr. Wesley Atherton. I'm calling from Saint Catherine's Hospital, in London. I need to speak with Damien, it's about his fiancée."

"This is Damien. What's wrong with Katherine? Is she sick?" He sounded appropriately concerned. He was probably a nice guy. I didn't want him to be a nice guy.

"Who's Katherine?" It was a woman's voice.

"Shh," Damien hissed. Muffled words were exchanged.

"Are you still there?" A bell was ringing in the background.

"Yes. Yes, I'm here."

"Do you need to get that?"

"No. Go on."

"There was a derailment late last night, near Camden Town. Katherine was on it and she sustained a head injury."

"But she's okay?"

The voices in the background were getting louder.

"She needed surgery. She's stable now but—"

"Julia!"

"How dare you!" a woman shouted.

I pulled the phone slightly away from my ear.

"It's not what it looks like."

"Don't insult me, Damien. It's exactly what it looks like! Christ, the girl answered the door wearing a sheet. Do you think I'm an idiot? Kate's in the hospital and you're—"

"We aren't having this discussion now. Kate's condition, it's serious, Julia," he said. "I have her doctor on the phone."

"Give me that! Hello? This is Julia Lawson, Katherine's mother."

"Julia, it's Wes. I tried calling you a few minutes ago to see if you'd spoken to Damien. When you didn't answer I thought that maybe I'd better ring him."

"I left my purse in the car when I ran up here. How's Kate?"

"She made it through surgery just fine. She's stable. They'll be moving her up to intensive care soon."

"Is she awake? Can I talk to her?"

"I'm afraid she's still unconscious. But that's nothing to be alarmed about at this point. Are you on your way to the airport?"

"Yes. I'll see you soon."

"I'm coming with you," Damien interjected. "It'll just take me a few minutes to shower and pack."

"Don't bother," I heard Julia say.

"You can't stop me. You know she'd want me there."

"She would want the man she thought you were there. But you're not him. You're not even close." Then the line went dead.

Chapter Three

I'd been up close to twenty-four hours. It was almost 9:00 a.m. and I was in the intensive care unit. My shoulder was throbbing and I was completely done in. Exhaustion had worked its way into my bones. The dull hum of the respirator would have been lulling if it wasn't so damned important. Katherine was still dependent on it to breathe. With just a glance in one direction or another I was able to stay apprised of all of her vital signs. Eric had come and gone. At this point, he was confident the burr holes would be sufficient. For that I was grateful.

Now it was a matter of watching and waiting. I hated waiting.

"Your mum's on the way. I'd kiss you on the lips like bloody Prince Charming and wake you up, but this ghastly ET tube is in the way, love." I lifted the hand I was holding to my mouth and placed a gentle kiss in its palm.

The nurses in the ICU were changing shift. I could hear them outside the curtained-off cubicle giving report. I knew visitors weren't normally allowed during this time, but no one asked me to leave and I didn't volunteer. I was just thanking God for that small favor when one of them pulled back the curtain.

"Dr. Atherton?"

"Yes?"

"I didn't mean to startle you."

"That's quite all right."

"There's someone asking for you."

"Do you know who it is?" I asked, running my hand through my hair then over the stubble on my face.

"He said he's a friend of the family's. He's in the waiting area around to the left."

"Thanks. Take care of my girl." I headed for the exit then proceeded around the corner to the waiting area.

"Dr. Atherton?" The gentleman stood as soon as he saw me. He looked to be in his late forties, perhaps early fifties. He was wearing a rather rumpled tweed coat, wire-rimmed glasses and had the distinct look of someone who had been up all night. For a moment I wondered what his excuse was.

"Yes." I offered him my hand. "Mr.—"

"Grant. George Grant. Can you tell me what's going on?" He removed his glasses and began to polish them furiously. "No one will tell me anything. I worked all night and came home to a message on my machine from Julia. All she said was that Katherine was here and to ask for you. I tried to call her back, but she didn't answer. I didn't have any luck with Katherine's mobile either."

I reached into my suit coat pocket, pulled out the phone, and saw that the battery had died. "Bugger, the battery seems to have run out." I sat down heavily in the chair next to Mr. Grant. "You're a friend of the family's?"

"Yes, Katherine was staying with me while completing her internship here," explained George. "Now, tell me what's going on! Is she all right?"

"I was out with Katherine last night. We had dinner and went to the theater. We took the Tube. On the way back, the carriage we were on, it derailed."

"At Camden Town?" asked George. "I heard about the accident on the radio. Two people died, one critically injured."

"I tried—"

"But that's past our stop!" George stood, placing the glasses firmly back on his nose. He turned to me, his eyes full of accusation.

I've never been one to beat around the bush, so I just came out with it, the cold, hard truth. "Yes. She was coming home with me. If it wasn't for me she wouldn't have been there."

"Good Lord." George sat back down.

"She sustained a head injury. She was operated on earlier. She's stable at the moment, but she's still in critical condition."

"You called Julia? You spoke with her?"

"Yes."

"Does she know about you and Kate?"

"She knows we're friends and that we were out together." I reached into my pocket and pulled out Kate's engagement ring. "Ever meet him?"

"No."

"He was cheating on her. Can you imagine that?"

"She told you that?"

"No. I called the stupid git to tell him about the accident. While I was on the phone with him, Julia arrived. Damien's shaggin' mate was there. It seems Julia put two and two together."

"I see." George removed his glasses again and pulled out his handkerchief.

"You do realize you just did that, right?"

"I think I might have missed a spot," said George irritably, scrubbing the lenses again. "What kind of a doctor are you?"

"I'm a psychiatrist." I leaned back in the chair.

George abruptly stopped what he was doing.

"It's not a compulsion you know, the thing with my glasses."

"Of course not."

"Just a nervous habit. Perfectly normal."

"Absolutely."

"Can I see her?"

"Of course. Though she is unconscious, you understand?" I cautioned before standing up and leading the way back inside the ICU and over to Katherine's bed.

I pulled open the privacy curtain; the second George laid eyes on her, the blood drained from his face.

"Maybe you should sit down." I offered him a nearby chair.

"She looks..."

"She's not."

George sat and I gave his shoulder a reassuring squeeze. "She's going to be all right. Look, I haven't had time to cancel my patients for the day. I need to go to the office and try to clear my schedule, get a change of clothes. You can stay for as long as you want. I'll be back as soon as I can be, yeah?"

"Of course."

Before leaving I stopped by the nurses' station and asked them to page me if anything were to change. I didn't want to leave Katherine's side, not for one bloody second. But I had other obligations to take care of. With luck, I'd be able to discharge my duties quickly. I indulged in one more long, lingering look before tearing myself away and walking out the door.

"I didn't expect to see you today," gasped my secretary. "I've just finished canceling your appointments."

"You heard about the accident?"

"It's all the buzz. How is she doing?"

"No change. I want to get back to her as soon as possible. Cancel what you can for the next three days. All of my outpatients should be able to be rescheduled. I'll do my rounds here if you can't get them covered, but try. All right?"

"Of course."

"I've covered for enough of the other guys. Call in some favors. Oh! And, can you see if Charles can bring me a change of clothes? Maybe for the next couple days? Though it's his day off." I looked down at the blood-stained clothes I was wearing. "Maybe it would be faster if I just found a nearby shop?"

"Wes, don't be silly." She held out her hand. "Give me your keys. I'll run over and get you a change of clothes, then I'll call Charles and update him on what's going on."

I gratefully dropped the keys to my house into the palm of her hand. "What would I do without you?"

"Let's not find out. Is your arm going to be all right?"

"It's just a dislocated shoulder. I'll be right as rain in a week. Thanks. Oh! And can you somehow manage to get this charged?" I pulled Katherine's mobile from my pocket.

"It's the same phone as yours. Just stick it on your charger, Wes. There's an extra in the top right drawer of your desk."

"Really?"

"How did you make it through medical school?" she asked as she walked back to her desk and picked up the phone.

"I cheated!" I declared with a wink before walking into my office.

It took close to two hours for me to finish tying up loose ends and for my secretary to return with a change of clothes.

Once she had, I headed back over to the hospital. There were showers there in the locker room adjacent to the operating theater and I was in desperate need of one.

I tilted my head up into the stream and let the endless supply of hot water sluice over my aching shoulder and down my back, rinsing off the last of the soap. I stretched my left arm gently forward, in front of my chest, testing its mobility and range of motion. Then I switched the jet to the massage option, turned toward the tile wall and leaned against it, resting my forehead on my right arm and positioning the jet so that the spray of water pounded against the knots in my mid-back.

"You slumming?"

I looked back over my shoulder. My old flame, Reese Wallace, was leaning against the doorway to the mens' shower, looking as sexy as ever. Reese and I had been lovers for about two years. Despite the fact that I'd been the one to end it, until meeting Katherine, I really hadn't started to move on.

I turned off the taps then nodded toward the towel that I'd left hanging on the wall. "Don't you knock?"

"Banged you a few times," she said saucily as she threw the towel at me. "Since the women's locker room is closed this week for repairs we came up with a system. There was a memo and everything."

"Yeah? Well, I tend not to read the memos from the surgical department."

"Did you see the men/women/vacant sign outside?"

"No." I ran the towel over my wet hair. "Was I supposed to flip it to men?"

"That's the general idea." Reese stepped closer. "Unless you're here to shower with me?" She tossed her long mane of dark hair over her shoulder. "I could use some help. You know, I'm very, very dirty."

I was trying to wrap the towel around my waist and failing

miserably. "As tempting as you are, no."

"Jesus, what did you do to your shoulder? Here, let me help with that." She started to secure the towel for me.

"You don't have to do that."

"Don't be ridiculous. Though I readily admit, I like undressing you far better than dressing you."

"It was dislocated. I was in an accident."

Reese stepped back and studied me for a moment. "Let's see, you're not flirting back, you're being modest." She slapped my chest, playfully. "You've met someone! Haven't you?" She looked down and smiled. "That's gotta be the reason I haven't gotten a rise out of you yet."

"Yes, I've met someone."

"I knew it! And you spent the night together. That's why you're showering here. Didn't even have time to make it home before work. But how the hell did you dislocate your shoulder? That's a new one!"

"I was with her all night, yes, but not like you think. She's a patient here, Reese. She's in critical condition up in ICU. We were involved in the Camden derailment. I've got to go."

She followed me out of the shower area and back into the locker room. I didn't care. Reese had seen me in the buff more times than I could count. When I reached the locker where I'd stored my clothes I loosened the towel and dropped it carelessly on the bench. She stood there silently, leaning against the wall while I awkwardly slipped on a pair of boxers and then tried to pull a T-shirt over my head.

"Wait." She walked over to me and held the shirt so I could slip into it.

"Thanks, I feel..."

"No problem. I'm happy you found someone, Wes." She smoothed down the front of my T-shirt then leaned in to kiss me on the cheek.

"Now I've just got to hold onto her."

"You will. Who in their right mind would let a prize catch like you go? If you need anything," she said as she grabbed a towel and headed toward the shower, "just whistle."

"Reese?"

"Yeah?"

"How have you been? You doing okay?"

She flashed a brilliant smile. It seemed forced, empty, sad. "Never been better, babe."

Once upon a time, I wouldn't have been able to let that go. I would have reached out and she would have reeled me in. I'd learned the hard way, no matter how ardently I tried, I couldn't erase Reese's emptiness. She wouldn't let me.

As soon as I finished dressing I made my way back up to the ICU. George was sleeping soundly in the chair, a book on his chest. The nurse that I'd spoken to before leaving was sitting comfortably at the desk, his feet propped up on the desktop, a magazine in hand.

"Ms. Lawson was extubated?"

"Yeah! Mr. Riley came by. Her intracranial pressure was down, things looked well, so bye-bye ventilator. Good news, huh?" He barely looked up.

"There was a change. You didn't call."

"It was a good change, not a bad change."

"Right."

"When was the last time you slept or ate?"

"I slept last night. Well, the night before. And I had dinner. I'm fine. You have any coffee?"

"I'll make a fresh pot. It won't be long before it's ready," he offered, standing up quickly and making his way over to the coffee station.

"Thanks."

The next few hours passed slowly. George was dead to the world, but I couldn't sleep a wink. When he finally came to, he seemed relieved to see me.

"What time is it?"

"It's just gone past four," I told him.

He looked at Katherine. "She's still unconscious?"

"I'm afraid so."

"Her doctor came while you were gone, but he wouldn't answer any of my questions. I wish she'd wake up."

"She will, soon. It'll be a while before Julia arrives. Why don't you go grab a bite to eat? The cafeteria is down on the first floor."

"Would you like me to bring something back for you?"

"I don't think I could eat anything."

He nodded. "I'll see you in a bit then."

I pulled my chair closer to the bed and stretched my legs out. Then I picked up the book George had left, and started to read aloud. It wasn't long before I was interrupted.

"Dr. Atherton? Katherine's mother just arrived," one of the nurses called out. "I'm buzzing her in now."

Chapter Four

"Mrs. Lawson?"

She was a bit taller than Katherine with shoulder-length brown hair and blue eyes. Her features were slightly more angular and she looked predictably exhausted.

"Yes."

Before I could offer her my hand, she moved over to the side of the bed and took her daughter's hand in hers.

"I came straight from the airport. Oh my God!" Her eyes flooded with tears. "Mommy's here, baby," she whispered to Katherine before turning her attention back to me. "How is she?"

"Better, actually. I think she's out of the woods, so to speak. She's breathing on her own again and the pressure in her head is down. That means that the burr holes and medications are working to reduce the swelling. That's good. We just need to be patient."

"She's so still. She hasn't woken up since the surgery?"

"No." I reached for the box of tissues and offered her one. The tears were flowing now and she'd started to stubbornly wipe them away with the back of her hand. "It may likely be a while yet. Mr. Grant has been here."

"I saw him downstairs. Actually, at the elevator. He's taking my luggage back to his place. I sent him home to get some rest.

And, speaking of rest, it looks like you could use some too."

I ran my hand through my hair, ignoring her remark about my needing rest. I wasn't about to go anywhere.

"Would you like some coffee?"

"I'd love some," she said.

I made a quick trip back to the break room, then returned with two cups. Julia accepted hers with a smile and sat down before going in for the kill. No mincing words.

"What were you doing out with my daughter?"

"I think you need to hear that from Katherine."

"Don't give me that. I'm asking you."

I took the seat next to her. "I met your daughter on the Tube one evening. She was the most beautiful thing I'd ever seen. She was radiant, fiery, quick tongued, totally unpretentious. I'm afraid that once I see something I want, I can be rather unrelenting."

"So you convinced her to go out with you on a date?"

"She told me she was engaged on more than one occasion. Katherine didn't consider it a date. It was just dinner."

"And that's different how?"

"My point, exactly!" I said triumphantly. "I thought it was a date. Why didn't she? Well, you've got me. She's your daughter."

"So, how long have you been *not* dating my daughter?"

"We've just had the one non-date."

"Let me ask you a question," said Julia, shifting a bit in her chair. "You meet my daughter, charm her into agreeing to a date, it's a train wreck, literally... And yet you're still here by her side. Why? You barely know her."

"I made her a promise."

"A promise?"

I shook my head. "It's more than that."

She waited patiently.

“Are you sure you want to hear this?”

Julia nodded.

“As we pulled into her stop I kissed Katherine good-bye. It wasn’t our first kiss of the night and I didn’t want it to be our last.” I paused, hesitant to continue.

“You asked her to go home with you?”

I looked away and swallowed down the lump in my throat. “Begged would probably be more accurate. Promised her she wouldn’t regret it. Convinced her, I did. Before the next stop we derailed. It all happened so bloody fast. There wasn’t any warning. We lost power. I had my arms around her, but I couldn’t hold on and keep her from falling.”

“You do realize this isn’t your fault.”

I turned back and looked her in the eye. “The wreck, no. But, the fact that she was there in that carriage at that time? That’s completely my fault.”

“I’m sorry,” Katherine said, pulling away.

“At least let me walk you back to your flat.”

She shook her head. “It’s close to the stop. I haven’t got far to go. I’ll be fine.”

“I insist. It’s late.”

“If I don’t walk away from you now I won’t have the strength to do it at all. Please, Wes. Just let me go.”

I had no choice. I steeled myself against the overwhelming disappointment and watched as Katherine walked down the aisle. I’d tried my best and I’d lost.

As soon as she stepped out of the carriage, I switched sides so I could follow her progress from the window. I saw her hurry toward the exit to the station. Then, when she was just about to round the corner, she hesitated and turned back. It was almost as if she were searching for the right window. I lifted my hand to the glass. Suddenly, Katherine was running back toward me. I moved, swiftly, arriving at the open doors just in time to gather her into my waiting arms.

"You came back."

"I realized I hadn't said good-bye."

"I'm better at hello," I said, taking her face in my hands and crushing my lips to hers in a passionate kiss. As I felt her arms wrap about my waist I lowered my hands, resting them on her hips and pulling her in closer still.

"Wes, my daughter is very stubborn. If she didn't want to go out with you, she wouldn't have. If she didn't want to go home with you, she wouldn't have agreed to it. No one pushes Kate around, and I mean no one."

I wondered about Damien. "Can't help but notice that Damien isn't with you. Is he coming?"

"I don't know. I actually hope he isn't. I've never been good at pretending." Julia shook her head. "I always thought he was the steady, reliable type."

"He's a fool."

"True. Your injury," she said, gesturing toward my immobilized arm. "I didn't even ask about it."

"It's nothing, just a dislocation. I'll be fine."

I reached for Katherine's hand, intertwining my fingers with hers.

"Is this all right?"

"Are you asking me for permission to hold my daughter's hand?"

"I find myself on uncertain ground here. I'm not a cad, Julia. Really I'm not. But I'm afraid you might think me one."

That made her smile. "I'm really not quite sure what to

make of you, Dr. Atherton."

"Wes."

"Okay. Wes. You look so familiar." Julia stood up and stretched. "I just can't place it."

"My father was fairly well-known, when he was alive. Perhaps that's it. I'm often told I look very much like him."

"You're Sullivan's son," she said, recognition dawning.

"That's right. You know of him?"

"I still have a couple of his paintings in my gallery. I'm ashamed to say that I've overpriced the pieces because I can't bear the thought of parting with them. He was a very gifted man."

"Yes, he was. Tell me, do you believe that certain things are predestined, fated to happen?"

"No. And before you ask, I don't believe in love at first sight, either. Your parents' love was legendary. While I believe that it was genuine, I also believe that kind of love is very rare. But, then, I'm divorced and bitter. What do I really know?"

"You're forthright, direct. I like that."

"I believe we shape our own lives, for better or for worse, by the choices we make."

I nodded. "Yeah. I'm sorry Katherine chose... That I..."

"Who's to say it wasn't a choice for the better?" asked Julia. "Her getting back on."

"I expect that will be up to Katherine."

"You're afraid that when she wakes up she's going to regret it."

"Yes."

Before she could respond, my mobile rang. "Excuse me, I have to answer this. Hello?" It was my secretary.

"Wes, sorry to bother you. I thought you'd want to know

that Bernie Friedman admitted Jennifer Carlton when he was on-call for you last night."

"What? Why am I just finding out about this now?"

"She was brought in around two this morning, right before Bernie's daughter went into labor, first grandchild. It was a girl by the way. He just called to let us know."

"Bollocks!"

"Bernie offered to see her today for you. She's over there, at Saint Catherine's."

"That's all right. Tell him I'll do it. Listen, it's almost five o'clock. Can you have some food delivered to the office? Dinner for two? I'll swing by and pick it up."

"Sure. Katherine's recovering I take it?"

"She's still unconscious, but she's stable. Her mum arrived from the States a short while ago."

"I see."

"Katherine's going to be fine, though. I can feel it. Thanks for asking."

Chapter Five

"Do you have Miss Carlton's chart?"

"Right here." The ward clerk handed it to me.

I opened the chart and flipped to the admissions summary. "She was picked up at Mornington Crescent station around midnight? How odd."

I was so keen to see Jennifer, the ward clerk's response was lost to me. Jennifer Carlton had become my patient a little over a month ago and I still wasn't quite sure why.

"How can I help you?" I asked her.

"I've already told you, you can't."

Her large, doe-like eyes seemed empty, haunted.

"Yet you've come back for a second appointment and my secretary tells me you've made several more."

Jennifer stood up and strolled over to the window. She was thin, delicate, vulnerable. Her hair was down today, its long dark waves spilling loosely about her shoulders. Her dress, as always, was simple yet tasteful. But underneath the calm exterior, she seemed distracted, even more so than the first time I'd seen her.

"I'm hoping that I can help you," she finally said.

"How?"

"I don't know yet. Is it all right if I just sit here for a few minutes and enjoy the quiet?"

"Of course."

For the rest of that session we sat in silence. It was how we'd spent our first session together and it ended up being how we spent the third and forth as well. Jennifer always arrived on time. She always came alone. And she always paid in cash.

I knocked twice, then opened the door and entered.

"Dr. Atherton!" Jennifer was sitting up in bed reading a paperback novel that she promptly tossed aside.

"Miss Carlton."

"I told you he would come, Will."

The man who had been keeping Jennifer company was impeccably dressed in a dark suit, white shirt and blood red tie. His hair was closely cropped and precisely parted. Although his finely chiseled features were reminiscent of Jennifer's, in contrast to her deep brown eyes his were a striking blue.

"William Carlton." He stood up and offered his hand. "I'm Jennifer's brother."

"Wesley Atherton."

His handshake was firm and confident.

"Will here used to be a spy," announced Jennifer. "He swears he's quit, but I'm not sure I believe him."

"Perhaps Jennifer and I should meet alone for a few minutes. Do you mind?"

"Not at all."

"You might as well let him stay, Doctor," Jennifer said. "He's probably got the room wired."

"The room isn't wired." Will checked his watch. "But I have a call to make. So I'll leave you two to chat."

"Don't go far. I want to go home. I didn't sleep a wink here last night. There are too many of them walking about at all hours, chattering incessantly."

"She didn't sleep the night before either," added Will.

"Well of course not. Could you? I'll sleep tonight though. The doctor here is safe. We'll get the rest sorted. Eventually. I think. You'll help me, won't you?"

"I'll help you," I assured her.

"I'm so tired."

As soon as Will was out the door I took the chair he'd previously occupied, opened up Jennifer's chart, and scanned the remainder of the admission note. "It looks like Dr. Friedman prescribed something that should have helped you sleep."

"I didn't take it."

"You didn't?"

She shook her head then pointed to the dustbin over in the corner. "When the nurse left I tossed it in there."

"Why did you do that?"

"The other doctor, he said it would help stop the hallucinations," replied Jennifer. "I'm not having hallucinations. What I see, what I hear, it's real."

"Tell me what you see, what you hear."

Jennifer's eyes darted about the room.

I leaned forward. "What are you seeing now?"

"I knew you would go to her, move toward the back."

A sudden chill ran through my body and made me shiver. Before I could stop myself the words tumbled out of my mouth. "Go to who?"

"Why, the girl. He laughed when I told him she had the power to save you. He didn't believe me. He believes now."

"Are you talking about Will?"

"I'm talking about the Reaper."

"The Reaper?"

"Death." Jennifer climbed out of her bed, walked over to the window and gazed out. "He makes those tracks look so appealing sometimes," she said wistfully. "He calls to me you know, whispering words and sweet promises. I hear him even now. I hear all of them. That's why I can't sleep."

"What are the voices saying, Jennifer?"

"That I'm not supposed to meddle. But sometimes I can't help myself."

"You said earlier that he makes the tracks look appealing. Are you having thoughts about harming yourself?"

"No," she replied, shaking her head. "I must figure out how to make it right. You're not going to let me go home tonight, are you?"

"I'm not sure you're ready to go home. Tell me about what happened in the Tube station."

She squeezed her eyes shut and shook her head. "I was trying to get someone to listen, but nobody would. It's so..."

"So what?"

"Frustrating!" she practically yelled. "If only they'd stopped it. They could have saved you all. But, I saved you. At least that's something. The rest is a jumble now. I'm too tired to make sense of it. I need to rest."

I hastily scribbled an order. "I'm going to have the nurse bring you a sleeping pill. I'll come back to see you tomorrow evening. Promise me you'll take the pill and stay until we can talk again?"

"I promise."

"Good. I'll see you tomorrow." I made my way over to the door, pulled it open, and instantly laid eyes on Will. He appeared to be waiting for me.

He was standing in the hallway holding two cups of coffee.

"Tomorrow will be our sixth meeting," I heard Jennifer say right before the door closed. "I'm paid up for six."

"Coffee?" Will offered one of the cups to me. "You're probably wishing it was something a little stronger."

"Are you and your sister very close, Mr. Carlton?"

"Please, call me Will. I'd say so, yes. She lives with me. I travel quite a bit. Jennifer takes classes part-time at the university and tends to the house."

"Can you tell me about her history?" I motioned toward the visitor's lounge and we started to stroll in that direction.

"What is it you want to know?"

"How long has she been ill?" I asked, before taking a seat.

Will chuckled, then he selected a chair directly across from me.

"Why do you laugh?"

He shrugged. "She said you'd be stubborn. That you wouldn't believe. What Jennifer has isn't a mental illness, it's a gift."

"Then why is she seeing a psychiatrist?"

"She wasn't seeing a psychiatrist, per se. She was seeing you. Trying to get close, suss it out. She told you why. She gave you a reason, told you she was there to help you. You didn't believe it. You still don't."

"She also told me you were a spy. I'm supposed to believe that?"

"I was with MI5. I've only been out a matter of months."

That took me aback.

"I do private security now," he added. "Look, I can appreciate that this whole thing is unsettling."

"Unsettling?"

"If it hadn't been for Jennifer, you'd be dead. My sister isn't hallucinating or paranoid. She's not psychotic. She may see and hear things that we don't, but that doesn't make them less real."

"There are a lot of people who would disagree with you there."

"She saved your life."

"You're telling me she knew there was going to be a crash and that I would somehow be involved?"

Will took a sip of his coffee. "It sounds bonkers, I know."

"Damned right."

"And being a shrink you probably hear a lot of crazy-sounding talk."

"I've heard my share."

He nodded. Then he stood and tossed the last of his coffee in the rubbish. "Well, hold on to your hat, Doc. If my sister's right, there's a whole lot more crazy to come."

The truly daft thing was that deep down inside, I knew he was right.

Chapter Six

I was completely knackered, but I couldn't seem to slow my mind down. Jennifer's words rolled round and round in my head. I desperately wanted Katherine to wake up, but I feared the regret I might see in her eyes. So for the next eight hours I did nothing but pace and drink bad coffee. I'd long ago switched to decaf and was just returning with a fresh cup when Katherine opened her eyes.

"Mommy?"

I hung back. Julia stood up and quickly moved to the bed. She leaned over and kissed Katherine on the forehead. "Shh, Mommy's here."

"Where?" Katherine seemed confused, her brow furrowed.

"You're in the hospital. There was an accident."

"An accident?"

Julia pulled the chair she'd been sitting in closer to the bed, sat back down and said, "Yes. Down in the Tube, the carriage you were on derailed."

"I remember it pulling out of the station, then...nothing."

"You hit your head. Wes called me. I flew right out. It's Wednesday morning, sweetheart."

"Where's Damien?"

"He isn't here."

"He isn't here? Does he know?"

"He knows. Your friend, Wesley, called him."

Katherine blushed at the mention of my name.

"So, is Damien coming?"

"I'm not sure."

"I don't understand, what did he say?"

Julia sighed.

"Mom? There's something you're not telling me! Why didn't Damien come with you?"

Katherine was beginning to look stressed. I stepped into view and smiled. "You're awake!"

"Wes has hardly left your side. I tried to convince him to go home and get some rest but he wouldn't hear of it."

"He is annoyingly persistent."

"It's one of my very best features," I said.

Katherine lifted her hand up toward her head.

Julia reached out to stop her. "You had a bleed inside your brain. They did some surgery."

"Did they shave off all my hair?"

I took her hand in mine and sat down on the edge of the bed.

"No, they didn't shave off all of your hair, just a little spot where they made the holes."

"Holes? I have holes?"

"Only two. They did it to relieve the pressure from the bleed. It worked like a charm, love. Can't even tell they're there."

"Honest?"

"I swear. I've been so worried. How do you feel?"

"I have a bad headache."

"Wes?" Julia looked alarmed.

"Her pressure and vitals are fine. I'm sure they have something ordered that can help with the pain. I'll go ask the nurse."

"I'll go. I've been sitting here for hours feeling helpless. It'll feel good to stretch my legs."

"What happened to your arm?" asked Katherine, once we were alone.

"It's nothing. It's just a dislocated shoulder."

I leaned over her and lowered my mouth to hers, stealing a tender kiss. "I promised you a really good kiss when you woke up," I said, pulling back a bit.

"Yeah, well I'd say that qualified."

"I can do far better than that."

"I remember."

"I'm not a patient man, but I'm reasonable. The other night with you? It was wonderful. Well, right up until the wreck, that is. What with you, and then Margaret and Henry."

"Who?"

"The older couple we were sitting next to."

"Are they all right?"

"No, love."

"They're in the hospital too?"

I shook my head. "They died, both of them."

"If you'd stayed in your seat—"

Katherine reached out for my hand and gave it a little squeeze. I returned the pressure.

"But I didn't. You came back."

"You met me at the door."

I nodded. "I want you to know that I remember it, the promise I made."

"Shh." She placed her fingertips over my lips. "I wanted to be with you. The truth is, I never wanted to leave."

"I shouldn't have asked you to come home with me, Katherine."

"No?"

I wasn't explaining this well. I'd had all this time to prepare, and I was botching it.

"Not because I didn't want it, or you. But because it may have given you the impression that it would have been enough for me, or all I wanted, that one night. And that's not fair. It wouldn't have been enough."

"It wouldn't have been?"

"Not by a long shot."

"What on earth am I going to do with you, Wesley Atherton?" she asked with a smile that instantly removed the weight of the world from my shoulders.

"Well, I have loads of ideas, but I don't think the nurses would approve and you have to keep your blood pressure down for a few more days."

She blushed. "Wes, Damien—"

"Damien. I was hoping you'd forgotten about him."

"She's awake?" The nurse pushed back the curtain surrounding the bed and turned up the lights.

"Yeah, I think she's had enough beauty sleep, don't you?" I teased.

"He's a silver-tongued devil," warned the nurse with a wink. Then she shook her finger at me and added, "Her blood pressure is stable. Don't elevate it too much!"

"What's too much?"

"Want me to see if we can move her to a private room?"

"That'd be brilliant." I smiled down at Katherine. "I bet

you'll be able to go home sometime tomorrow."

"We better make our flight arrangements, then," interjected Julia.

The nurse shook her head. "No flying, not for a good ten days at least. I'm sure the doctor is going to recommend you stay in London until your six-week follow-up. I'll call Mr. Riley and see about that move."

"Make it a king-sized bed, non-smoking," I called out to her as she walked away. "She's right, by the way, no flying for you. Not for a while. I just meant you could probably leave the hospital."

"Oh," said Julia. "We'll find a hotel then."

"Don't be ridiculous. You and Katherine will stay with me. It looks like I arrived just in time. How are you feeling, dear?"

"George, I appreciate the offer, but you can't put all three of us up in your tiny flat," Julia objected.

Katherine winced in pain and closed her eyes.

I bent down and whispered in her ear, "What is it, love?"

"Headache. I was remembering something. There was a woman. A woman in the station."

I swallowed and waited patiently.

"It's so bright," moaned Katherine. "I think I'm going to be sick." She covered her mouth with her hand.

I quickly examined the monitors. "Her pressure is going up, everybody out."

"What is it? What's wrong?" asked Julia, alarmed. I couldn't blame her, I was alarmed too.

"We could use some help over here!" I grabbed an emesis basin from a nearby shelf, then turned to Julia. "Could be just too much stimulation, could be a simple migraine, or it could be worse. Please step out into the waiting area. We'll work to get this under control."

Julia started to protest but I interrupted her. "Trust me. I'll take care of her. We need to let the medical staff do their jobs."

Julia nodded and reluctantly left the ICU with George.

Katherine's nurse rushed over. "What's going on?"

"She's photosensitive, complaining of a headache. Her vitals are all elevated."

"But the intracranial pressure seems to be holding steady," she observed.

"Give her some pethidine."

"There aren't any orders for pethidine. I'll page Mr. Riley."

"I'll write the order!"

I walked over to the nurses' station, picked up Katherine's chart and opened it to the top sheet of doctor's orders.

"She's not on your service. You can't be writing orders for her and you shouldn't be looking at that!" She reached for the chart. I pulled it away.

They had secured the latest lab results to the front of the order sheet so Eric would be sure to see them during rounds. There it was, plain as day, circled in red, a positive pregnancy test. Did Katherine even know?

"You didn't see that!" The nurse took the chart away from me.

"I bloody well did!"

"Well, pretend you didn't. Eric will tell her and then she'll tell you herself." She smiled. "Congratulations, by the way."

"I've got Riley on the line!" the woman behind the desk called out.

Katherine began to retch. I moved quickly, returning to her side. "I know it hurts," I told her, holding the emesis basin under her chin while I rubbed her back. Nothing came up. As soon as the spasm subsided I set the basin down, grabbed a washcloth and plunged it into the pitcher of ice water that was by her bedside. "Here you go. I want you to lean back." I folded the wrung-out cloth into fourths and gently laid it on her forehead.

"I'm sorry," she whispered.

"Whatever for? Don't be ridiculous."

"This has got to be your worst date ever."

The nurse approached with a syringe. "Mr. Riley ordered some PRN pethidine for the pain. I'm going to put it in her IV. He's just finishing rounds on the tenth floor. He'll be coming to check on her. I told him her ICP was fine but he's ordered another scan. He wants to be sure."

"Did you review her latest lab results with him?"

"It's all right," she assured me.

"You'll start feeling better shortly, love. Let's take some slow, deep breaths and try to relax. Breathe with me. All right?"

After several minutes Katherine removed the washcloth and searched out my eyes. "I don't like hospitals, Wes."

"We'll get you out of here as soon as we can."

"Sorry to interrupt. I'm Dr. Riley. I did your surgery." Eric offered his hand to Katherine. "I'm gonna do a quick exam. You're welcome to stay, Wes, if that's what the lady wants." He started to pull the curtains surrounding Katherine's bed closed.

"I'll go tell your mum that your pressure's back down. I'm sure she's worried."

"Thanks," Katherine said.

"I'll come out and join you in a minute," added Eric.

I walked out of the ICU and immediately laid eyes on a very brassed-off Julia.

Chapter Seven

There was a tall, well-built man standing across from her, arms folded in a defensive posture across his chest. My guess? Damien.

I swallowed down the lump in my throat, walked up to the man, and offered my hand. “Damien? We spoke on the phone.”

“Yes. You’re Katherine’s doctor?”

“No. I’m *a* doctor. I’m not her doctor.”

“He’s a friend, as am I,” interjected George. “I don’t believe we’ve been introduced. George Grant.”

“You’re the one she’s been staying with.”

“Yes, quite.”

Julia turned to me. “How is she?”

“She’s going to be fine. Bad headaches aren’t unusual. Her pressure is back down. Eric, Mr. Riley, gave her some medication for the pain. She’s doing better.”

“I want to see her,” said Damien.

Of course he did.

Eric joined us. “Mrs. Lawson?”

“Yes!”

“I’m Mr. Riley. Katherine is recovering nicely. I believe the headache is just that. To be on the safe side, we’re taking her down to CT and we’ll do a comparative scan. She should be back up within an hour."

"I want to see her," demanded Damien, stepping forward.

"And you are?"

"Her fiancé. I have a right to see her."

"You don't have any rights," said Julia. I had a feeling this was about to get ugly.

Eric lifted his hand to scratch the back of his head. He was a surgeon. His way of dealing with a problem was to cut it out. Any minute now he was going to make a run for the nearest exit.

"She'll want to see me," said Damien with confidence.

"Let's get the scan done first," I suggested. "Then we'll see what she's feeling up to."

Julia folded her arms across her chest. "The sooner you insist on seeing her, the sooner you're going to force me to tell her you're sleeping with somebody else."

Damien turned to face her. "You'd risk upsetting her?"

"I'll let you sort this one out, Dr. Freud." That did it. Eric slapped me on the back and then predictably walked away. George was off in a corner polishing his glasses. As absurd as it was, I was left to handle the mess.

I inserted myself between the two of them. "This isn't the time or the place for this."

"He's right, Julia. We need to put aside whatever differences we have and get along for Katherine's sake," said Damien.

"Actually that's not what I was saying at all. I'm not suggesting Julia dismiss her feelings."

"So, what *are* you saying?"

"The two of you want to have this out, I'll let you use my office. But you're not going to do it here, now."

Julia blushed. "You're right, of course."

"I'll ask Katherine if she wants to see you," I told Damien.

"Thank you." He smiled. It seemed almost smug. With each second that ticked by I liked the wanker less and less. I started to walk back toward the ICU.

"I appreciate you going to bat for me," he called out.

That made me pause. I didn't want him thinking I was his ally, or his friend. "Just so that we're clear, I'm not doing this for you. I'm doing this for Katherine. If she wants to see you, fine. Personally, I'm hoping that she doesn't. She deserves better."

"Damn right!" said Julia.

Damien sighed. "Look, I know I made a mistake."

I held up my hand. "Don't apologize. To be perfectly honest with you, I'm glad you did. Really. One man's mistake is another's good fortune. I'll let you know what she says."

"Just who the hell are you again?"

"Wesley Atherton, your competition." I didn't even take the time to register his response. As soon as the words were out of my mouth I turned and proceeded through the door, shutting them all out.

Katherine's face lit up the moment she saw me. I made my way over to her bed. She shifted over a bit, so I could sit beside her.

"Medication's working?"

"Like magic," she said. "I feel a little woozy."

"They're going to be taking you downstairs so they can get more pictures of that pretty little head of yours. Did Eric explain?"

"Yes. He said it's just to make extra, extra sure. I'm having a hard time staying awake."

"That's all right. Go to sleep if you want. I do have a bit of news for you though."

Katherine's eyes widened. "Something bad?"

"Damien's here, well, he's out in the waiting area. If you want to see him, I can arrange it."

"Does he know we—"

I smiled, sadly. "George introduced me as a friend."

"A friend," she repeated.

"You know I want to be more."

She nodded. "You do kind of wear your heart on your sleeve."

"I don't want to push you. If you want me to bring him in, to step aside, I will, for now. I won't like it, but I'll do it."

"What am I missing, Wes?"

"What do you mean?"

"I hope that's not your poker face. I don't know, maybe it's the medications. But before you came in I got the impression Mom was about to tell me something. Am I wrong?"

It wasn't the medications. Despite them, Katherine was both perceptive and persistent. She wasn't going to let this go. I didn't want to be the one to tell her, to hurt her. But I didn't want to lie to her either.

"Your mum and Damien had a bit of a row. That's why they didn't fly out together."

"About what?"

I was going to have to say it. "She stopped by Damien's on the way to the airport."

"Yes, and?"

"He was with another woman."

Katherine turned away from me.

"If you don't want to see him, I'll keep him away from you. If you want me to beat him up, I can do that too, but you've got to give me a couple weeks because of my shoulder."

"I'm not ready to see him yet."

"Yet. You said yet."

"I have to face him eventually."

"No you don't, you could write him a note, or send him an e-mail."

"An e-mail?"

"Oh, bugger it! You're going to forgive him and go back to him, aren't you? Be a picture-perfect family."

I took her engagement ring out of my pocket and held it out to her. "Is he really what you want? Because if he is, if he truly is, then I'll back off. Please tell me he's not."

"I used to be so sure that he was."

"And then?" I felt a glimmer of hope.

"And then I met this guy, on the Tube. You said family. You know. Don't you?"

I nodded. "Yes, I saw it in your chart. It doesn't change anything."

Katherine looked away. "How can you say that?"

I turned her head back toward me so that I could look her in the eye. This time I said it with more conviction. "It doesn't change anything."

For a long moment we sat there in silence.

"Okay, I'm a stupid git. Of course it'll change some things. But it doesn't have to change what's happening between us, not if you don't want it to."

"Give him the ring. Tell him I need a few days. Tell him I'll talk to him in a few days."

"Do you need a few days?"

"To face him, yes, but not to decide. I made that decision down in the Tube station. Maybe even before then, when you first kissed me. Or, during dinner. Or possibly even some time the night before when we stayed up all night, just talking on the phone."

"Would you consider staying with me when you're released? George's flat sounds impossibly small. I have plenty of room and promise to dote on you."

"I can't commit to anything."

I knew she couldn't and I wouldn't ask it of her, not now. "I'm not looking for a promise, Katherine. I'm only wanting a chance."

"That I can give you."

I reached out to caress the side of her face. "So, we're going to see where this takes us, yeah?"

"Are we crazy?"

I smiled. "Certifiable, I'm sure."

"Wes? They're ready for her in CT," said the nurse.

I leaned down and kissed her softly. "I'll be here when you get back," I promised as they wheeled up a trolley.

I braced myself for what was to come and exited the ICU.

"Let's talk."

I said the words just as I walked past Damien. Whatever was going to be said between us was going to be said in private.

Damien followed me down the hallway. The second we turned the corner he grabbed me from behind and pushed me up against the wall.

"You're trying to steal her away from me, aren't you?"

"Thought I was pretty straightforward about that. Look, you want to hit me? Go on. I wouldn't blame you a bit. Might bring you some satisfaction, but it won't change a thing. In the end she won't choose you."

The fact that I gave him permission to hit me seemed to

either confuse him or take the fun out of it. He stepped back.

"Katherine and I have a long history. How long have you known her, a couple weeks?"

"A few days." I offered him my card. "You may have a long history, but something important is missing in the relationship, or it wouldn't have come to this. Deep down you know that. Call on Friday."

"You told her, didn't you?"

"I had no choice. She asked what was wrong and I couldn't lie to her."

He stepped back and laughed ruefully. "That's great, just great."

He paced for a moment in front of me before asking, "Have the two of you...?"

"No. Not yet."

"Not yet. How do I know you're telling the truth?"

"I guess you don't. But I am."

"What did she say?"

"She asked me to give you this." I held out the ring. "And she said she needed a few days."

He palmed the ring. "It's my own damn fault. I'm gong to lose her, aren't I?"

I answered him honestly. "I think you already did."

Damien nodded sadly, turned away and walked down the hall toward the elevator. After pushing the button he turned back to face me.

"You think you can make her happy?"

"I know I can."

Chapter Eight

For the next hour I sat in Medical Records, trying to finish some paperwork that I'd put off. But it was no use. I couldn't focus. My mind was racing. I'd just returned a call from Charles, my butler, when the clerk called out to me.

"Wes? It's the ICU on line three."

I reached across the table and picked up the phone.

"Dr. Atherton here, is everything all right?"

It was her nurse. "They moved Katherine to a regular med-surg bed up on ten. The CT looked fine. She's in 1012."

"Brilliant!"

"I've already let the family know. They told me where you were."

"Should have done that myself. Thanks for everything."

Flooded with relief, I rang off then set out for the tenth floor.

"Did you hear? Everything looks fine according to Mr. Riley!" Julia said as I entered the room.

"Yes. It's wonderful news." I walked over to Katherine's bedside. "How's the headache?"

"Much better. Practically non-existent."

There was a tray of food in front of her. It appeared to be untouched. "You haven't eaten."

"I'm feeling a bit queasy still and the green Jell-O? Not so appetizing."

"Maybe some broth?" suggested Julia.

"You know what? You should all go home and get some rest. The doctor said I'm going to be fine. You heard him!"

"She has a point, Julia. You're exhausted," agreed George. "We could grab a quick bite, and then you really should get some rest."

Julia held up her hands in surrender. "When you two start ganging up on me I know it's time to throw in the towel. Besides, we still need to finish that argument about where we're all going to stay."

"No. No arguing. It's been decided. You'll stay with George. I'm going to stay with Wes. There's not enough room for both of us in George's flat and Wes has promised to spoil me."

"But, Kate—" began Julia.

"Mom, it makes sense. He's a doctor. If something goes wrong he'll take care of me. He'll be there for me, just like he was that night. It's decided."

"My stop is just one away from George's on the Tube. You can come whenever you want," I added.

Julia looked at me. "I'm counting on you."

"I won't let you down."

She sighed. "We are just talking a few days. I'm sure we can arrange for follow-up back home."

"Right," I agreed. "Just a few days."

Both Julia and George said their good-byes, leaving with a promise to return the next morning.

"Are you going to kick me out, too?" I asked, as soon as they were gone.

"Wes, you've got to be exhausted."

"I have one patient I'm hoping to discharge in the morning, after that my schedule's clear for the next few days. I can rest then."

Katherine shook her head. "No, you can't rest then. That's when the spoiling is supposed to commence. Remember?"

"Ah, yes, of course. Move over."

Katherine shifted over in the small bed. I climbed on top of the covers, rolling onto my side so that I faced her. "How do you *really* feel?"

"Tired. Is that normal? I've just slept for two days."

"First off, it wasn't two whole days. Second, your body is healing and it's craving real rest. What I meant was, how are you feeling emotionally."

Katherine closed her eyes for a moment. "Overwhelmed," she finally said.

"That's understandable."

"If I tell you something, promise you won't think I'm crazy?"

I leaned up on my elbow. "What is it?"

"When I got off at the station I was so confused, so torn, even a bit ashamed."

"Ashamed?"

"I wanted you, Wes."

"I wanted you, too, so very much."

"But I felt that I had an obligation. That I'd chosen my path, made a commitment. My father, he cheated on Mom all the time."

"And you didn't want to do that."

"I saw what it did to her."

"I'm sure it took a toll on you as well."

"I remember thinking that my mother stayed in a bad marriage for years out of a sense of obligation and here I was about to enter into one for the very same reason."

"You felt obligated because you'd accepted his proposal."

"Yes. Who knows? Maybe Damien felt obligated to propose in the first place. We'd started dating early on in high school. Everyone expected us to get married. We were comfortable with one another. But we weren't passionate. Am I making sense?"

"Perfect sense, love."

"Okay. So this is where it gets weird. There was a woman in the station."

"At Mornington Crescent?"

"Yes. She seemed upset about something. She came into view just as I turned the corner. She was talking to a security officer at the bottom of the stairs, arguing with him. She seemed close to tears. She reached for me as if she wanted to grab me. The officer held her back. But she shouted out something."

Katherine shook her head.

"What?"

"Time's running out. Go back. Hurry! Wesley needs you!"

"She said my name?"

"She couldn't have, right? But I swear in my head, in my heart, that's what I heard. Right then, I made a choice. Everything seemed so clear at the time. I knew."

"What?"

"I'm not sure. At the time it made sense, but now I can't remember. All I can remember is that I *wanted* you and I wanted, no, I *needed* to be with you."

I couldn't help myself. "You wanted me, huh? Tell me how much."

Katherine rolled her eyes. "Did you even hear the other part?"

"Yes. I did." I placed a kiss on her nose.

"And?"

"You know, I asked your mum if she believed in fate. I found myself thinking, I'm not the kind of man who goes after another man's wife or fiancée or girlfriend. I'm not. And, I certainly didn't believe in love at first sight before—"

"Ms. Lawson? I'm Dr. Wallace."

As soon as I heard Reese's voice I looked over my shoulder.

"I'm interrupting. Carry on, I'll come back tomorrow," she said, obviously surprised.

I quickly rose to my feet. "Reese. It's all right. Come in."

She seemed to struggle with a moment of indecision before approaching the bed and extending her hand. "Ms. Lawson, Mr. Riley requested that I pay you a visit. If this isn't a good time, I could come back in the morning."

"No, this is fine," said Katherine. "I'm really hoping I can leave tomorrow. Are you covering for Mr. Riley?"

"No, I'm an obstetrician." Reese turned to me. "Would you excuse us for a moment?"

"It's all right, he knows about the baby," said Katherine.

"Yes, well then. Here's my card. Call my office in the next week or two and we'll get you scheduled for your first exam."

Katherine glanced down at the card.

"Any questions?" asked Reese.

"I don't think so. I'm sure I'll have questions. This is...wow." Katherine placed her hand over her still-flat stomach.

I smiled. "You're going to have a baby."

Katherine took a shaky breath. "Yeah. I'm going to have a baby."

"Well," said Reese, interrupting the tender moment, "you've got my card." She turned and hurriedly made her way to the door to leave. Just as it was closing she paused and added, “Congratulations, Wes. I know this is something you’ve always wanted. You deserve it.” Then she was gone.

“Be right back.” I couldn’t leave it like that. I followed Reese out into the hallway. She was standing just outside the room, her back against the wall, Katherine’s chart wrapped in her arms and held in front of her chest like a protective shield.

“Reese?”

She was staring into space, a far-away look in her dark brown eyes. When she turned to look at me I had to resist the urge to step back in surprise. The vulnerability and openness of her expression startled me. But I didn’t step back, I held fast and waited.

“I never even said I was sorry, did I?” asked Reese.

“No. No, you didn’t.”

“I am. I think about it a lot, how I messed everything up between us. But, you know what the really twisted thing is, Wes?”

“No, Reese, tell me.” I shoved my hands into my pockets.

Her eyes were brimming with tears. “I think I’d do the same thing again. I’m fucked up, aren’t I?”

I stepped closer to her, removed my hands from my pockets and used the pads of my thumbs to wipe away the tears that had begun to spill from her eyes. “Are you asking for my personal or professional opinion?”

She chuckled at that. Then shaking off my tender gesture she winked at me. “Surprise me, Wes, you know how much I love surprises.”

I sighed as I watched the practiced façade fall back into place. “How about I go for honest? Think you can handle that?”

She traced the waistband of my jeans with her fingertip. “Babe, you know I can handle whatever you dish out.”

I reached for her hand, took it in my own, and held it between us. “I think you have issues with trust and intimacy, Reese. You’re terrified of being vulnerable, of being rejected, of being hurt. But, the problem is that if you don’t open yourself up, if you never let anyone in, you’re going to stay like this. You’re going to remain alone and you’re going to remain unhappy. I don’t want to see that. I’ve seen glimpses, Reese.”

She licked her lips, tossed her hair over her shoulder and in a low voice said, “I remember opening up for you. Remember how good we were? Remember how I made you feel?”

“I’m talking about an emotional connection, Reese, and you know it.” I let go of her hand. “Want to know how you made me feel? Like I was just a fuck. A good fuck, but a fuck.”

“Heck, Wes, you’re selling yourself short. You were a great fuck.”

I looked down and shook my head. “But, I could have been a lot more.”

“And you will be. Just not with me.”

I looked up at her.

She shrugged as if she didn’t care. “I’m glad, truly. I’m not cut out for all that, Wes. Keeping the baby would have been a mistake. If I’d told you before, well it’s water under the bridge, isn’t it?”

“Yes, for us, that’s true. But, Reese, promise me you’ll think about what I said?”

“I’ll think about it. You better get back to your girl.”

I nodded, then turned and walked back into the room.

“Sorry. Now, where were we?”

“Do the two of you have some kind of history?” Katherine asked.

Before I could respond, someone knocked on the door.

“Come in!”

Charles opened the door and cautiously peered inside.

"Charles, you made it 'round rather fast! Let me introduce you to Miss Lawson."

Charles bowed slightly in Katherine's direction. "It's a pleasure to meet you, Miss Lawson."

"Call me Katherine. You're a friend of Wesley's?"

"I'm Dr. Atherton's butler. I managed to acquire everything you requested, sir. Will there be anything else?"

"He was my father's butler," I clarified.

"And now yours," added Charles. "Thank you for the opportunity to actually do something useful. Will there be anything else?"

"You have servants?"

"Servant. One." I self-consciously ran my hand through my hair. "And, I didn't employ him. I inherited him."

"He has class issues," offered Charles, in a quiet voice.

"I am expecting to take Katherine home tomorrow."

"I'll make sure the house is ready," said Charles. "Do you have any special requests, Miss Lawson?"

"Requests?" Katherine's IVAC began to beep. "Wes? Is there something wrong with the IV?"

"No, love. You've just run through the bag of fluids. This was the last bag. We can disconnect you now."

I shut off the pump and the beeping stopped. "Let Charles know if there's anything special you'd like to have. He'll stock the fridge. Better to have things on hand than for me to have to run out to the store in the middle of the night in search of chocolate and pickles!" I slapped Charles on the back then went to wash my hands in the sink.

Katherine laughed. "I'm only two weeks along. I'm not having any cravings. Please, don't go to any trouble. I don't need anything special, really."

"I have a feeling that spoiling you is about to become my primary duty," said Charles. "Tell me, what is your favorite flower?"

"Tulips. They are without a doubt one of my favorite things about spring."

I dried my hands then pulled on a pair of latex gloves. "Let's get this out, shall we?"

"Are you sure it's all right?"

"If you'll excuse me, I have much to do before tomorrow." Charles hurried out the door.

I couldn't help but smile. "He's a bit squeamish. Sit up and move to the end of the bed."

I began to unfasten the tape that held the IV lines in place. Then I handed Katherine a cotton gauze pad and gently pulled out the needle. "Apply pressure to the site for a moment. I feel bloody useless with this arm in a sling." I draped the lines over the IVAC pump.

Katherine looked down, then she shook her head.

"Are you all right?"

She'd yet to start applying pressure to the IV site and a bit of blood had seeped out.

"Katherine?"

She started to slide off of the bed. I managed to catch her with my good arm.

"Katherine!" I set her back on the bed. "Lie down, love. What's going on?"

"Just a little dizzy."

"I've got you." I retrieved the gauze pad and applied pressure to the small puncture wound.

"I feel so strange."

"You'll be fine. You're weak as a kitten at the moment, but

you'll be fine."

"I feel like I'm still falling."

I climbed into the small bed and spooned up against her. "Close your eyes and rest for a bit. If you fall, I'll be here to catch you."

Katherine closed her eyes. "They both think that the baby is yours."

I wrapped my free arm around her. "I know."

Chapter Nine

Eric woke me up with a gentle shake. It was morning and the room was filled with bright sunshine.

"I'm pretty sure this is against the rules," whispered Eric, gesturing between Katherine and me.

I carefully unwrapped myself from Katherine's warm body and eased myself out of the bed. "I'm surprised to see you this early."

Eric shrugged. "I had an emergency during the night. I thought I'd make rounds before going home." He nodded toward Katherine. "I'm going to let her go today. She'll need to come and see me in a few weeks for a follow-up. And she should see an OB. I asked Reese to stop by. Do you know if she made it?"

"Yeah, she came by. It was a little awkward."

"Sorry. Guess I wasn't thinking."

"It's all right. We'll manage."

"I'll go start on the discharge paperwork. It'll take fifteen minutes give or take, then I'll come back and remove Katherine's drain."

"Sounds good."

"There's someone waiting outside the door for you, by the way. He asked that I let you know."

"Who is it?"

"Don't know him."

I followed Eric out. It was Will Carlton.

"Morning," he said.

"How'd you find me?"

Will just smiled. "I was hoping I could take Jennifer home this morning. She didn't sleep well last night."

He pursed his lips and looked down at the floor. It appeared as if he were trying to choose his words very carefully. Finally he looked up and said, "I'm afraid Katherine's not out of the woods yet, not by a long shot."

"She's fine. Everything's checked out. In fact, she's being discharged."

"Jennifer said that death is knocking. It won't be deterred or denied. It's coming. You must be on your guard. Do you understand?"

"Is this the crazy talk that you warned me about?"

"Don't dismiss this. Both the girl and the child are in danger."

He knew Katherine was pregnant.

"Do you have access to Katherine's medical records?"

The elevator across from us chimed. The doors opened to reveal Jennifer, dressed in a gown and robe.

"Pigeon, you were supposed to wait for me in your room," Will said, placing an arm around her shoulders.

"I want to go home, Will. I can't rest here."

"I know."

"Did you tell him?"

"I was trying to."

"They're in danger, Doctor. He's angry, angry because he was cheated." Jennifer's eyes darted up and down the empty hallway. She tilted her head slightly to the left and paused for a moment, listening in silence. “It’ll have to be you. You’ll need to protect her. I’ve already done too much to upset the balance. Three strikes and you’re out, they say. I’ve been a naughty girl and naughty girls get punished. He’ll take Will. It’s going to have to be you.”

“Jennifer, are you still hearing voices?”

“Only when they talk to me.” She said it so reasonably, so matter-of-factly. “There are too many here to ignore. Too many are tied to this place. It would be quieter at home.” She turned her head abruptly, toward the closed elevator doors. “I’ve bloody well warned him. That’s enough! Go back to your room!”

Will put his arm protectively around her and leaned down to whisper something in her ear. Jennifer looked up, a shaky smile on her face.

“I’m sorry, sometimes it gets to be a bit much. The constant…” she lifted one trembling hand to her head and tapped, harshly, against the side of her temple, a tone of desperation creeping into her voice, “…flood of information. I don’t know what to do with it. Please! You need to help me set things right again. Will you do that? Will you make it all go away?”

“Jennifer, it sounds like the hallucinations are still bothering you. You’re not stable. I’d like to try adding a medication that will make the voices go away. Will you give it a go?”

“I’ll take it if you want me to, but it won’t make them go away. They’re not hallucinations. They’re ghosts. I see them everywhere. I hear them.”

“Jennifer—”

“I understand your doubt. You’re a man of science. You don’t see the oxygen molecules in the air, but you know they’re there.”

“Oxygen molecules are real, Jennifer. They can be seen. Not

with the naked eye perhaps, but—"

"They surround you, and yet you never notice, never see them. What if there's more you don't see?"

I caught the eye of a nurse that I vaguely recognized as she walked by.

"What is it, Doctor?"

"Can you escort Miss Carlton back to her room down on two south? I'm going to be discharging her shortly and she wants to start gathering her belongs."

"I can take her," volunteered Will.

"I'd like to speak to you for a moment if you don't mind."

"Not at all."

"Follow me."

Will followed me down the hall and into the doctors' lounge.

"You won't help her by feeding into her delusions," I told him as soon as the door closed.

Will crossed his arms in front of his chest. "What if it's not a delusion?"

"You want to help your sister? Then try to orient her to reality."

Will sat down on the sofa and looked me in the eye. "I'm taking her home. I'll make sure she gets the medications and I'll stop validating her sightings."

"I'll call down a discharge order and the prescription. If you need me, call my service. Otherwise I'll see her in my office at the regular time next week."

Will stood up. He reached into his breast pocket, pulled out his business card and handed it to me. "I wager we'll be seeing one another before next week," he said. Then he was gone.

I returned to Katherine's room and crawled back into the bed, stretching out alongside of her. She moved toward me, her body seeking out my warmth. "Katherine, love, time to wake up."

"It's your turn to feed the baby," she mumbled pushing back on me slightly, her bottom pressing up against my dick.

Katherine's breath hitched, then she released a moan that made me instantly hard. I was about to pull back, put some distance between us, when she slid one bare leg on top of mine, trapping me in place.

"Certainly hope you're dreaming about me, love," I whispered to the small section of back that peeked out from her hospital gown. I placed a kiss between her shoulder blades.

"Wes," she whispered.

I was already excited, but the simple sound of my name on her lips, the intimacy of the situation, excited me even more. The closeness of her, and the way her body seemed to call for mine, even in sleep. I found myself wanting to wrap my arm around her, to cup her breast in the palm of my hand.

"God, I want you."

Katherine stirred. I moved back, giving her room. She rolled over to face me, her eyes opening ever so slowly.

"Hi, beautiful."

She smiled. "Morning. How's the shoulder?"

"Fine. Well, better." I closed my eyes and tried to will my erection away. "How did you sleep?"

"I slept well. Are you sure you're okay?" She placed her hand casually on my stomach.

My eyes popped open.

"Yes, fine."

"You sure?"

She'd started to trace an invisible pattern around and below my belly button. I placed my free hand over hers. "That's not helping."

The corners of Katherine's mouth slipped into a satisfied smile. She shifted so that her lips barely grazed the shell of my ear and whispered, "That might depend on your point of view. What is it you want, Dr. Atherton?"

"You're teasing me!"

"Who, me?"

"Or, torturing me is more like it!"

"I am not torturing you. You big baby."

"No?" I took her hand in mine and slid it down to cup my cock. "Look what you've done. What do you expect me to do with—"

My brain was entirely short circuited by a playful squeeze.

"You want me."

"Very much," I admitted. "Do you want me?"

"Yes." She licked her lips. "Yes, I want you."

"I was so afraid that you would regret it, agreeing to come home with me." I lifted her hand and held it to my heart.

"You promised me I wouldn't. I'm going to hold you to that."

"Demanding one, you are!"

"Whatever will you do with me?"

"Do with you? Let me assure you, I've got plans for you, Miss Lawson. Great. Big. Plans."

Charles opened the door as we walked up.

"Let me take that, sir." He reached for Katherine's suitcase. "I'll unpack for Miss Lawson. May I fix you a drink? Dinner is almost ready."

"Dinner?" I followed Charles into the living room.

"Yes, sir. I assumed you'd prefer to dine in this evening." He walked over to the bar where there were two crystal glasses sitting on a small silver tray. Then he picked up the bottle of scotch and began to pour. "I have an assortment of juices and soft drinks for Miss Lawson, decaffeinated, of course."

"Water will be fine," said Katherine. She was standing in front of the large fireplace that dominated the far wall, staring at the painting hanging above the rich mahogany mantel. Undoubtedly, she'd seen replicas of it before.

"My mother," I said. "It was the first time she ever posed for him."

"It's beautiful." Katherine accepted a glass of water from Charles. "She was beautiful."

"It would seem that the Atherton men have a knack for finding beautiful women." I took a sip of my scotch. "The glow of your skin in the firelight is breathtaking."

Katherine looked back over her shoulder at me and smiled coyly. "Are you flirting with me?"

"Yes." I sat down on the black leather sofa opposite the fireplace. "Come and join me?"

"We hardly know one another. What am I doing here?" Katherine asked, sitting next to me.

"I don't know. It feels right, though, doesn't it?"

"Yes. It feels right."

"Are you hungry?"

"No. You?"

"Not yet."

"Think I could squeeze in a bath before dinner?" she asked, fluttering her eyelashes playfully.

"Excuse me, sir." Charles stood just outside the entrance to the living room.

"Yes?"

"Miss Lawson is unpacked. I wasn't sure what time you

wanted to dine. I prepared a simple Osso Bucco with risotto. It's in the warming drawer."

"I think we can take it from here, then. Miss Lawson is going to bathe before dinner. Thank you for everything."

"Will you need me in the morning?"

I shook my head. "Take the morning off as usual."

"Very well, sir."

Katherine stood up, walked over to the baby grand piano in the corner of the room, and gently brushed her fingers across the keys.

"Do you play?" I asked her.

"Me? No. Will you play something for me when your shoulder is better?"

Before she could protest I removed the sling and tossed it onto the sofa. I rotated my shoulder carefully, stretching it out. "It's almost there."

I crossed the hardwood floor and sat down on the piano bench. Katherine came to stand behind me, gently placing her hand on my wounded shoulder.

"You were trying to hold on to me," she said, as I began to play.

"Wish I'd done a better job of it."

"You play brilliantly." Katherine slid her hand from my shoulder to the nape of my neck.

I paused, then quietly turned to face her. "Come here." I spread my knees apart, opened my arms and pulled her into an embrace.

"Your arm is supposed to still be in the sling."

"Sod the sling. I've been dying to do this." I rested my forehead on her stomach. "Tell me you're not going back to Damien."

"Damien who?"

I looked up at her, searching out her eyes. "I'm on shaky ground here. I feel like I'm standing on the edge of this precipice and there's a part of me that just wants to jump, feet first, and damn the consequences."

"And the other part?"

"Well, he remembers what happened the last time I got burned. You know, that first step can be a doozy. And, if there's no one there to catch you..."

"Go on."

"I didn't expect this, us. Tell me you're not going back to Damien."

"I'm not going back to Damien." Katherine cupped the side of my face in the palm of her hand.

I released the breath I'd been holding and nodded. "Right then. I'm going to give you fair warning. I intend to keep you here."

"What are you going to do? Tie me up and hold me hostage?" She laughed.

"Would you like that?"

"No!" she protested a little too loudly. "Well, maybe. I've never tried it before."

"Don't make plans for Saturday afternoon, I want to take you someplace."

"Where?"

I stood up and reached for her hand so that I could lead her upstairs. "It's a surprise. Ready for that bath?"

Katherine followed me up the white marble staircase. "There are three bedrooms up here. I've turned one into an office of sorts. This is the guest room." I flipped on the light.

"Can I be honest with you about something?" she asked, still standing out in the hallway.

"Yes, of course."

"Okay. I'm thinking, guestroom? Why doesn't he want me in his room?"

"I didn't want to push, or presume." I took her face in my hands and kissed her softly on the lips. "I would much prefer you stay in my room. I'll move your things." I opened the closet door to find it essentially empty.

"What's wrong?"

"Seems Charles didn't put you in here after all."

Katherine headed down the hall. "This one?"

"The next one, on the left," he replied.

Katherine passed through the doorway and let out an audible gasp.

"What is it?"

My decidedly masculine room, the space where I spent most of my time, had been subtly transformed. Charles had scattered small candles on the shelving across from my bed that housed the television and stereo. There were more on the bedside tables, the side table next to the sofa where I stacked books and magazines. They were just about everywhere. All of them lit.

"I swear it didn't look like this when I left."

Katherine walked over to the antique four-poster and picked up the long red silk nightgown that Charles had laid out on top of the dark brown chenille duvet.

"Is this Charles's idea as well?"

"He picked it up, but the idea was mine. Not that the hospital gown wasn't attractive."

Katherine hugged the nightgown to her breast, and sighed. "Candles. Silk nightgowns. I think I'm falling in love with Charles."

"You bloody well better not be!" I unceremoniously pulled

the nightgown from her grasp.

"So, you're the jealous type? Good to know."

"Bath's in there."

Katherine walked through the door, then leaned back out. "It's a pretty big tub, plenty of room for two."

"Has anyone ever told you that you're a horrendous tease?"

"No."

"Well, you are!" I swatted her on the bum, then followed her into the bathroom. "I've strict orders to take care with your blood pressure for a bit longer."

"So, don't increase my blood pressure."

I tossed the nightgown over my shoulder, then rolled up my shirtsleeves. "Love, if I don't increase your blood pressure, I'm doing something drastically wrong."

There was a fresh arrangement of white tulips on the bathroom counter. "Charles went to a lot of trouble to make me feel comfortable. To make me feel at home."

I put my arms around her and pulled her close. "Maybe you are home," I said, leaning down to kiss her.

I woke with a start. It was still dark outside. The bedside clock told me it was nearly morning. Katherine was sound asleep. Last night, after her bath, we'd shared the home-cooked meal Charles had prepared. She'd insisted on loading the dishes into the dishwasher while I returned a few telephone calls. We'd climbed into bed with plans to watch a movie, only Katherine had promptly fallen asleep.

The outline of her face was barely visible on the pillow next to me. Quietly, I slipped out of the bed. The hardwood floors were cold, the air in the room colder still. I padded barefooted over to the bathroom, closed the door, then used the toilet.

Upon leaning over to flush, I noticed it, the sound of water trickling into the bath. I turned on the light to the shower stall to illuminate the space then checked the tub. It contained about a foot of water and a steady stream was continuing to trickle from the faucet.

After tightening down both taps, I reached into the tub, and untwisted the stopper. The water started to drain. Satisfied, I moved to the sink to wash my hands. Then, just as I was about to reach for the hand towel I heard the trickle again. The stopper had fallen back in place. This time I unscrewed it, pulling it out completely and setting it on the tub's edge.

My attention was drawn to the sound of movement just outside the door. Despite my efforts to be quiet it seemed that I'd woken Katherine. I opened the door, expecting to see her up and about. Only she wasn't, she was still in bed.

"What's wrong?" she asked, sitting up and shielding her eyes from the light. I flipped the switch, cloaking the room once again in darkness. Then I returned to the bed.

"Nothing, love. Just went to the loo. Go back to sleep."

"Okay," she replied, the tone of her voice indicating she was already drifting back off.

I pulled the covers up, snuggled back into them and closed my eyes. "Thought I heard you get up. Must have been a mouse."

She bolted upright, scaring the hell out of me. "You have mice? Can mice climb?"

I rolled over. "It's an old building. If there is a mouse, it's not going to bother you. It's more afraid of you than you are of it."

The sun was coming up now. In the dim light I could see her leaning over the edge of the bed, scanning the floor. "I doubt that," Katherine murmured.

I couldn't resist, I walked my fingers across the comforter

and ever so lightly brushed one against her forearm.

Katherine shrieked. It was a blood-curdling, girly scream. She spun to face me. I did my best to look innocent, apparently to no avail.

"Oh, you're in trouble now, mister!"

"Shoulder!"

Katherine squinted her eyes and began to mercilessly tickle me, lightly fingering my stomach and ribs. "So, stop moving your shoulder."

"Stop!" I laughed, fighting to still her hands. Finally I managed to grab her wrist. "Ow!" A twinge of pain shot through my shoulder.

Katherine climbed on top of me, and straddled my hips. It was a provocative posture and the ease in which she did it seemed to make it even more so. "You don't look like you're really in pain."

"Oh, but I am." I tilted my hips up, grinding my growing erection into her pussy. I let go of one wrist, then slowly moved her hair back over her shoulder.

Katherine closed her eyes.

My hand drifted, fingers leisurely trailing down the column of her neck and across her shoulder, to the thin strap of her gown.

"I think you should spend your entire day nursing me back to health."

"You think you'd like that?"

I hooked my finger under the silk and slid the strap from her shoulder, revealing the curve of her breast.

"I think I'd like that very much."

Just as one mouthwatering nipple popped into view the telephone rang.

"Bugger! I told the service to only call for emergencies."

"Whoever it is, fix them fast." She snatched the bedside phone from its cradle and handed it to me. "Here."

"Dr. Atherton... What?... No, it's all right. I imagine he was quite insistent. Put him through."

It was Damien.

"Will she see me?"

"It's rather early, Damien, the sun's barely up."

I glanced up at Katherine. She looked almost panicked.

"I'm worried about her. How is she?"

"Katherine's doing better." I reached for her hand and gave it an encouraging squeeze. "She was discharged from the hospital late yesterday."

"Thanks, I'll call Grant's."

There was little point to beating around the bush.

"She's staying with me. Let me check and see if she can come to the phone." I placed Damien on hold. "You want to talk to him?"

"No. Yes. I don't know. I should though, right? I mean, no sense putting it off. Except, well, as long as I put it off I don't have to...you know."

"Deal with it?"

"Exactly."

"You're babbling, love."

Katherine bit her lower lip. "Maybe I should do this in person? I don't want to hurt him, Wes."

"There's no getting around that, I'm afraid. Losing you is going to hurt. There's also the baby."

She placed her hand over her stomach and nodded. "I'll talk to him. Would you mind if I asked him to come here?"

"No, but he might prefer someplace more neutral. If he does, I can drop you somewhere and wait in the car."

I handed Katherine the phone. She climbed out of bed and took the call off hold.

"Damien? Yes, I'm here. I agree, we need to talk." She listened for a short while then added, "Sometimes love isn't enough."

I climbed out of bed and slipped on a robe.

"I'll start the coffee, give you some privacy," I whispered before heading for the door.

Katherine nodded.

"Oh, Damien, please don't cry. I'm all right. Really, I'm fine. Come over tonight and we'll talk. Yes, around seven will be fine. Wes!"

I turned to look back, my stomach a mass of knots.

"The address?"

I grabbed a pad of paper and hastily scribbled it down for her.

"We all make mistakes," I heard her say just before I rushed out.

One thing I knew for certain, I didn't want to be one of hers.

Chapter Ten

"Would you like some tea? Wes and I were just going to have some."

"I'd love some," Julia answered.

"Grant didn't come in?" I asked.

"He had some errands to run. Wow!" Julia walked to the center of the room then stepped back and studied the series of large still lifes that hung on the east wall. "Dupont, Clark, Baronkopf."

"Show off," Katherine teased.

"You have some beautiful pieces. Do you paint?" Julia asked me.

"No. I'm afraid that's one talent of my father's that I didn't inherit."

"Cups?"

"Over there, love."

Katherine lifted a cup and saucer out of the cabinet. When I turned back to Julia, she dropped it. The fine bone china shattered on impact, sending shards across the marble floor. Katherine crouched down and immediately began to gather up the broken pieces.

"Ouch!" One of the shards sliced open her fingertip. She stood up, then swayed.

"Kate!" Julia called out in alarm.

I managed to catch her and ease her into a chair.

"All right?"

"I think so, I just felt dizzy all of a sudden."

Julia sat down next to her. "Could the dizziness have to do with the head trauma? Should we be worried?"

"I don't think so," I assured her.

"Is this the first time it's happened, sweetie?"

"There was one other time, at the hospital. I'm fine, Mom." Katherine turned to me and asked, "It's normal, right? Nothing to be alarmed about?"

"How's the noggin?"

Katherine knocked on the side of her head. "Fine."

"How many fingers am I holding up?"

She rolled her eyes. "Three."

"You can see them clearly?"

"Clear as a bell."

"Any pain in your abdominal area?"

"Why would she have pain in her… You're pregnant?"

Katherine swallowed, then nodded.

"And the baby is Damien's?"

"Yes."

"He knows?"

"No, I just found out myself. I asked you over so I could tell you. Damien's going to come over tonight."

"Oh, sweetheart."

"I can't see myself making a life with him, Mom."

Suddenly I felt like an intruder. "I'll leave you two to chat. Leave the mess. I'll clean it up later."

"You don't have to leave." Katherine reached for my hand

then she turned back to face Julia. "I'm going to have this baby."

"Kate, have you really thought this through?" asked Julia, worry etched on her face.

"I'm trying to take this one step at a time."

"You are *not* taking this one step at a time." She shook her head. "I'm worried, Katherine. You two barely know one another. I was already afraid you've been rushing things with Wes. Now you're talking about having a baby?"

"Julia—"

"Don't get me wrong, Wes. I like you. Really, I do. And, I can see the passion between the two of you. I'm not so old that I can't remember what it's like, to feel a strong sexual attraction to someone."

Katherine blushed and let go of my hand.

"It can be intoxicating. It can tempt us into doing things we wouldn't normally do."

"I'm terribly sorry. Please, excuse the interruption."

It was Charles.

"It's quite all right, Charles," I assured him, feeling a bit grateful for it. "The water's boiled. How about we have the tea?"

"Allow me, sir." Charles walked over to the kettle and took over preparations.

"Charles! This is my mother, Julia Lawson," introduced Katherine.

"The pleasure is all mine, madam." Noticing the shattered cup on the floor Charles quickly retrieved the broom from the pantry. "Shall I serve in the living room?"

"We thought we'd just sit here. You can join us," suggested Katherine.

"That's not how it works, Miss Lawson, but thank you. How many will there be for dinner this evening?" Charles dumped the broken shards into the dustbin.

"Julia, can you stay?"

"George is expecting me back for dinner."

"Just the two of us."

The telephone rang and Charles answered it. "Atherton residence." After listening for a moment he turned to me. "It's your service, a Mr. William Carlton is on the line. Seems there's a bit of an emergency."

"Thanks for coming." Will opened the door and waved me inside. "I don't want to leave her alone for long," he explained.

We climbed the stairs quickly.

"Tell me again what happened?"

"Everything seemed fine. We were watching a movie. Halfway through we took a break and I ran downstairs to make some popcorn. When I returned Jennifer was lying in the tub, still clothed. The water was as cold as ice. She's completely non-responsive. I had to physically pull her out."

"Where is she now?"

"In bed."

The first thing I noticed upon walking into the bedroom was that the bed was empty. The covers were on the floor.

"Shit! Help me!" Will ran toward the bathroom. I entered a split second later. Jennifer was back in the tub, floating face up in the water, her lips slightly parted and almost blue from the cold. The palms of her hands were upturned, her eyes completely vacant.

I knelt in front of the tub. "Thought you said you'd removed the wet gown?"

Will reached for his sister.

"Hold on," I told him. "Slow down."

He took a deep breath and rubbed his hand over his face.

"I did. I had removed it. I left it in the sink. She must have put it back on. She's hypothermic. We've got to get her out of there."

"Jennifer? Look at me!" I commanded.

No response.

"I've never seen her like this!" Panic was creeping into Will's voice.

I reached in and lifted Jennifer's hand out of the cold water. Once her arm was held straight, at a ninety-degree angle to the surface of the water, I let go. Her arm slowly and fluidly returned to its prior position.

"Lay a towel out on the floor," I suggested. "Then we'll fish her out."

Will grabbed a long bath towel and laid it out in front of the tub.

"Her presentation is inconsistent. Her movements are still fluid. You saw how easily I repositioned her. She obviously climbed out of bed, put her wet gown back on and climbed in here." I stood up and reached for her feet.

Will hooked his arms under Jennifer's shoulders and together we lifted her out of the tub and onto the towel.

"Let's get this off of her." I moved her into a sitting position and lowered the straps of her gown. "Then we'll get her into bed. We need to get her body temperature back up."

Will raised Jennifer's hips so that I could remove the gown. Then he carried her, still unresponsive, to the bed.

"Now what?" asked Will. He picked the covers up off of the floor and arranged them over Jennifer.

"She's been eating and drinking today?" I rubbed my injured shoulder. The lift had taken a toll.

"Yes. She was perfectly fine earlier. I've never seen her like this, I tell you. Never," insisted Will. "Did you re-injure your shoulder?"

"It's all right." I sat down next to Jennifer, then picked up one of her hands, placing it between mine. "Jennifer, I want you to look at me. Can you do that? Look at me."

I watched as ever so slowly her eyes tracked over until they met mine. "That's it, stay with me now."

"She was so cold," whispered Jennifer, "so cold and wet. Don't be afraid of her, she only wants to help."

"Help with what?" asked Will.

"Help to save the baby." Jennifer rolled onto her side. "She doesn't understand. I have to make her understand. I'm so tired, so very tired."

"Just rest, love." Will pulled the blanket up, tucking it in around his sister. "Just sleep. It'll be all right. We'll figure this out. Dr. Atherton is here to help."

"Actually," whispered Jennifer before succumbing to sleep, "I believe we're still supposed to be helping him."

"Thanks for staying. I'm sorry I was gone longer than expected." Charles was sitting at the kitchen table, polishing a large silver tray. "Want a beer?"

"I work for you now. We shouldn't be drinking beer together."

I ignored him and pulled two from the fridge. "Is that mine?"

"Yes, and you've really let it go! You should let me do more. Look at the tarnish on this?" Charles held up the tray. "It's disgraceful!"

"I should be ashamed. Catch." I tossed him the beer. "I'm

sure that there's a special place in Hell for people like me, an especially nasty corner where they keep all of us that fail to polish the silver."

"*You* don't have to polish the silver." He opened the bottle and took a long swallow. "Sara Chase's assistant called. She hasn't received your response for the Black and White Ball. It's tomorrow night."

"Bugger! I forgot all about it."

"No worries. I responded for you and a guest. I imagine Miss Lawson will enjoy it. She'll need a dress, though; there wasn't anything appropriate in her luggage. I'll select something suitable and bring it 'round tomorrow. And I'll retrieve the car from storage. It's been a while. I hope it's still in working order."

"I have a car, Charles. I can drive us."

"Nonsense, this way you can enjoy the champagne. I'll pick you up at eight o'clock."

"Where's Katherine?"

"Sleeping."

"Sleeping?" I turned toward the kitchen clock. "Hasn't it just gone half past eight?"

"She was probably tired after all of the crying." Charles began to peel the label off of the bottle.

My stomach clenched and a sense of dread washed over me. "What happened?"

"Damien happened."

"Shit! I completely forgot. I'm an idiot!"

"Well, fortunately for you, he's an even bigger tosser. I may have overstepped a bit, but in your absence I had to use my best judgment."

"What did you do?"

"Showed him out the door, in a manner of speaking."

"Come on, let's have it."

"He was yelling at her, Wes. He called her a whore, then I heard a slap, and she cried out. I was concerned for her safety so I interrupted them."

"He hit her? He hit her and you just showed him to the door? What's the matter with you?"

"I didn't *just* show him to the door, I also quite possibly broke his nose. I probably should have said that I grabbed his head and shoved it into the door before opening it and letting him out. I think I might have done that twice actually."

"What did Katherine say during all of this?"

"Nothing. She was shaking like a leaf and on the verge of crying but she choked it back. After he left she merely said goodnight and walked upstairs. She puts up a strong front, that one. The blood cleaned up quite nicely though. So no worries on that front."

"I'm not worried about the soddin' paint and floors. I'm worried about Katherine."

"I went to check on her just a few minutes before you came in. Seems she finally cried herself to sleep. I could hear her through the door. Didn't want to disturb her. I'm sorry I lost my temper, but if you would have been here—"

"I'd no doubt have done the very same thing." I tossed my empty bottle in the rubbish, walked over to the door and as I pushed through it I said, "I'm glad you were here. Goodnight, Charles."

Chapter Eleven

The sun was bright. In the two days since Katherine had been released from the hospital it had vacillated between rain and clear blue skies.

We drove in companionable silence. Katherine was sitting quietly in the passenger's seat, staring out the window. She was dressed casually in a pair of jeans that she topped with a simple pink sweater and matching knitted cap. She wore her hair down so it loosely framed her face, accentuating her natural beauty.

We stopped at the light and she turned to look at me. "What?"

"You're bloody gorgeous, you know that?"

She brushed off the compliment. "I have holes in my head."

"That pout is going to be my undoing." I leaned toward her and licked her bottom lip with the tip of my tongue before lightly nibbling on it. And then I kissed her. I couldn't help myself. It was a soulful kiss, deep and full, slow and sensual, full of promise.

The car stalled as my foot came off the clutch, ending the kiss abruptly.

"Bugger!"

Katherine erupted in laughter.

"You think that's funny, do you?" I quickly restarted the

engine, then eased it back into gear.

Katherine nodded. “God, it feels good to laugh!” She placed her hand over her stomach.

I waited until the laughter died down. Then I asked her the question that had been on my mind all morning. “Did you tell him?”

“No.” She looked away. “I just couldn’t get the words out, could hardly get any words out. I need to though. I will. It just...didn’t go well.”

“Do you want to talk about it?”

“How much do you charge?”

“For you? No charge.” I pulled off to the side of the road.

Katherine sighed. “Wes, what are we doing?”

“What do you mean?”

“Is this a date? Are we dating?”

“Do you want to date?”

“You can’t answer my question with a question. It’s against the rules.”

“There are rules now? I think I missed the part where we voted to have rules.”

“So much in my life seems up in the air, uncertain. Maybe my mother’s right. Maybe we’re rushing things.”

I swallowed. “What does your heart tell you?”

“What does *your* heart tell *you*?”

“Okay. How’s this? I think what we have is the beginning of a relationship, maybe *the* relationship. The one I’ve been waiting for.” I paused and took a deep breath before taking her hand in mine and holding it over my heart. “Since I’ve met you I feel different. I feel more alive.”

“Really?”

“Really. Just thinking about kissing you? Well, it makes my

heart beat faster. I don't know exactly how this is going to turn out any more than you do. But I so want to find out. Don't you?"

She nodded. "Yes."

"But?" I turned off the car's engine and opened the door. Katherine stepped out and walked around to meet me.

"When I tell Damien, he's going to try even harder to get me to go back to him. He's going to pull out all the stops. It's going to make this, us, hard."

"That's all right. Let it get hard. Anything worth having—"

"I'm going to be having another man's baby, Wes. Can you really handle that? Are you sure you even want to?"

"I'm a right stubborn bastard. I think I inherited the trait from my dad. Never much cared about what other people thought. When I see something I want, I go after it, I fight for it, and I generally win. Honestly, love, from the moment I laid eyes on you—"

"You didn't know I was a package deal."

"I know now."

"What's in the trunk?" Katherine peered over my shoulder as I opened the boot.

"Just these." I held up a bouquet of white roses.

Smiling flirtatiously she stepped forward, ever so slightly batting her eyelashes and feigning a Southern accent. "Why, sir, are those for me?"

"Sorry to disappoint. That's where we're going." I pointed across the street. "I come to pay a visit every two weeks. Mum loved flowers."

"Would you prefer I wait in the car?"

I linked my arm with hers and escorted her across the street toward the large stone church. "Don't be silly. My parents would love to meet you."

"This is Highgate?" she asked as we approached the iron gate.

"You've been here before?"

"No, but I've seen pictures."

The grounds of the cemetery were green and lush with vegetation. I reached for Katherine's hand.

"There are some very famous people buried within these walls." I gestured toward a particular grave. "There's one of my very favorite stories."

"Tell me."

"Mrs. Elisabeth Rossetti, or as she was better known, Elisabeth Eleanor Siddall. She was a famous model."

I dusted off the top of a nearby headstone, and sat down.

"It says she died in 1862. She was still quite young."

"She was only nineteen when Walter Deverall, the artist, discovered her. He spotted her through the window of the hat shop where she was working. She captivated him completely."

"Sounds like you might have a thing for her yourself?"

"Wouldn't you like to know? Anyway, you've probably heard this all before."

Katherine shook her head. "No, go on."

"Deverall was part of a secret group of young artists called the pre-Raphaelite brotherhood. They were rebels of a sort. They took exception to what the Royal Academy thought was art. They painted what they wanted."

"And what was that?"

"They all wanted to paint her. Deverall, Sir John Everett Millais, Wesley Holman Hunt and Dante Gabriel Rossetti."

"Rossetti. She married him."

"They fell in love soon after she completed her most infamous pose. It was for a painting called *Ophelia*."

"I'm certain I've seen it."

"She and Rossetti lived together for a number of years. Eventually they married."

"They lived together? That must have caused quite a scandal!"

"They were, in many ways, quite unconventional. Sadly, it wasn't a happy marriage. Rossetti was unfaithful and often flaunted it. Lizzie was almost constantly ill and became profoundly depressed."

"It's no wonder."

"She fell pregnant, but the child came prematurely and was stillborn. After that, her depression became worse. She took laudanum, which was common in the day. She began to have episodes of psychosis. There were times she believed the child was actually alive, crying for her."

"How tragic!"

I stood up, went to Katherine and wrapped my arm around her shoulders.

"One day, Rossetti returned home to find her dying. She had overdosed on the laudanum. Some say she committed suicide. Others say it was an accidental overdose. Mostly, I think she just wanted the pain, the overwhelming sense of despair, to stop."

"Such a sad story." Katherine leaned in closer to me and rested her head on my shoulder.

"Come on, my parents are across the way in another section."

We walked in silence until their graves came into view.

"I miss them both," I said, laying the roses on top of the headstone. "She was hands down his favorite subject, you know. Seems he never tired of painting her."

I stepped back and smiled.

"What were you thinking just then?" asked Katherine.

"Reliving an old memory. I'd walked in on them once when they were working."

My mother laid in repose on the red velvet chaise, her pale blonde hair almost white in the glare of the late-afternoon sun.

"Don't move!" my father told her. "It's just the human body, son. You've seen me paint nudes before."

"Yes, but you're usually wearing clothes and that's Mum!"

"I'm not going to sell it. It's merely for my own pleasure. I paint her nude all the time like this. We find it very erotic."

"A son does not need to know these things. Why can't you be uptight, rigid and sexually repressed like most parents?"

"I tried it once." My father continued to work on the canvas. "I didn't like it."

"Sullivan!" Mum scolded.

"Hush, Margo! Don't move a muscle. Your position is perfect." My father sighed, then put down his brush and turned to face me.

"We love you, Wes. I know that we're not perfect. We've made some mistakes and we'll probably make more. I understand that in some ways I'm an embarrassment to you and I'm sorry about that, but this is who we are, son."

"You're sorry but you won't do anything about it?"

"Would therapy help?"

"Yes, that would be brilliant. You and Mum can talk to someone, a professional."

"I was thinking more along the lines of you, actually." My father stepped back and studied the canvas from a different angle. "Your mother and I seem quite happy. It appears you're the one that's a little distressed. Dammit! I'm losing my light! Was there something else?"

Katherine laughed. "No! That didn't really happen!"

I held up my right hand. "Swear to God!"

"How long have they been gone?"

"Dad's been dead just a bit over a year. Mum passed away two years before. He was never the same after that. She took a part of him with her. He stopped painting the day she died."

"She was his muse."

"I haven't been back to the house since he passed. It's just sitting there, all of the memories tucked safely inside."

"You own the house you grew up in, now?" asked Katherine, casually leaning against a neighboring headstone.

"Only child, I inherited everything. The house, the land, the money, the art and Charles, mustn't forget Charles."

"What do you mean?"

"Charles's father, Malcolm, had been our butler for years. Charles and I essentially grew up together. I became a doctor. Charles became a valet. When his father retired he took over as butler for my parents. My father didn't want Charles to be without work and he didn't want the house or I to be without Charles. I know he meant well."

"It's awkward though?"

"We were friends. I don't like having him serve me. In fact, I hate it."

"You aren't friends anymore?"

"We had a falling out. We hadn't spoken in months."

"What changed things?"

"You. What happened. Time is too short for pettiness, don't you think? I want to make amends."

A cold gust of air suddenly whipped through the graveyard. Katherine looked up toward the sky and I followed her gaze.

Big, dark rain clouds had moved in from nowhere, blotting out the sun.

"Looks like we'll have to call off our picnic."

"We were going to have a picnic?"

The sky above us opened up. Rain began to pour down, hard and heavy.

"Come on!" I shouted, removing my coat so that I could hold it out over the both of us.

Katherine didn't seem to care. She stood there, head tilted toward the sky, eyes closed, arms outstretched. It was as if she were welcoming the rain, calling to it, begging it to bless her. Her eyes flew open at the low ominous roll of distant thunder and instantly sought out mine.

"Let's go! We should make a run for it! You're already soaked through, you crazy bint!"

"Crazy, am I? Is that your professional opinion, Doctor?"

A streak of lightning flashed across the sky followed by a loud crack and a deep rumble. Katherine lifted her hands up and stood there, catching the water in her open palms.

"Oh, it's glorious! Did you see that, Wes? It's incredible. We never get rain like this in California!"

I watched as she turned in a circle, taking in the atmosphere from every direction. Her clothing was drenched, every speck of exposed flesh dripping wet. As she turned toward me she caught me staring and smiled. I stepped closer to her. Some tiny beads of water hung from her long dark lashes and as she blinked they fell gracefully onto her face, joining the rivulets of water that ran down her cheeks. She was glowing, glistening.

"You're radiant."

It's what attracted me to her in the first place, that inner light. Even in the midst of the darkest of storms, Katherine shone.

She began to walk backward toward the direction of the car.

“Are you coming?”

Was she kidding? I would have followed her anywhere at that moment.

We quickly made our way out of Highgate and down to the car. I unlocked the passenger door so Katherine could slide in first, then I made my way around to the driver’s side.

Another clap of thunder sounded as I slammed the door shut. Katherine’s eyes were fixed on the rear-view mirror, a look of shock on her face. I turned to look behind us and saw nothing.

“What is it? You’re suddenly as pale as a ghost.”

She shook her head. “Nothing. I thought I saw someone, a woman. One second she was there, the next she was gone.”

“She was probably making a dash for her car. Christ, you’re shaking like a leaf. Let me get the heat on.” I started the car and turned on the heater. “We’ll get you home and out of those wet clothes.”

The drive back took a bit longer due to the rain.

“You’ve been quiet. Lost in thought?” I asked as we pulled up in front of my house.

“A bit.”

“Race you to the door?”

“You’re on, pal!” Katherine released her seatbelt and sprang from the car.

“Not fair! That’s cheating!” I quickly jumped out of the car, grabbed the picnic basket from the backseat, then ran to catch up to her.

“I am victorious! Go me!”

"What's that?" I opened the door then lifted my hand to my ear. "The judges have ruled? Sorry, love, you've been disqualified for the false start back there."

"No way, mister!" Katherine looked down at the puddle rapidly forming in my entryway. "I'm drenched."

"Don't move."

I locked the front door, pulled off my boots and socks, then shed my coat, letting it all fall to the floor. There was another roar of distant thunder. Katherine's back was to the door. I stepped closer to her, then leaned down, lightly brushing my lips across hers.

"I swear, the rain tastes like wine on your lips," I whispered, resisting the urge to deepen the kiss.

I crouched down on one knee to remove her boots. Then as I climbed back to my feet, I pulled the T-shirt I'd been wearing up over my head. Before I had time to toss it onto the growing pile of clothes, Katherine boldly reached out for me, slipping a finger inside the waistband of my jeans and pulling me toward her.

She unfastened the buckle of my belt then paused, her hand at my zipper. I lifted my hand to cup the side of her face and searched out her eyes.

"Lift up your arms," I told her, gathering up the edge of her sweater and raising it. We lost eye contact for the briefest of moments as I pulled it over her head. Her cap came off as well. I carelessly tossed them aside.

"Wes."

I placed my hand around Katherine's neck and, ever so slowly, slid it down, gliding it over her damp flesh, heating it, warming her.

A sigh escaped her lips as I brushed my fingertips across the tops of the full mounds of her breasts.

"White lace." I reached down to palm one. "It looks so innocent, pure, virginal. I'm having horrible, nasty thoughts."

"Are you now?" she asked in a breathy voice as I lowered my hands to her zipper.

"Oh, yeah." I pulled her wet pants past her hips and watched them fall to the floor, then I quickly shed my own jeans. "You have no idea how much I want you right now."

I crushed my lips to hers in the heat of passion. The lace of her bra scratched against my chest as I pressed my body flush against hers. She parted her lips, and I slipped my tongue inside, boldly exploring the warm, wet cavern, holding nothing back.

Katherine released an intoxicating moan into my mouth that made me want her even more.

I slid my arm around her waist and then snaked my hand inside her matching lace knickers to caress her bottom. My kisses followed the path to her neck and I nibbled gently at her pulse point. She was trembling with need and in truth, so was I.

"Tell me you're cold."

"I wasn't shivering from the cold." She was flushed with arousal.

"I'm going to go get your robe. I've got to get some distance." Before I could step back, she reached down between us, the back of her hand brushing across the front of my boxers.

"Or what?"

I moved in close, pressing my rock-hard cock into the softness of her belly, my face just a hairsbreadth away from hers.

"I spontaneously combust from all this pent-up sexual tension."

Katherine's breath hitched.

"Or I throw you onto the cold marble floor and have my wicked way with you."

"I vote for—"

I placed my fingers over her mouth to silence her.

"I'll be right back with a robe. Then I'll start a fire and get the chill out of the air."

It took me only a few moments to dash up the stairs, put on a dry pair of jeans and grab the robe I'd promised.

I returned to find Katherine in the living room. She was bending over to turn on a lamp, her back to me.

"Here you go, love." I held the robe out, behind her. Its hem brushed up against the calves of her legs.

When it did, Katherine let out a terrified scream. She spun around and her scream rippled, echoing throughout the room.

"Christ!"

"Sorry, you startled me," she gasped placing her hand over her heart, trying to catch her breath.

"Didn't mean to. Here, slip this on." I held out the robe. She wasn't moving. "Katherine?"

She was looking past me, over my shoulder. I turned. She was staring at the large mirror that hung on the wall in the entryway.

"What is it?"

"Nothing. It's..."

"Yes?"

"It's nothing."

We were stretched out on the floor of the living room in front of the fireplace on a blanket, the remains of our picnic still spread out before us.

"Biggest childhood fear?" I asked her.

"That my parents would divorce. They fought a lot. It happened by the way. They were divorced before my father died. You?"

"That I would grow up and that my parents would remain children. It happened too, by the way." I rolled onto my back.

"Liberal or conservative?" she asked.

"Liberal."

"Me too! But, wait, you can't be liberal, you have too much money."

"Right. So I can afford to be liberal."

"How many women have you slept with?"

"How many what? How would I know?" I laughed.

Katherine didn't look amused.

I quickly sobered. "Oh, come on. It's not like I've kept a list, love. Do you remember every bloke you've ever shagged?"

"There's just been Damien."

From the moment I'd first met her, I knew she was younger than me. And I knew that she and Damien had been high-school sweethearts. It stood to reason that he'd have been her only lover, yet the simple fact caught me off guard.

She turned away and shook her head. "I must seem so immature to you, so naïve. I'm just finishing my masters program. You have a house, an established career. You're a doctor. That means lots of years of school."

"So?"

"So, you've probably had hundreds of lovers. A world of experience."

I smiled. "I'm pretty sure it hasn't been hundreds." I reached for her chin and gently guided her head back until she faced me once again. "How old are you?"

She swallowed. "Twenty-four."

"I'm thirty-five. Does it matter?"

She shook her head. "It's not the age difference."

"It's all the women you imagine I've been with."

"I don't want to disappoint you like I..."

"Like you what?"

"This wasn't the first time Damien cheated on me, Wes." The confession was spoken so quietly, it was barely audible.

"Maybe not. But it was the last. You're not going to disappoint me."

"How do you know?"

I leaned forward and kissed her with all the passion that she made me feel. Katherine's lips parted and my tongue slipped inside the warmth of her mouth to tangle with hers. I eased her down onto the blanket, rolling on top of her. Spontaneously her legs separated and my hips dropped between them. I was hard and I knew beyond a shadow of a doubt that she could feel it. Slowly, I pulled back from the kiss.

"Any more questions?"

"Favorite color?" she asked, almost breathless.

"Green. The color of your eyes."

A bell chimed once, then I heard the sound of the front door opening and closing.

"Be right back." I climbed to my feet just as Charles came around the corner.

"Sorry I didn't have a chance to bring this 'round sooner. The car needed a bit of work." He had a long garment bag draped over one arm.

"I completely forgot," I confessed, suddenly remembering the party we'd discussed the night before. "Perhaps we should skip it. I haven't even mentioned it to Katherine."

"Well, mention it," said Charles.

"Tonight's the annual Black and White Ball. It's a big charity bash," I started to explain.

"You should go. Really. Don't stay home on my account."

"I responded for you as well, Miss Lawson," interjected Charles.

Katherine shook her head vehemently. "I don't have anything to wear that's even remotely appropriate."

Charles held up the garment bag. "Yes, you do. I'll ready your bath and lay out your dress."

"You bought me a dress?"

"Technically, Dr. Atherton purchased the dress. I hope you are pleased."

"We don't have to go if you aren't feeling up to it."

Charles held up the bag. "It's Chase Couture."

"Get out!" gasped Katherine. She climbed to her feet, excitement evident on her face. "Really?"

Charles nodded. "Really. I'll lay your things out in the guestroom, sir. That way Miss Lawson can get ready in private and make a grand entrance."

The decision was made.

Chapter Twelve

"Stop fussing. Your tie is perfect," scolded Charles.

"It may look perfect, but it's choking me." I studied my reflection in the grand entryway mirror. "Yes, it seems the poor man suffocated to death. But the knot was tied rather well, don't you think?" I mocked.

"Oh! Very well, come here." Charles waved me over.

I turned toward him and froze. "Never mind."

"What? Now you can breathe just fine?"

"No, actually, I believe Miss Lawson has completely taken my breath away."

"I'll start the car and wait for you, sir. Take your time. There's champagne in the living room."

"What?" asked Katherine. She'd stopped halfway down the staircase. Her blonde hair had been combed back into a sleek French twist. The long sleeveless gown was of a thick black matte jersey that hugged her every curve. She wore opera-length black gloves and no jewelry. The neckline in the front was modest, conservative.

"Oh, you've got a little..." I pointed toward my own front teeth.

"Oh my God! Where? That is so me! I should have known I'd never pull this off!" Katherine picked up the skirt of her black gown and rushed down the remaining stairs so she could check her teeth in the mirror.

At the first glimpse of her back I became completely undone. Her dress was essentially backless and it dipped low, dangerously low. Without thought I reached out and traced the length of her spine with my index finger. "You're perfect, love."

"Why did you do that?" demanded Katherine, her tone sounding a bit angry, maybe even hurt. "Do you have any idea how nervous I am?"

"You are without a doubt going to be the most beautiful woman there. You look exquisite. You are exquisite. You have nothing to be nervous about." I lifted her hand to my lips and kissed her fingertips.

"Really?" Her anger was quickly melting.

"Really. But something is missing." I picked up the velvet box that was on the entry table, opened it and took out an earring. "Allow me." I clipped it onto her left lobe.

"What?" she asked spinning around to look in the mirror. "Oh!"

She leaned in to take a closer look. The long, exotic earrings were made of gold and encrusted with tiny seed pearls and bright green stones.

"Hold still, there's another. There."

"Please tell me you didn't buy these for me, Wes. They're too extravagant."

Charles had purchased a black velvet wrap to go with the gown. He'd left it hanging over the banister of the staircase. I retrieved it.

"They were my mother's. My father gave them to her. When they initially met my father was a struggling artist. After his first successful show in Paris he had them made."

Katherine turned around and I draped the wrap over her shoulders, then placed a soft kiss behind her ear. "Pearls and peridot. The moon and the sun. During the Middle Ages, people wore peridot to gain divine inspiration."

"She was his."

"Yes. Can I tempt you with a toast?" I walked into the living room and set to work on the cork.

"I really shouldn't. Pregnant."

I turned the label around and showed it to Katherine. "Non-alcoholic. Charles is nothing if not thorough."

"What shall we toast to?" Katherine raised her glass.

"To taking chances?"

Katherine nodded, touching the side of her glass to mine before taking a sip. "Blech!"

"It's bloody awful!" I laughed.

"Tastes like bad cider."

We set our glasses down.

"Ready for our date?" I offered her my arm.

"Date? This is not a date," she protested, shaking her head just like she had that first night we were out.

"It's not?"

"No!" she insisted.

I opened the front door.

Katherine gathered the wrap around her shoulders, then smiled up at me. Rain blew into the entryway. It was cold and still pouring outside, but despite that, suddenly I felt warm inside.

"*This* is much more than a date," she said. "It's a very special beginning."

I popped open the large umbrella Charles had left to shield Katherine and myself, then we ran for the car. Charles was waiting for us and opened the car door as we approached the old 1951 Silver Wraith Rolls-Royce my father had loved so much. As soon as we were safely inside Charles took a seat behind the wheel.

"Wait a moment." I leaned forward, peering out into the night.

"What is it, sir?"

It was Damien, standing out in the rain across from the house.

"I don't bloody believe it! Stay here, I'll be right back."

"Let me, sir," suggested Charles, following my gaze.

"No. I'll take care of it." I stepped out of the car and popped open the umbrella. Swiftly, I crossed the street, dodging the larger puddles and stepping up to the curb.

"Rough night to be out, mate." I lifted the umbrella a bit, offering Damien some shelter from the rain. "How's the nose?"

"Broken."

He'd yet to make eye contact with me and his voice was empty, devoid of any emotion. I could smell the alcohol on his breath. He wasn't wearing an overcoat, he had no umbrella and his clothes were soaked through. He seemed oblivious to the cold or the pouring rain for that matter. He just stood there, staring, his eyes haunted, his face etched with pain.

"What are you doing here, Damien?"

"Just needed to know it was real," he said, slowly turning to look at me. "It's true, isn't it? It doesn't matter what I do. Neither one of us will have her. Not you. Not me."

"Damien, it seems you've been drinking."

"Of course I've been drinking! Wouldn't you be? First I lose Katherine, and then he shows up. He made me watch it over and over again."

"Watch what?"

"No matter what I do, the end is always the same! I can't change it. It's hopeless. There's no choice, really. The baby is going to die."

Damien turned to walk away, but I reached for his arm. "Wait! What baby? What are you talking about?"

"My baby." A bolt of lightning streaked across the sky casting a momentary glow around us.

I held fast onto Damien's arm, took a steadying breath and waited for the loud roll of thunder that followed to subside.

He looked suspiciously over his shoulder, then leaned forward and whispered, "Is he still following me? Do you see him?"

"Who?"

"Him!" Damien looked up into the night sky; he was almost frantic. "He's found me. He said he'd always find me. His face may look human, but he's not. He's up there now, taunting us, laughing! Can't you hear?"

"I don't hear anything, Damien. Nothing but the rain and the thunder."

He sounded psychotic. Just as I was about to suggest we step inside he pulled away from me. Suddenly he was calm, collected.

"I need to know you're going to take care of her, Wes. Can you promise me that? Tell her I'm sorry for everything I've done, for being weak. I don't think I'm gonna make it through this."

"Damien, are you thinking about hurting yourself?"

"No. I may be a lot of things, but I'm not a coward."

"Let me call you a taxi," I offered, escorting him across the street and through the gate surrounding my house. "I'll call you tomorrow. We'll talk, okay?"

Damien nodded.

"Go stand under cover." I pointed to the awning over the doorway. "I'll call you a taxi. No sense standing out here in the rain."

Silently he began to walk toward the steps.

"And stay away from the booze. Go back to your hotel and sleep this off." I pulled the gate closed, then headed back toward the car.

"Hell is naked before him, and destruction hath no covering," Damien shouted out.

I turned back around. He was standing in the middle of the walkway, focused again on the sky, the rain once more pouring down on him.

He's not my responsibility, I said to myself. But it felt like he was. He was hurting and I was in part to blame for that. I pushed the feeling aside and climbed back into the car.

"What is it? What's wrong? Why is he just standing out there in the rain?"

"Why am I completely surrounded by crazy people?" I pulled out my mobile and dialed a local taxi service.

"That's easy, because you're a psychiatrist. You're probably like a magnet for the insane."

I shot Katherine a sideways glance, then held my hand up while I placed the order for the taxi. When I finished I turned to face her.

"You knew this was going to be hard. He's devastated that he lost you. And to make matters worse, he's completely pissed."

"He's angry."

"Probably, but what I meant was that he's drunk, love. Look, the taxi's coming. Let's go, Charles. We're going to be late."

"What did Damien say?"

"Nothing really."

As I watched the raindrops hit the window and slide down, a sense of guilt and betrayal washed over me. I had just out and out lied.

We drove on in silence. A few seconds passed.

"Raise the screen, Charles."

The privacy screen ascended.

"He said things, lots of things that didn't make any sense. But he said something that frightened me."

"What?"

I found myself avoiding eye contact. I didn't want to alarm her, but I didn't want to deceive her either. You can't build a lasting relationship on a foundation of lies and deception.

"It's silly, really. It can't be of any consequence."

"Wes?"

I interlaced my fingers with hers. "He said that the baby is going to die. His baby."

"He actually said that? Are you sure?"

"Positive. Are you sure you didn't say something to him about the baby? Or, maybe you called someone back home who might have said something?"

Katherine suddenly looked exceedingly pale. "I need some air."

I quickly rolled down each of our windows a tad. The cold night air rushed in. It was both bracing and soothing. Katherine took in several deep breaths, then shook her head.

"No. Not a soul. The only other person who knows is Mom. She wouldn't say anything, she's furious with him." Katherine placed her left hand protectively over her stomach. "This just doesn't add up. I've known Damien for a really long time, Wes. I've never thought of him as a violent man. I can't imagine he'd do anything to hurt the baby."

"Could just be the liquor talking." I waited a moment. I didn't want to press, but I had to know. "Charles said he slapped you last night. Sometimes, people act uncharacteristically when they're under stress."

"He's a commercial pilot, Wes. Before that he flew fighter jets for the Marine Corps, F-18's. I don't think I've ever seen Damien drunk. He's steady and dependable. Well, except for the cheating. He's one of those guys who thrives on pressure."

I looked at her and carefully chose my next words. "Has he ever hit you or threatened you before?"

"No. Never."

"Has he ever hurt anyone that you know of?"

Katherine shook her head. "Not that I can think of. Do you really think he knows about the baby and that he might try to hurt it, or me?"

"I don't know what to think at this point. I know one thing, though. After he's had a chance to sober up, I'm gonna ask him some questions. Meanwhile, I don't want you to be alone. He knows where we live. Promise me you won't be stubborn about this?"

"I won't be stubborn about this," promised Katherine. "But you live there, Wes. I'm just a guest."

Charles rapped on the window and it made me jump. I hadn't even realized the car had stopped. I certainly hadn't heard Charles get out. I swallowed down any retort and instead reached for the handle of the car and pushed the door open.

I'm just a guest.

The words rang in my ear. Hadn't I told her I wasn't running away? I reached into the car for Katherine's hand and helped her out. Charles escorted the two of us to the large porte cochere before turning back to pull the car off to the side drive.

We walked to the door, Katherine's hand resting comfortably on my upper arm. As we approached the entry, I could hear the music and laughter from within. There were other couples filtering in at the same time, announcing their names to the doormen. “Atherton,” I said.

“Ah, yes. Dr. Wesley Atherton and guest,” confirmed the doorman.

“Actually, this is Miss Katherine Lawson, the woman in my life.” I lifted her hand to my lips, kissed her fingertips then escorted her through the front door.

“Do you think I’m ridiculous?”

“No, I think you’re wonderful. Let’s make it an early night. I want to take you home and show you something really important.” I lifted two glasses of champagne from a tray as it went by and handed one to Katherine. “We’ll find some sparkling water to fill it. Promise.”

“What is this really important thing you’re going to show me?” She stepped closer to me, searching my eyes.

I leaned down and whispered in her ear, “I’m gonna show you just how much you mean to me, Miss Lawson.”

“Wes! There you are. Did you get my message?”

I pulled out my mobile and checked the display.

“I left it on your office voicemail.”

“Oh, no. I haven’t checked my voicemail. Bernie! Let me introduce you. Bernard Friedman, this is Miss Katherine Lawson. We’re on a holiday of sorts this weekend.” I wrapped my arm around Katherine’s waist. “I’m only answering emergency calls.”

“The board met last night, Wes. You’ve been nominated for Medical Director. Once more, it seemed pretty clear that if you’re willing to accept, the job is yours. Congratulations!”

“What?” I was gobsmacked.

“Congratulations?” Reese walked up with a nervous Laura in tow. It was clear Reese had had more than her share to drink; she’d probably started even before the party. The dress she’d chosen was daring, even for her, a deep red with a plunging neckline that showed off her ample breasts, and a slit on either side that flashed plenty of leg. She reached out and placed her hand on my forearm. "So, you're already sharing the news, huh? Most couples wait a few months, to make sure the sprog's really gonna stick. But, you've never been patient, have you, Wes?"

Katherine blushed. Suddenly all eyes were on her.

"Cat got your tongue?" asked Reese, reaching for the lapel of my jacket.

Katherine grasped her wrist. "That's a lovely ring you have." She lowered Reese's hand and studied it closer.

Reese tossed her hair back over her shoulder and swallowed down the last of her martini. "It was a present," she said, haughtily, "from Wes."

"We were actually congratulating Wes on his Medical Director nomination," said Bernie.

"Oh." Reese looked at Katherine with an expression of feigned innocence. "I guess I've made a bit of a slip-up, haven't I?"

"Well, you've got all sorts of things to celebrate tonight!" said Bernie. "No sense in pretending we didn't hear, is there?"

"No, I suppose there isn't," said Katherine.

"Mind if I steal her for a dance, Wes? I promise to return her safe and sound."

"Just don't let any other blokes cut in. Her next dance is spoken for."

"I think I'll take you up on that cup of coffee you suggested earlier, Laura. I believe you're right. I've had a few too many martinis," admitted Reese.

Laura set her own glass down on a nearby table. "I'm sure I can find you one. One cup of coffee coming right up."

As soon as she was gone Reese relieved me of Katherine's

glass of champagne and quickly drained it. “Take me out to the garden.” Reese stepped closer to me and snaked her hand around my waist.

“That’s not going to happen.”

I spied Jennifer weaving her way through the crowd toward us. I was surprised to see her there.

“Jennifer?”

“You’re looking devastatingly handsome tonight, Dr. Atherton.”

She turned her attention to Reese. “I don’t believe we’ve met. I’m Jennifer Carlton.”

“Jennifer this is Dr. Wallace.”

“What a lovely dress!” Jennifer leaned close to Reese. “You’ve just got a little…” She discreetly swiped her knuckle across the underside of her nose.

It was only then that I noticed the minute trace of white powder at the edge of Reese’s left nostril.

“You really should be more careful,” Jennifer added in a hushed whisper.

Reese glanced at me, then wiped at her nose.

“If you’ll excuse me. I must borrow the good doctor for a minute or two.” Jennifer hooked her arm through mine and led me over toward the bar. “Let’s get a drink, shall we? You’re going to need it.”

Chapter Thirteen

"I'm surprised to see you here tonight. How are you feeling?"

"I'm fine. I came with Will. He recently revamped the security for the entire grounds. I've managed to lose track of him, but that's not important, it's you I came to see."

"How did you know I was going to be here?"

"Elisabeth told me. She's been trying to reach you."

"Elisabeth Cramer?" I asked scanning the room for my old school chum.

"She didn't tell me her last name. I don't think she's here. At least I haven't seen her."

"About your height, glasses, short, dark hair?"

"No. That's not right."

I frowned. "Well, what did she look like?"

"My height and build, yes, but this one has long, auburn hair. Sometimes she's quite clear and then there are other times when she—"

"Seems a bit confused?" I finished. "Does she want to see me as a patient?"

"What? No. Not confused, transparent or is it translucent? Anyways, sometimes you can see through her. You know who she is. She used to live in your house. It was a long time ago.

But you dreamt of her, painted her that summer when you were fifteen. Well, not actually her, she was long dead, but flattered nonetheless."

Jennifer signaled the barman. "One scotch and a club soda, please."

I stepped back and accepted the scotch. On the surface she appeared completely intact. Her hair was impeccably coiffed, a beautiful array of Victorian-like curls piled high on her head. She wore a lovely white chiffon gown. It was strapless, fitted through the bodice, and then fanned out into a long, flowing skirt. Her makeup was subtle. Her eyes clear and focused. Her speech, steady.

"Dr. Wallace, she meant something to you once. I'm sorry that it has to be this way."

"What way?"

"She's in a lot of pain. She's lonely. She's not going to find happiness in this life. Don't be sad, there's nothing you can do to save her. If not this, now, then it's going to happen next week. Car crash. At least this way it will count for something. It'll distract him for a bit. Give us time to think, plan."

"Plan?"

"She's doing cocaine again by the way," she said as she turned her head slowly and narrowed her eyes. "And she's flirting with Stanley!" hissed Jennifer. "I must go rescue him. Remember what I said, it's important."

"What part?" My head was spinning from attempting to track our conversation. "Perhaps Will should—"

"For heaven's sake, must I spell everything out?" she asked in a hushed whisper. "Keep Katherine out of the water! Now, go about enjoying the party. Mingle! Look natural! Don't let on that you know. And for God's sake, stay on your toes."

"Right." I knocked back the scotch.

"You all right?" It was Will. He stepped up to the bar and ordered a drink.

"Do me a favor, will you?"

"Anything for you, Wes."

I leaned closer to him and quietly said, "I don't know how you're getting your information. But I insist that you stop."

"Stop what exactly?"

"Digging into my personal life and sharing what you find with Jennifer. It's completely inappropriate and she's incorporating what you're telling her into her delusions."

Will shook his head. "I haven't told Jennifer a thing. I looked into your background, yes. But only after Jennifer started seeing you."

"You didn't tell her about Katherine being pregnant?"

"No."

"Did you tell her about Reese and I?"

"Dr. Wallace? No."

"What about Elisabeth Siddall?"

"Who?"

I set my glass down on the bar and repeated, "Elisabeth Siddall."

Will scratched the back of his head. "I'm drawing a complete blank."

I caught the barman's eye and pointed to my now-empty glass. "She's the one I painted that summer, when I was fifteen."

"Oh, right. The redhead who was the object of all of your upper-school masturbatory fantasies," nodded Will.

"According to who?"

"Your therapist at the time."

I pinched the bridge of my nose. A headache was forming.

"You accessed my therapy notes?"

"Let's just say they fell into my lap. Interesting parents, by the way."

"You expect me to believe that you didn't share any of this with Jennifer?"

"I didn't. I give you my word. Besides, I don't have to share anything with her. I told you. She just knows things."

"Shit!"

"What?"

"She's talking to Katherine."

They stepped out onto the veranda and I lost sight of them.

"Excuse me, I think I better go find my date."

Just then Reese stumbled by and grabbed my arse. "I'll be waiting in the garden," she said a bit too loudly.

Carlton's eyebrows shot up.

"I wasn't heading out to meet her in the garden."

"Of course not."

"I'm going to find Katherine," I said loud enough that Reese would be able to hear.

"Right."

"Why am I even explaining this to you?"

"No idea, mate."

It took me a few minutes to cross the ballroom. When I stepped out onto the veranda I noticed that the rain had stopped. The air was crisp and cool. I moved to the edge of the railing, assuming I'd find Katherine in the courtyard below.

A scream pierced the night air. My eyes were immediately drawn to the large fountain that sat out in the courtyard. Reese stood in the middle of it, her dress gathered up around her thighs, laughing. "Come on in, Laura, the water's fine!" Katherine was running toward them, the long skirt of her gown grasped in her hand.

The fountain was approximately ten feet in diameter; the perimeter of the base was made so that people could sit along the edge. In the center was a large flat marble surface with water sheeting down. By the time Katherine approached, Laura had already slipped off her shoes, lifted her light pink A-line skirt and was kneeling on the edge trying to talk sense into Reese.

"Reese! Come on out of there. What are you doing? This is crazy," Laura called out to her.

"Laura!" laughed Reese. "The fish! They tickle! Look, there are hundreds of them." As she leaned forward to inspect them more closely she lost her balance. "Oomph!"

"Reese! I am so regretting being your friend right now."

"You're not my friend, Laura. I don't have any friends," she said bitterly as she tried to get up. "Well, don't just stand there! Help me! My dress is caught on something, a drain maybe."

Jennifer stood on the staircase. She turned and looked up at me. It was as if my world suddenly came to a screeching halt. Time stood still for a second as flashes of our conversation replayed through my mind. The wind outside picked up, blowing the loose leaves on the ground about my feet. Thunder rolled in the distance, a portent of more rain yet to come.

Will passed me by, racing down the stairs.

For a moment it was as if I were drowning, trying to move but struggling to push through the resistance of the water. I watched as Laura gathered her skirt and stepped into the fountain, first with her right foot and then her left. A sense of dread washed over me. Katherine had one knee on the bench and was extending her hand in an offer to help.

"Be careful the bottom is probably slippery. Hold onto my hand if you need to. Shoot!" Katherine looked down into the water.

"No!" I shouted. Sprinting down the stairs, I bolted toward them. "Katherine step back! Will! Grab her!" I yelled out, pointing to Laura.

There was a loud clap of thunder. A bolt of lightning streaked across the pitch-black sky, illuminating the courtyard. I watched in horror as the arc of lightning seemed to reach down toward the transformer that was located outside the garden gate. Sparks began to fly as one of the power lines detached, the wind carrying it down. Like a snake it slithered through the night air in search of its prey. I wrapped my arm around Katherine's waist, pulling her clear of its path. I watched over my shoulder as Will unceremoniously tugged Laura toward him, scooping her up into his arms and lifting her clear of the water.

"What are you doing?" Laura began to struggle against him, but her question was cut off by the scream behind her. She turned toward it, and then just as quickly turned back, burying her face in the chest of the man that held her, safely, in his arms.

"Oh, God!" cried Katherine turning away from the image, clinging to me.

"Wes!" shouted Eric. He ran down the stairs and pointed to a tray stand in the corner of the courtyard.

"Right!"

I quickly pushed the tray that held a variety of plates and glasses onto the ground and then smashed the stand against the side of the building, breaking off the wooden legs. I tossed one of the legs toward Eric as I ran back over to the fountain. Reese was now floating, facedown, near the edge, hundreds of lifeless goldfish and small koi surrounding her perfectly still body. "Try to get these under her arms. See if we can pull her out."

Sparks continued to fly and there was a large crackle. My

eyes were momentarily drawn to the large transformer. Just as I was about to turn my attention back to the task at hand it exploded, shrouding the entire house and grounds in darkness.

"The power's gone off! Help me get her out!" I tossed the wooden leg aside and reached into the water. "Laura, we need you!"

Eric reached in and helped me pull Reese out. "I saw an AED hanging on the wall outside of the kitchen. Laura?"

"Get it," she directed. Eric took off at a run. "And call 999!" Laura stripped off the cardigan she was wearing. "Wes, do we have a pulse?"

"I'm not getting one."

"Step aside. I could use more light." As if on cue, some of the lights flickered back on.

"There must be a back-up generator," I said.

Laura positioned Reese's body and began the rescue breathing.

After a couple of breaths she paused. There was no effect. "Beginning CPR," she announced, methodically following the familiar protocol. As she knelt over Reese's body and positioned her hands over her chest, Eric ran up.

"I've got it!" he said, setting the device onto the ground alongside the body.

"Give me the electrodes." Laura spread open the top of Reese's dress. "For Christ's sake, get these people out of here!" she added, stubbornly wiping the tears from her eyes.

A crowd had begun to form at the top of the stairs. Will walked toward them. "Please, everyone, give us some privacy. Please."

I watched, in shock, while Laura accepted the first electrode from Eric and positioned it about halfway between Reese's right nipple and collarbone. Laura picked up Reese's hand, removed her ring and handed it to me.

"I'm sorry, Wes."

I slowly turned to face Jennifer. Tears filled my eyes. I tried to stubbornly blink them away.

"She's not dead," I managed to choke out, my voice thick with emotion.

"Yes, she is," she said, looking several feet above Reese's body.

I shook my head, not wanting to believe it.

Jennifer stepped closer and reached for the lapel of my jacket. "She says not to worry. She doesn't want to come back. Living here for her was just about getting through the next moment, and the one after that. She's happy now, at peace."

"No."

"She needs you to take care of something."

Tears were now rolling down my cheeks. "What?" I asked.

"There's a dog. Now that she's gone she's afraid there will be no one to look after him."

I shook my head. "Reese doesn't have a dog."

"I need more light!" shouted Laura as she struggled to plug the pads into the connectors.

Someone handed me a flashlight. I stepped closer and lifted the light as high into the air as I could.

"That's it! That's good. Clear!" Laura pressed the button, delivering the first shock. "Damn! Nothing! Everyone, clear!" Again, nothing. "Continuing CPR. Eric, you do the breathing. We'll rotate after four. Where are the damned paramedics?"

I squeezed my fist around the ring. The conversations around me seemed to recede into the background. I closed my eyes and was flooded with memories.

"You're giving me a ring?" asked Reese. "Why? Doesn't that seem, I don't know, serious?"

"This is serious. I want to get married."

"What? Where the hell is this coming from? Wes, I admit it, we've got a good thing going here."

"But we could have more. I know I could love you, if only you'd let me. We could be a family, Reese."

"A family."

"I saw the test results this morning, after you left for work. I was returning a call and I needed a pen."

She rounded on me, furious. "You went through my things?"

"No, I didn't purposefully go through your things. Look, I don't want you to have to do this alone. I want to do this together."

Reese began to laugh as she got up, walked over to the liquor cabinet and pulled out a bottle of vodka. "What? Are you going to make an honest woman out of me, Wes? Do the right thing? And, here I thought chivalry was dead."

"Reese! Put that away. It's not good for the baby. You know that. We need to talk this through."

"There's nothing to talk about." Reese, knocked back a shot. "I got rid of it last week."

"What do you mean?"

She poured herself another drink. "I had an abortion."

"An abortion?"

"Oh, don't look at me like that!"

"You didn't think I'd want to know?"

"It was my decision. This doesn't have to change anything. The two of us have fun together. Come on. Let's go upstairs and play. Pretend you never saw those test results. We'll go on just like before, okay? What have we got to lose?"

I looked down and studied my shoes for a minute.

"Wes?"

"I can't believe you didn't even tell me."

"Good grief! It wasn't about you, Wes!"

I jumped to my feet, walked over to the sofa, grabbed my coat and quickly put it on. "It bloody well was about me. I can't do this anymore. How can you be so empty?"

Reese defiantly placed her hands on her hips and tossed her hair over her shoulder. "If we're not gonna fuck tonight, you might as well go. I'm not in this for the hearts and flowers."

"I feel sorry for you, Reese."

"Yeah? Well don't!" For a second she looked as if she were going to cry.

"You want to know what we've got to lose? Nothing. I know I've never had you, not really. But, I trusted you. Now, that's gone. And so am I."

"What? This is goodbye?"

"I won't be back. Take care of yourself, Reese."

"Don't you want your ring?"

"Keep it," I said before closing the door.

"Call it," said Eric quietly as he placed his hand on Laura's shoulder.

"No!" She repositioned her hands over Reese's chest.

"It's no use, Laura."

I felt as if I were going to suffocate, as if my heart were being squeezed. I flipped open my mobile and dialed Charles.

"I'm in the courtyard. I need you." I barely recognized the sound of my own voice.

"Wes? What is it?" he asked.

"Why did you have to get drunk! You stupid, stupid bitch!"

Laura began to scream at the lifeless form.

I didn't answer Charles. I just hung up and went to Laura. The instant my hand touched her shoulder she stood up and flew into my arms. The professional control was gone, stripped away. All that was left was a grieving friend. I didn't know what to say, so I said nothing. Instead I just held her and let her sob.

The ambulance pulled up, siren blaring. I vaguely heard Eric introduce himself and begin to give a report. Laura pulled back and managed to compose herself.

"Thanks. I'd better go talk to them," she said. Then she was off.

At some point I became aware that Katherine had slipped her hand inside of mine. I watched as the paramedics covered Reese's body. I dropped the ring into my coat pocket and I walked over to the fountain, Katherine's hand still in mine, and looked down into it.

"The earring fell in," Katherine said. "I was reaching for it and you stopped me. Why?"

I looked past Katherine. Jennifer was standing there, eyes on me. "You wouldn't believe me if I told you." I reached past the now-dead fish, retrieved the earring and handed it back to Katherine.

"You realize that if you hadn't stopped me—"

I held up my hand and shook my head. I couldn't bear to hear the words. There'd been too many close calls, too many deaths. And, I was beginning to believe, really believe, that Jennifer was right. There were going to be more.

"A dog?" I asked her.

Jennifer nodded. "You'll get on just fine."

It was raining again. Charles had discreetly lifted the

privacy screen. Katherine and I were riding in the backseat in silence. And it was a silence that had gone on for too long. I wanted desperately to explain, but the awkwardness of the situation kept me from it.

"You were lovers once?" Katherine finally asked, hesitantly.

I nodded, then turned to look out the window. Tears were falling now, and I didn't want her to see them.

The stubborn bint wouldn't let up. She gently turned my face back toward hers then kissed them away.

"Shh," she soothed, her fingers gently stroking the hair at the nape of my neck.

"I'm sorry."

The car came to a stop. I pushed Katherine away and managed to pull myself together before Charles opened the door.

"Charles, I'd like you to go back and drive Laura home," I told him, extending my hand to Katherine and helping her out of the car. "She was quite distraught. She shouldn't drive herself."

"Of course. I'll head back right away. Will there be anything else?" He escorted us to the front door, holding an umbrella over our heads.

"Tomorrow Katherine's family is coming for dinner."

"Very well, sir." Charles unlocked the door, held it open for us, then locked us safely inside.

The house was dark when we entered and I made no move to turn on any lights. The anonymity of it felt comforting. I went through the familiar motions of setting the alarm and hanging my coat up in the entry closet before wordlessly heading for the stairs. I'd gone up about halfway before realizing Katherine had yet to move.

"Are you coming?"

The light from the street bounced off the entry mirror, illuminating the outline of her body. Katherine shook her head and placed her hand over her heart. "I'm sorry. I don't know what to do, what to say."

"You don't need to say or do anything. Just come." I held my hand out to her. "Just be with me."

Katherine climbed the stairs, took my extended hand and let me lead her to the bedroom. Once inside I struck a match and lit a few candles. I then walked over to my dresser, pulled on the end of my bow tie and cursed. "Damn it! I can't get this knot out!"

"Let me."

Katherine walked over to me and gently pushed my hands aside.

"You don't need to coddle me," I protested, feeling weak and vulnerable and hating it.

"It's not coddling to help someone you care about when they're in need." She easily unfastened the knot, then slid the tie from around my neck.

"Do you?" I asked her, stilling her hands and searching out her eyes.

"Do I what?"

"Care. For me?"

Her brow furrowed. The question seemed to trouble her. "Yes, I thought you knew that, Wesley. I care very much."

I took her face in mine and leaned down, resting my forehead against hers, then I made my confession. "I was never in love with her, but she meant something to me. She should have meant more. She just... She wouldn't..." I pulled away.

"What?" She reached out and began to unbutton my shirt.

"Bare herself to me." I said it softly, looking her in the eye. "Let me see her. Let me know her. I needed that. I need that."

Katherine stepped back, reached under her arm and released the side zip of her dress, letting the fabric slip from her body to pool at her feet. Her breasts, now uncovered, beckoned to me in the flicker of the candlelight. I'd never seen such a beautiful canvas and was instantly awash with shame at my desire. It somehow seemed inappropriate. I turned away.

The sound of the mattress springs drew my eyes to the dresser mirror. I could see her clearly, sitting on the edge of the bed. She'd stepped out of her pumps and was sliding off her stockings.

"You don't have to..."

She stood up and came to me.

"Shh." Katherine hooked her fingertips in the top of her knickers, then slid them down the length of her long, graceful legs.

"Just come to bed, Wes," she whispered as she let her hair down and shook it out. I watched her unmake the bed, then crawl between the sheets. For a moment I wasn't sure what to do.

"Undress," she said. "Come to bed."

I removed my clothes. Taking my time. Folding them. Hanging them up. "I don't want your pity."

"You don't have it." She lifted up the edge of the sheet and patted the side of the mattress.

I climbed in alongside of her. "What do I have?"

"Me. You have me." Katherine reached up, slipped her hand around the back of my head and gave me a sweet and tender kiss.

The second her lips touched mine I felt like weeping. She was being completely giving, completely open. I rolled her onto her back and deepened the kiss, sweeping my tongue along her bottom lip. She invited me in then, surrendering herself to me, letting me take what I needed. I leisurely explored the inside of her mouth. The kiss was exquisite, almost painfully tender.

"You must think I'm a horrible monster, to want you, to need you like I do even now." My voice was filled with emotion, emotion that I didn't want to be embarrassed about.

"No," she whispered. "You're not a monster. You're a man." Katherine reached down, wrapped her hand around my cock and positioned it at her entrance. "Wes, you're a good man."

"I feel like I've been waiting forever for this moment and it's all wrong."

Katherine brushed the head of my cock along her already wet slit. "I want this. I want you. I want to feel you inside of me. That can't be wrong."

"Christ! You're so wet."

Katherine tilted her hips up in an invitation I couldn't resist. One smooth thrust was all it took. I'd never felt anything so exquisite. I was totally surrounded by her. Her arms were wrapped around my neck, her legs were wrapped around my hips, and her heart, it was almost as if her heart had somehow managed to wrap itself around my very soul.

I rested my forehead against hers and, after giving her a second to adjust I began to slowly thrust in and out of her. Repeating that timeless dance of mating, of coupling, of making love, of loving. As the realization crossed my mind I lost control, spilling much too soon inside of her.

"I'm sorry," I muttered, feeling like a prat. I began to pull out of her.

"Don't move," she said, wrapping her legs around me even more tightly. "You just stay right where you are."

"I can do better than that, really."

"There's not a doubt in my mind," she assured me. "And you'll have the opportunity. There will be lots of opportunities.

Right now, just let me be with you."

I closed my eyes and nodded. We held one another for a long time. How long, I wasn't sure. Eventually I started to fall asleep. I rolled off of her then and she let me, saying nothing. I pulled her close, spooning up behind her, my hand resting comfortably in the crook of her hip.

"Stay with me," I whispered.

"I'm not going anywhere."

"Promise?"

She placed her hand on top of mine. "Promise."

Chapter Fourteen

I couldn't sleep. I was way too preoccupied. After Katherine drifted off, I began to replay all of the things Jennifer and Will had said to me over the past few days. I had to admit the threads of truth were coming together, forming a macabre tapestry. As I lay in the darkness I wondered if, perhaps, I could have prevented Reese's death. But, that was absurd. It was just an accident. Wasn't it?

The knowledge that I could have easily lost Katherine and that the possibility of danger remained was haunting me. I resisted the urge to wake her, to tell her.

To tell her what? It seemed that everything was moving so bloody fast. If I were to be honest I'd admit that I'd felt off balance since the second I'd looked into her eyes that day in the carriage on the Tube. The carriage. Suddenly my life, like it, was careening out of control.

Frustrated, I finally gave up on the idea of sleeping, eased out of bed, put on my robe and walked down to the office to check my e-mail. The room was uncomfortably cold. I turned up the thermostat and booted up my computer. The monitor came to life, then it started to flicker.

"Don't die on me." I tapped the side and the screen went black. "Great."

I tried once more with the same results before padding downstairs. I picked up the basket of mail that had collected during the week, carried it to the kitchen, then made myself a pot of tea. I drank down the first cup while sorting through bills. That chore done, I retired to the living room, built a fire in the fireplace and curled up on the sofa with some journal articles that I'd put off reading for months. The hours passed quickly.

As the sun began to rise I stood up and stretched. "Figures. Now I'm starting to feel tired."

I moved over to the piano, pulled out the bench, sat down and began to rifle through a book of sheet music. My mind again drifted, inevitably, to Katherine. It had felt so wonderful, having her beneath me. I'd come embarrassingly quickly, but it was still good, still memorable.

I could feel my cock beginning to harden. I looked down. "Yeah, you better do better next time. Remember to give the lady a good seeing to and... Oh, God, I'm talking to my dick. It's official, I've become my father."

"Morning. Couldn't sleep?"

I looked over my shoulder. Katherine was standing in the doorway to the living room, with a throw wrapped tightly around her body. Her long blonde hair was tousled and her eyes were still heavy from sleep. She walked up to the piano and leaned on the gleaming black lacquer top.

"Had some thinking to do."

Katherine reached out and cupped the side of my face. I closed my eyes, then turned slightly, placing a kiss in the palm of her hand.

"Thank you for last night."

I looked up, surprised. "Seems I should be thanking you."

She walked over to the window, the morning light softly illuminating her in an almost ethereal glow. Katherine looked like something sent from heaven. I stood and moved behind her, brushing her hair over one shoulder, revealing her ear and neck. I bent down and kissed her tenderly.

"It's starting to snow," she murmured.

It was true. Outside, snowflakes were drifting gently toward the ground.

Katherine gathered the blanket more tightly around her. "Now there's something you don't see every day. Not where I come from."

"Doesn't it get boring with it always being the same perfect temperature day after day? Sunshine. Sunshine. Occasional early morning clouds followed by more sunshine?"

"Well…no."

"What would it take to convince you to stay here, in London?" I pulled back the blanket she'd wrapped around her and kissed her shoulder.

"What would it take to convince you to move to California?" she asked, tilting her head to the side, offering me better access.

"California, huh?" I nibbled on her earlobe. "Are you naked under there?"

I pulled her back against me, pressing my growing arousal into her bottom and rotating my hips. Without hesitation, she returned the pressure, making my cock harden even further.

"Possibly."

I slid my hand back up, my fingertips grazing the outline of her breast. I grabbed a fistful of her hair, wrapped it around my hand and pulled back gently. Katherine's chin arched up, exposing her neck, baring it for my pleasure. She was mine for the taking. She moaned as I began to nip at the soft, sensitive spot just behind her ear. "Drop the blanket," I commanded, my voice already rough with desire.

"I'm standing in front of the window."

I swept her up in my arms, walked the short distance to the

center of the living room, then set her back down on the area rug in front of the fireplace.

"Drop the blanket," I repeated slowly, looking steadily at her.

Katherine released her hold on the blanket, letting it slip to the floor.

"I want you. No, I need you." I reached out with my right hand and ran it down her neck, past her collarbone, and over her breasts and stomach. Then I slid both hands around her and began to knead and caress her bottom. "Is the fire behind you too hot?"

"No. It's nice. Warm."

"Step up onto the hearth." I guided her back a step, then up, never breaking eye contact. "That's a good girl, love."

I reached for her hands, placing one on either side of the mantle. "Hold on here, and here. Don't let go."

"What are you going to do?"

"I'm about to redeem myself," I promised before lowering my mouth to one breast and latching on, suckling voraciously while I palmed the other.

Katherine's breath hitched in surprise as I pulled on her with my mouth and tongue.

I moved from one breast to the other. "It feels so good," she gasped.

I couldn't help myself. I smiled, delighted by her sounds of obvious pleasure. After releasing her nipple I looked up at her.

"You know, they're just going to get more sensitive." I flicked my tongue over the hardened nub to illustrate the point.

"More sensitive?"

"Oh, yes. More sensitive. Rounder. Fuller. Mine."

"I think they're supposed to feed the baby," said Katherine, quietly. Her mood appeared to be shifting rapidly from aroused to self-conscious.

I dropped to my knees in front of her. "Learning to share is important," I said, somberly. "When the baby comes, I'll share. I promise."

"Wes!" Katherine's face turned crimson. She let go of the mantle and covered her breasts with her hands.

"Uh-uh-uh." I shook my head. "Hands back up where they belong."

I remembered then how much younger than me she was, how much less experienced. "Don't be embarrassed," I told her. "You're beautiful, so incredibly beautiful."

She swallowed, her expression uncertain.

"Open up for me." I placed my hands on her ankles, guiding her legs farther apart. "I have to taste you." I used my fingers to separate her folds then leaned down, my mouth watering in anticipation. "You're so wet."

"Wes, I..." She released her hold on the mantle and laced her fingers through my hair.

"You smell so delicious." I slowly dragged my tongue up the length of her wet slit, lapping up the generous amount of cream.

"Oh, God," Katherine moaned, her legs quivering. "I think you should stop."

Stop? I'd just gotten started. I looked up, my eyes locking on hers. "If you want me to stop, I will. But I don't want to stop."

"You don't?"

"No." I pulled back slightly. Using just the tip of my tongue, I teasingly flicked her now fully engorged clit. "You like that, you want more."

Her body was flushed and trembling in need. I dove back in, taking her swollen nubbin between my teeth, tugging on it gently. When I heard her gasp I latched my mouth onto her completely, sucking hungrily on the sensitive bundle of nerves. I could feel it as the evidence of her arousal poured out and onto my chin.

I slipped two fingers inside and began to slowly thrust them in and out of her sopping channel, stroking her slick walls. "Tell me what you want. Let me please you."

"I just want you."

"You have me, love."

"I want more of you," she admitted, the first wave of an orgasm approaching.

I grinned, and added another finger.

"Any part in particular?" I gently curled the fingers of the hand moving inside of her forward, searching for the spot that would ensure her release. At the same time I pressed down, firmly, on her lower abdomen.

"Oh, God!" Katherine's breathing was becoming more and more ragged. She guided my head closer to her cunny. I latched back onto her clit and her upper torso arched forward. Katherine's head was thrown back as her orgasm first broke through. She exploded, her knees buckling.

"Wes!" she cried out.

I stood up, and in one fluid movement lifted her into my arms then deposited her onto the floor. I rolled back onto my heels, wiped my mouth with the back of my hand and gazed down at her.

She was glowing, her hair was tousled, her breathing winded and her skin flushed. She looked wanton as she gazed at me through lust-filled eyes. I'd never seen anything so spectacular, and it was in that moment, I knew for certain. I knew I could never be without her. I knew I'd fallen irrevocably in love with her.

I untied the sash of my robe and slipped it from my shoulders. Katherine reached out and wrapped her hand around my cock. I positioned myself over her then leaned down and kissed her softly, deeply, allowing her to taste herself.

Katherine's legs wrapped around my hips. She draped her arms around my neck and held on tight as I slid into her. We began to move together. The pace felt practiced and familiar. I thrust into her slowly, rotating my hips on each downstroke.

Katherine closed her eyes and bit down on her bottom lip.

"Everything all right? Feeling all right?"

"Better than all right," she admitted, her eyes darting away.

"Look at me." I pushed into her deeply, making her breath hitch. "This is where I belong."

She moaned as I pulled out, angling my hips so that the top of my cock dragged across her still swollen clit.

"That a good moan?"

Katherine smiled and nodded encouragement, so I repeated the motion, picking up speed, intensifying the rhythm. I felt her orgasm approaching, her thighs quivering, her cunt clenching around my swollen cock.

"You're so close." I was determined to hold on and draw out her pleasure. "Come for me, baby. I want to make you come."

I bent down and crushed my lips to hers in a possessive kiss. It was almost bruising in its intensity at first. I felt a frantic need to show her how much I desired her.

"I'm... Oh, yes!" Katherine screamed in ecstasy as she ran her hands up the length of my back and threaded her fingers through my hair.

It was the sound I had been waiting for. I let go of the last thread of control I'd been holding onto so desperately, coming long and hard, shooting my seed deep into her waiting womb.

"Wes! Wake up!" Katherine whispered, shaking my shoulder.

"Sleep more."

"I think someone's in the house!"

I sat up, suddenly wide-awake. I sat still for a second then leaned over, placed a chaste kiss on Katherine's lips and laid back down, determined to go back to sleep. "It's fine."

"What do you mean it's fine? Wes!"

"Nasties don't make coffee, love. It's Charles."

"Charles? You don't suppose he saw us, do you?"

"Probably."

"He's going to assume..."

I leaned up on my elbows and ran my foot up and down the length of her calf. "...that we had really great sex," I finished.

"It was great, wasn't it?"

I heard the kitchen door swing open.

"Think we can sneak upstairs?" Katherine whispered.

"This is my house. I'm not sneaking anywhere." I looked back just in time to see Charles walk past the living room. "Morning, Charles!"

Charles paused, stepped back and looked into the room. "Ah, you're awake. Shall I prepare breakfast, sir?"

"Absolutely. I'm starved. How about you, love? Did you work up an appetite?" I ran my finger up the side of Katherine's arm.

"Wes!" She batted my hand away, then turned back toward the door.

"He's gone." I lowered Katherine to the floor and kissed her shoulder. "I want you again. Can you feel how hard you make me?"

"He'll hear."

I nudged her legs apart with my knee. "I promise to fuck you quietly."

"No!" She started to scoot away.

I wrapped my arm around Katherine's waist and held her firmly in place.

"No?"

"First of all, you are not quiet."

"And?"

"And there's no door. He could walk right by and see us."

"Right." I tossed the blanket that was covering us aside and moved to get up. "Looks like I'm going to have to fire Charles."

"You can't fire Charles."

"What is this about?" I asked her, stretching back out alongside of her. Katherine glanced away and worried her bottom lip.

"Talk to me. Was it not really good for you earlier?"

"Are you kidding? It was wonderful, that's not it."

"Then what?"

"I guess I'm not used to being so casual about sex. I'll be going back to California next week. And... Oh, God! Let me up!" she cried out as she scrambled from underneath me, grabbed the blanket and flew up the stairs.

I followed her, my robe in my hand, and arrived in the bathroom just seconds after she did. She was sitting on the floor in front of the toilet, the blanket discarded next to her.

I could hardly believe what she'd just said. "You're planning on going back next week?"

Katherine nodded as she stood up, flushed the toilet and went over to the sink to splash some cold water on her face. "That's the plan, isn't it?"

"Well, I don't like the bloody plan!" I shouted.

"I'll be able to travel by then."

"As a matter of fact, I think the plan sucks! I didn't agree to that plan." I picked the blanket up off of the floor and tossed it onto the counter.

"I don't live here, Wes."

"What about your internship program?" I challenged.

"It was only a six-week program. I'll have missed too much to continue, I think." Tears spilled over and rolled down her face. "And, why are you yelling at me?"

I hastily put on my robe and secured the sash.

"Because I'm angry. Because you're leaving me. Because this isn't casual. Because I've fallen in love with you. You promised, Katherine! You said you weren't going to go back to him!"

"Could you repeat that?"

"You said you weren't going back to him."

"Before that."

"I'm angry, and hurt. I'm not a goddamned machine, you know. I have feelings."

"After that."

I replayed what I'd said in my head, then I looked her in the eye and smiled. "I'm in love with you. I don't want you to leave."

"I don't really want to leave! I tried not to fall in love with you, really I did."

"It's not your fault, I'm irresistible."

A sob escaped her throat.

"Christ!" I opened up my arms. "What a ridiculous pair we are."

Katherine stepped into my embrace and rested her head against my chest. After taking a deep breath she looked into my eyes, and said, “Things are moving so fast. I’m afraid.”

“Me too.” I leaned down and kissed her gently on the forehead.

Katherine laughed. “You’re supposed to be the older and wiser guy with all the answers.”

“Really? I could have sworn the casting call was for a devilishly handsome bloke who possessed a certain rakish charm.”

Katherine moved over to the sink, and picked up her toothbrush. Our eyes connected in the mirror. “Say it again?”

I walked up behind her and encircled her waist with my arm. “Katherine,” I whispered against the shell of her ear as I held her gaze. “I love you. I don’t want you to leave. I know this is new. I know this place is foreign to you. I know I’m relatively foreign to you. But, we’ve started something special here. Something I don’t want to lose. Just say yes. Say you’ll stay. Say you’ll give us a chance.”

Katherine brought her toothbrush to her mouth and began the ritual of brushing her teeth. I walked around to face her, wondering what was going on in her head. As she rinsed her mouth I hopped up on the bathroom counter.

“You want me to stay in London?”

“Yes.” I placed my hands on her hips and pulled her closer so that she stood between my legs. “More specifically, I want you to stay here, in this very house, with me.”

“Move in. You want me to move in with you?”

I nodded and let my eyes roam lustfully over her naked body, imagining how it would be to have her anytime, all the time. Perhaps my open scrutiny was too much. She reached for the blanket.

“How’s the tummy?” I asked taking the blanket from her and draping it over her shoulders.

"Still queasy. Isn't it too early for morning sickness?"

"Not necessarily." I noticed for the first time the sound of dripping water and glanced over Katherine's shoulder toward the bath. "It's been four to five weeks since your last menstrual period. That's about right. Looks like we've got a leaky faucet in the bath. I have to remember to mention it to Charles."

"Yeah. I said something to him. The tub managed to fill almost halfway a couple of times in the past few days."

I hopped off the counter and walked over to turn off the tap that was leaking a steady stream of water into the tub.

"You won't be alone, Katherine." I sat down on the tub's edge. "I want you to know that. I'll be here, for you and the baby."

Katherine took a deep breath. Tears spilled from her eyes and rolled down her cheeks. "Do you think maybe you could..."

"I could what, kitten?" I prompted as I rolled up the sleeve of my robe and reached back into the water to unstop the tub.

"Do you think that maybe..."

I didn't quite hear the rest. It was as if, suddenly, I was encased in a thick agar. I turned my head, slowly, my attention drawn downward. My field of vision narrowed as I looked down to see a tangle of long auburn hair entwined around my fingers. The rush of my own blood filled my ears, momentarily drowning out Katherine's words. Then the vacuum I found myself in filled with deafening silence. My gaze shifted to the face of the woman lying in the tub and as my eyes slipped into focus I realized that her lips, slightly blue and trembling from the cold, were moving. She was trying to tell me something.

My mind reeled in shock, as I struggled to make sense of it all. I closed my eyes, trying to will the image away, trying to rein in my rising panic. My heartbeat and breathing wavered for a second. But that second took its toll. My chest constricted and reflexively I gasped for air.

"Christ!"

Jumping up, I quickly retracted my hand from the water, splashing the front of my robe in the process. Within the blink of an eye I had pushed Katherine across the room and tucked her behind me, shielding her with my body.

"Mouse?" Katherine peered over my shoulder, looking toward the tub.

I shook my head slowly, blinking and trying desperately to get my now-out-of-control heart rate to slow down. I took a careful step forward, then another, until I was able to see the interior of the bath and confirm that it was empty. I watched as the last bit of water circled around the drain and with a slight suction sound disappeared.

I turned around to look at Katherine, uncertain how I was going to explain my erratic behavior.

"You were saying?"

I walked out of the bathroom waving her toward me.

"You saw her."

Katherine walked back into the bathroom and stared down into the tub.

"Who?"

"Oh, thank God! Wes, I've seen things, felt things, over the past couple days. Things I knew couldn't be real." Katherine slid down onto the floor. "I've been so scared. I thought I was going crazy!"

I rushed back into the bathroom, dropped onto the floor alongside her and gathered her up into my arms.

"I thought it was the accident, something not right in my head," she continued tapping on her forehead and looking up at me. "Please, tell me you saw her. Tell me I'm not going mad."

I reached out and wiped away her tears. "If you are, then we're both going mad." I stood up and helped her to her feet.

"Come with me."

Katherine followed me into the bedroom. I retrieved her robe from my closet and then helped her slip it on. "I want to show you something."

"Okay."

Katherine followed me down the hall into my office. As soon as we crossed the threshold she saw it, the replica that I'd painted as a boy, the replica of Beata Beatrix.

"That's her! That's the woman I've been seeing. Who is she?"

"Elisabeth Siddall." I numbly stared up at the painting. "You're telling me you've seen her?"

"In the cemetery, in your living room, in the bath, but only for a split second, the barest of a glimpse," murmured Katherine. "You saw her, too?"

"Yes."

I walked around my desk, turned on my computer, and waited for it to boot up. "Just now, floating in the bath, her Ophelia pose."

"And people think California is strange," muttered Katherine, taking a seat in the chair positioned in front of my desk.

Suddenly the hair on the back of my neck bristled and a cold chill passed through the room.

"She's here," said Katherine.

"Where?" I quickly scanned the room. "Christ, this is crazy."

Katherine stood up and closed her eyes. "I don't know. But the cold, there's always that cold and... Can you hear it? The baby crying?"

I listened intently. "No."

She shook her head. "It's gone. It stopped."

"This is insane." I opened up my address book.

"You said that already. What are you doing?"

"Looking for a phone number."

"We should do an Internet search. We can't be the only people to have seen her."

I picked up the phone and dialed. "The thought of a mouse sent you into complete hysteria, but an apparition comes out of nowhere, and look at you. You're as cool as a cucumber."

"Rodents are evil," she declared, pulling her feet up off the floor and tucking them safely underneath her bottom. "So are insects, except for butterflies and ladybugs."

"Hello, Will? It's Wesley Atherton. I want to speak with Jennifer."

"Damn! That means I lost the bet. Why do I even bother?"

"Bet?"

"She said you'd be calling today."

"Hello?" Jennifer picked up. "Wes? You can hang up now, Will."

"Yes, Jennifer, it's Dr. Atherton."

"You're not my doctor anymore. I only paid up for six. And, since you call me Jennifer, I think I'd like to call you Wes or Wesley. We're going to be working together after all."

I leaned back in my chair and rubbed my eyes. "Right now, I don't care what you call me."

"She's made contact with you. You believe me now, don't you?"

"I'm not sure what I believe."

"She won't hurt you. Don't worry, either of you."

"But something is trying to?" I asked, then immediately winced. "Never mind, I shouldn't have asked that."

"No. You're on the right track. You're sensing it now, aren't you? You can feel it getting closer?"

I wasn't sure what I was feeling.

"Don't forget about the dog, Wes. It's already afternoon. The poor pup is starving. What time would you like us, by the way?"

"For?" I opened my desk drawer and began to search for the set of keys that I still had to Reese's apartment.

"Dinner. I'd like to come by the house. She died in that house; her presence should be strongest there. Look in the bottom right drawer."

I pulled the drawer open and stared down into the interior, immediately spotting the keys.

"Seven," I said, palming them. "Come at seven."

Chapter Fifteen

"What's that?" asked Charles.

I closed the door then gave the puppy I was holding a scratch behind the ears.

"Charles, this is a dog."

He stood there, his expression completely neutral, staring at the pup.

"Is it housebroken?"

He followed me down the hall.

"Don't know. He was Reese's. I have his stuff in the boot, but there's not a lot of food. By the way, we're up to six for dinner tonight."

"I had shopped for four. People will be arriving in just a few hours."

"Next you'll be complaining that I never take you anywhere and don't look at you in the same way anymore," I teased, pushing through the kitchen door.

Katherine had changed into a pair of old, faded jeans and was wearing one of my white dress shirts, the sleeves rolled up. Her hair was pulled back in a ponytail and it swung back and forth, enticingly, along with her hips as she bounced and writhed to the music that was blaring from the CD player. The vision made me stop dead in my tracks. My eyes tracked the seductive swivel of her hips. "Get Spike some food. Get whatever else you need for tonight," I said. Then I turned to Charles and added, "Do you mind? She's a bit shy."

"Might I suggest that you consider restricting your liaisons to the bedroom?"

"What fun would that be, Charles?"

"Like father like son," he muttered before turning to leave.

I reached for his sleeve. "Tell you what? I'll restrict myself to that counter." I pointed to the far countertop that Katherine was working on. "And the floor."

Charles rolled his eyes.

"And, possibly the breakfast table," I added before letting him go and approaching Katherine.

"Hey, there." I wrapped my arm around Katherine's waist and pressed my erection into her bum. "You're a great dancer."

"Bet you say that to all the girls, you big flirt." Katherine looked back over her shoulder. "Who's this?"

"This is Spike."

I held up the wiggling puppy.

"He belonged to Reese. We're adopting him. What are you making?"

"Brownies, for dessert tonight." She picked up a dishtowel and wiped off her hands. "He's really cute. I just need to pour the batter into the pan and pop them in the oven."

"Wait a sec." I set Spike down on the floor and stepped closer to her.

"What?"

"You've got a little chocolate right..." I leaned in and with a sweep of my tongue lapped up the smudge on the corner of her mouth. "Some naughty little girl has been tasting the batter." I placed a hand over her breast and began to gently knead it. "No bra." I nibbled on her bottom lip. "Are you trying to drive me crazy?"

"Is my sinister plan working?"

I nodded. "Oh, yeah. It's most definitely working."

Reaching back, I tugged on the rubber band that had been holding her hair in place, letting it spill around her shoulders and down her back.

"You have the silkiest hair." I kissed her softly on the lips. "Turn around."

"What?"

I spun her around so that her back was once again to me and then I molded my body to hers.

"The sight of you, can you feel what it does to me?"

"Yes."

"Do you want me?" I unbuttoned the top button on her jeans and slid down the zipper.

"Yes." She pushed back against me, grinding her ass into my cock. I slipped my hand inside her knickers, seeking out her wetness, separating her folds and running my fingers up and down the length of her slit.

"Tell me."

With my free hand I quickly unbuckled my belt, opened my jeans and freed my aching cock.

"I want you," she gasped.

I turned her around, lifted her onto the counter and quickly removed the clothing that had fallen about her ankles. "Lean back against the cabinets then bring your feet up here on the counter."

She did exactly as I asked.

"That's it, baby, open yourself up for me." I licked my lips in anticipation, then leaned down and brushed them against her inner thigh. "God, you're going to taste so good. You're without a doubt the best thing I've ever had in my mouth."

I latched onto her clit, pulling the hardened bundle of nerves into my mouth, making her come almost instantly.

"Wes!" she cried out, lacing her fingers though my hair. "Inside of me. Now."

I pulled back and grinned up at her. "Demanding chit, you are."

Katherine lowered her legs and reached out to grab hold of my T-shirt.

"You ain't seen nothing yet, mister. Come here."

She pulled me close, reaching out with her tongue to lap boldly at my mouth and chin.

"Fuck, baby."

"I want you so much," Katherine moaned as she slipped her tongue into my mouth.

I lifted her up off of the counter. On instinct she wrapped her legs around my hips and her arms around my neck. Finally I broke off the kiss. "Let go."

Katherine let her legs slide to the floor. She was trapped between me and the table. For the briefest of moments, her eyes sought out mine in question. Then she reached out and slid her hand up and down the length of my erection.

"I want to see that beautiful bum." I turned her around and ran my hands possessively over her bottom.

"Wes, I..."

"Shh." I leaned over her, my chest against her back as I slid my hand down over her bottom, my fingers again separating her folds. I slipped two inside of her. "I want to take you from behind. I want to take you hard and fast and deep. I want to make you scream my name. I want to know you're mine."

Katherine was leaning across the table, supported by her elbows, her bottom exposed. I began by placing hot wet kisses along the length of her spine. She wiggled in pleasure and a fresh flood of juices coated my fingers.

"Tell me you're mine." I demanded removing my fingers and burying my cock deep inside of her.

"Oh, Wes!"

I pulled almost all the way out before thrusting in again.

"Say it."

"You're so deep," she moaned pushing back against me, meeting me thrust for thrust as we picked up speed. I felt it as her insides began to flutter around me.

"That's it, baby. Come for me. Let me feel you squeeze my cock."

She clamped down on my next downstroke, maximizing the friction. She was so fucking wet. So fucking tight.

"Oh, Wesley!" she cried out, another orgasm sweeping through her body.

"Say it, please," I begged, spilling everything that I had into her. "Tell me you're mine."

Katherine collapsed across the table.

"I'm yours," she said, dreamily. "Only yours. Always yours."

I reached down and gently brushed her hair over to one side. Then I whispered into her ear. "I love you."

Katherine sighed. "I love you, too."

The music had stopped. The only sounds left in the room were our heaving breaths and Spike's excited panting as he ran about our feet.

"You realize we just had sex in front of the puppy?" asked Katherine as I eased out of her. "Some Mom I'm going to make. We've probably traumatized him."

I swatted her bottom playfully. "Nonsense." I looked down at Spike and refastened my jeans. "Spike looks quite happy. Leave it to Reese to have a pervy puppy."

I sat down on the floor and invited the dog into my lap. “Listen, mate, just so we’re straight, you see anyone else doing that, you go in for the kill!”

“Getting possessive, are we?” Katherine sank down next to me on the floor. “I don’t think my legs are working anymore.”

I pushed Spike off my lap and gathered Katherine up in my arms. She sighed contentedly.

“Sleepy?”

“A bit. Maybe Spike and I should take a nap?”

“Your mum won’t be here for a couple hours yet.” I climbed to my feet then helped Katherine up. “Go rest. I’ll finish up in here. But, no dogs in the bed or on the furniture.”

“Don’t let him scare you. He’s really nothing but a softy deep down inside.” Katherine scooped the pup up, then retrieved her discarded jeans. “He’s all bark and no bite.”

Spike barked, seemingly in agreement.

“Traitor!” I yelled after them.

“Hello, Charles,” said Julia. “Sorry we’re a bit early.”

“No need to apologize. I’ll let Dr. Atherton and Miss Lawson know you’ve arrived.” He stepped aside and invited them in. “May I fix you a cocktail first?”

I quickly made my way down the stairs. “Julia, you look fetching. Wonderful to see you again, George.”

“Where’s Kate?”

“Upstairs. We heard the doorbell. She’ll be down in a minute or two.” I showed Julia and George into the living room. “Now, about those drinks.”

“Yes, what can I get for you?” asked Charles.

“A scotch would be nice,” replied George, sitting down. He

looked around the room. "Wes, you have a lovely home."

"Mrs. Lawson, what can I get you?"

"White wine?"

"I took the liberty of selecting a nice white Bordeaux from the cellar this morning. I'll go get it," offered Charles.

"Ah, here's Katherine."

"You're looking a little tired, sweetheart," said Julia as she walked up to Katherine and smoothed down her hair. "Are you getting enough rest?"

"We didn't sleep well last night." Katherine curled up on the sofa. "There was an accident at the party, someone died."

"Dear Lord," gasped George as he removed his glasses and began to polish them. "How awful."

"Was he someone you knew?" Julia asked me.

"Was a woman, actually." I quickly poured George and myself a scotch. "Here you go, George."

"Thank you," he replied.

Charles returned with a tray of stuffed mushrooms and the chilled wine. After pouring Julia a glass he set the mushrooms down on the coffee table and then quietly slipped away.

"She was an old girlfriend," added Katherine.

"I see," said George.

An awkward silence fell over the room.

I poured Katherine a club soda. "Mostly I'm grateful that Katherine escaped getting hurt."

"Were you almost hurt?" Julia looked alarmed.

"No!" Katherine accepted the club soda and took a sip. "Reese had a bit too much to drink and she climbed into the fountain. There were strong winds, what with the storms, and a power line was knocked loose. She... Excuse me!"

Katherine quickly set her glass down and ran from the

room.

"Don't know why they insist on calling it morning sickness," I muttered before dashing out of the room after her.

Katherine was in the guest bathroom. I knocked.

"Are you all right?"

It was a foolish question; I could hear quite plainly that she wasn't. After a moment or two she opened the door.

"Sorry."

I smoothed down her hair. "You've got nothing to be sorry for."

I walked the few steps down the hall and pushed open the kitchen door. "Charles, can you bring out a few crisps and some ginger ale?" I turned back to Katherine and held out my hand. "The salt will help. Maybe you should go lie down?"

She shook her head. "I'll be all right. I'm just going to run upstairs and freshen up."

I walked back into the living room just in time to hear George say to Julia, "So, Damien is the father?"

"Katherine will be back down shortly. She's been struggling with nausea all morning, I'm afraid."

Charles entered with the glass of ginger ale and a small bowl of crisps.

"Charles, where's the package I asked you to get when you went out to the house?"

"In the dining room, sir." He set the items on the table.

"There's something I'd like to show you," I told Julia, retrieving my drink, then offering her my arm. "We'll be but a moment, George, if you don't mind."

He reached for one of the mushrooms and waved us off. "Not at all."

I escorted Julia across the hall and into the formal dining

room. The long mahogany table was already set for dinner. The instant we entered, Julia's eyes were drawn to a painting displayed at the far end of the room. She walked up to it, leaning in to study the piece with a practiced eye.

"It's for you."

Julia turned quickly to face me. "What? No! I can't accept this. Wesley, this has got to be worth a fortune. It's exquisite."

I looked back at the familiar painting. My mother, Margo Atherton lay in repose on a red velvet chaise, her almost white blonde hair draped over the arm. Her body arched up as if seeking out the touch of an invisible lover. The chaise was positioned in front of a large set of windows and through them the late-afternoon sun poured in, dappling her pale skin in a golden luminescence. One delicate hand was held next to her head, the second draped, lazily across her stomach. Her lips were smiling in playful amusement and her eyes, her eyes conveyed her utter and complete happiness.

"I walked in on them the day he was trying to finish this. I was mortified."

"I didn't know he did any nudes of your mother." Julia turned on a nearby light.

"He never sold any of them. There are close to a hundred. This, however, is my favorite. It's very precious to me, and that's precisely the reason that I want you to have it."

"I don't understand."

"I'm in love with Katherine, Julia. Rather madly in love with her, I'm afraid. Perhaps I should say we've fallen madly in love with one another. I've asked her to stay on, here."

Julia's eyes flashed in anger. "And you thought you'd buy her with a painting?"

"No." I shook my head. "No. That would imply she's yours to sell and that's not true, is it? She's already agreed, Julia. We're committed to giving this a go. Katherine's priceless. Until

I met her, I had thought this to be my greatest treasure. I want you to keep it, to take care of it for me."

"Please, don't hurt her," said Julia, softly.

"I won't, I promise. I'll do right by her, Julia. I'll take good care of her."

She sighed and shook her head. "She's so vulnerable now and she's not very experienced. Damien's the only real boyfriend she's ever had."

"I know this is fast. But, it's real and it's good. It's bloody brilliant, actually."

"She's going to have a baby."

"I know that. I have a big house and a bigger heart."

Julie smiled. "You've got it bad."

I nodded. "I happily admit defeat. I've never been with someone like her. She's amazing." Julia leaned over and kissed me on the cheek.

"I'm happy for you, sweetie. I'm happy for both of you. Of course, you realize what I'll do to you if you screw this up?"

"I've got an idea."

"Almost a hundred, you say?" she asked, turning back to face the painting.

"Of the nudes, yeah." My mobile rang. "Excuse me."

"Get her out!" hissed the voice on the other side of the line. "She's not safe there. No! No! Please!"

"Damien? Is that you? I've been leaving messages for you all day. Are you all right?"

I heard a sudden crash, followed by a groan. "Damien? Bugger!"

"What is it?" Katherine walked into the room.

I rang off then quickly redialed the number. "It sounded like Damien was in some sort of trouble, I don't know. Hello?

This is Dr. Wesley Atherton, I was just speaking with a patient in your hotel and we were cut off. I'm concerned he's ill, too ill to answer the phone. Could someone go check on him and call me back? I don't know the room number. Damien..."

"Flynn," interjected Katherine.

"Flynn. My number is 07769584097."

It took them almost twenty minutes to call me back. I reached for Katherine's hand. "I'm sorry, I've got to go check on him. He told security he didn't need any help but..."

"But they weren't convinced?"

"They said he looks pretty bad, might be running a fever. I got the lecture on how they respect their guest's privacy, then he let Damien's room number slip. It was purposeful, I'm almost sure of it. I won't be more than an hour. Charles will come with me in case I need help."

Katherine opened the door to the hall closet. "I should go with you."

I turned to look at her and was struck by a fierce need to protect her. She looked so fragile and feminine in the chocolate brown suede skirt and cream-colored silk blouse, its soft fabric accentuating the curve of her full breasts.

"No." I reached into the closet and pulled out my leather coat. "I'll take care of it. You wait here. I'll be back in a jiff, you'll see. If Will and Jennifer arrive before we return, just fix them some drinks and be your charming self." I leaned down and kissed her, quickly, on the mouth.

Charles held the door open. "Would you like me to drive?"

"What kind of a kiss was that?" I heard her ask, quietly, just as I was walking through the door.

I paused, turned around and walked purposefully back into

the house. I wrapped my arm around Katherine's narrow waist and in one fluid movement pulled her inside the large entry coat closet, shutting the door and shrouding us in darkness.

"That was a proper kiss," I whispered. "That's the kind of kiss you give in front of your girlfriend's mother, especially when said girlfriend has expressed discomfort with public displays of affection and her former fiancé is sick and in need of a bit of quick rescuing."

"Oh," she said. "Why are we in the closet?"

"So that I can give you an improper kiss." My hand crept up to cup her right breast. "I should warn you. I told your mother I'm in love with you and that I intend to keep you."

"You told her?"

"Yes." I brushed my lips across hers and lightly traced the outside of her partly open mouth with the tip of my tongue, coaxing her lips farther apart. "Now, shut up and give me your tongue."

Katherine slipped her tongue inside and I sucked it fully into my mouth. I could feel her surprise as her breath hitched, but I paid that little mind. Instead I continued, massaging her tongue, sucking it in deeper and then releasing the pressure slightly and backing off.

Harder. Deeper. Faster. Trying to replicate for her, in some small way, the intense pleasure and raw emotion that I felt when I was buried deep inside of her. The sounds of her whimpering in need and the sensation of her nipples hardening as I swept my fingertips over them gave me the desired feedback. I was on the road to redeeming myself. I let my hands slide down over her waist and when they reached her hips I pulled her toward me and abruptly ended the kiss. Katherine staggered slightly in the dark. She wrapped her hands around my biceps to hold on and steady herself.

"Little weak in the knees, kitten?" I asked, feeling quite

smug.

Katherine nodded.

"Tell me, what kind of a kiss was that?"

"That," she replied, still a bit breathless, "was a great kiss."

"So, I take it I've officially atoned for that shamefully inadequate kiss out there?"

"Almost," she replied as she reached up, again seeking out the warmth of my mouth. I held her back.

"Greedy vixen. Tend to the guests now. I promise I'll tend to you later." I opened the closet door and swatted her playfully on her bottom. Before she could respond I was out the door with Charles.

Chapter Sixteen

We were led into Damien's room by hotel security.

"Good Lord!" exclaimed Charles.

Damien lay on the floor dressed only in a pair of black trousers. He was curled up on his side with bruising evident on his torso. The man was sweating profusely and shaking uncontrollably. I made my way over to him and tried to quickly assess the situation. Damien was mumbling almost to himself, his lips barely moving. "Not gonna do it. Not gonna hurt her. Not gonna do it."

"Damien, I want you to look at me."

He'd yet to move. It was as if he hadn't even noticed our presence in the room. He was unable to focus or respond. His eyes were jittering back and forth in minute, involuntary movements and his pupils were dilated. A puddle of vomit lay just a few inches from his face. His body glistened with sweat and the front of his pants were wet. I felt for a pulse and watched for a few seconds as Damien panted, his breathing shallow and seemingly constricted.

"His pulse and respirations are both elevated. We've got to get him to a hospital. Think we can get him into the car? St. Catherine's is less than a mile away."

"I'll get a rollaway bed from the storage room at the end of the hall," offered the security guard.

"Let's sit him up first, then we'll lift him together."

"Was he beaten by someone, do you think?" asked Charles.

I hooked my arms under Damien's and pulled him to a sitting position. "Hold him up." I walked around back. "Christ!"

"What is it?"

I knelt down to examine Damien's back more closely. It was covered with large angry red welts, swollen and hot, some of them oozing.

"Looks like insect bites of some sort. But, they're so big and so many of them. Charles, tell the guard to get towels and ice, quickly."

"Will do."

"What the hell happened here, Damien?"

"Not gonna do it. Not gonna hurt her. Not gonna do it," he continued to mumble over and over again.

It took less than five minutes to get him transferred from the room onto the rollaway bed and into the back of my car. We'd laid a cold, wet towel across his back and placed a garbage bag filled with ice on it.

Charles was driving. I dialed my mobile while watching Damien closely. "Laura? It's me. I'm on my way in with a sick friend. It looks as if maybe he's been bitten by something."

"Bitten by something? Does he know what?"

"He's pretty out of it. His heart rate is over one thirty, respirations over twenty, he's been vomiting, and he's diaphoretic."

"Have you checked his pupils?"

"Yes, they're both dilated and nystagmus is patently evident. He's shaking, Laura, almost seizing. He seems delirious."

"How close are you?"

"We'll be rounding the corner. I'm going to pull into the ambulance bay. Have someone waiting."

"I'm on my way out."

As Charles pulled into the parking area I saw Laura; she was waiting for us with two men. She was practically bouncing on her toes with nervous energy.

I climbed out of the car.

"Any change?"

"None."

The two men lifted Damien onto a trolley and rushed him inside.

Charles and I followed. A & E was fairly deserted. We waited on the other side of the curtain while Laura rattled off a long list of orders. Finally she pushed the drape aside.

"They're intubating him now. What the hell happened to him?"

"Don't really know," I told her. "We found him in his hotel room."

She brushed an errant stand of hair out of her eyes, pushed her glasses back up and shook her head. "Wes, when I was with the Peace Corps I spent a lot of time in Mexico. The symptoms and welts are consistent with a scorpion bite. Lots of scorpion bites. I'd guess this was done by fifteen or twenty at least."

"Scorpions?"

"Laura, check this out," someone called out.

Laura walked back over to the bedside. "What?"

"I'm getting a bizarre reading on the ECG."

"Let me have a look."

"See this? Then there are these tiny Q waves."

"And an accelerated junctional rhythm."

Charles leaned over and whispered, "What's that mean?"

I shook my head. "I don't exactly know."

"His rate's between sixty and one hundred beats per minute." Laura continued to scan the monitors. "I want to see the interleukin levels. If I'm right it'll be elevated. Get an IV going and start those medicines I ordered. We need to get him some relief."

I noticed that Charles was watching her intently.

"She's so confident," he murmured.

I looked back and forth between them. I hadn't seen that look on his face in ages. "Did something happen between you and Laura?"

Charles grinned. "A gentleman doesn't kiss and tell."

Laura rejoined us. "He's stabilizing. We're going to have to admit him and continue to carefully monitor the situation, though. I'm going to keep him on the vent as a precaution. He's out for now. I've never seen so many bites."

"You really think that's what it is?"

"The presentation is consistent, Wes."

"But it makes no sense."

Laura shrugged.

"Will you call me when he's extubated? I want to try to talk to him as soon as possible."

"Of course," she replied. Then she removed her glasses and approached Charles. "Hello, Charles."

"Hello yourself," replied Charles.

"I'm off at seven." She smiled up at him sweetly. "That's in just a few minutes."

"I'm working tonight. Dr. Atherton is having a dinner party."

"Oh, of course. I'm sorry." She turned her attention back

toward me. "I'll call you when he's extubated, Wes." She hurried away toward the emergency room exit, obviously flustered.

"Go on." I gave Charles a nudge.

He bristled a bit. "Go on, what?"

"Go after her. It's clear she fancies you. Invite the bird to dinner tonight. You always make extra. Skinny thing like Laura can't eat much."

"I'm not inviting her to dinner. It would be awkward."

"Awkward?"

Charles nodded.

"Don't be daft. You cook. You set the food on the table. We all sit down and eat. What's awkward about that? People do it all the time."

Charles dug his hands into his trousers, shook his head. "Not with their servants. I'm not your wife. I'm not your guest. I'm your butler."

"I'll tell you what you are. You're a snob. You accuse me of having class issues? You're supposed to follow my orders, are you not?"

"Yes."

"Go invite her to dinner!"

Charles took a few steps, then hesitated.

"Go!" I said, giving him a little nudge.

"Laura! Wait!"

When Charles and I returned home Will and Jennifer had just arrived and were still standing in the entry.

"Can I take your coats and offer you something to drink?" Katherine was asking them.

"Sorry I'm a bit late, I had a sick friend to attend to," said

Wes.

"I'll hang up your coats," offered Charles.

"But you're not late at all, we've just arrived," said Jennifer. Holding her hand out in front of her, she walked slowly to the stairs. "She was so sad here."

"Who?" I asked.

"Elisabeth. She died here. But you knew that." She turned to face Katherine. "You've seen her."

"How do you know?"

"I see her, too. Has she spoken to you?" Jennifer's gaze seemed to be tracking something as it moved about the room.

"No. Has she spoken to you?"

Jennifer nodded.

A chill passed through me.

"She's here, isn't she?" asked Katherine.

"You're getting better, better able to detect her. Open yourself up. She doesn't want to hurt you, just the opposite."

Katherine leaned against the nearby banister. "What does she want?"

Before Jennifer could respond, Charles returned. "What can I get you all to drink?"

I wrapped my arm around Katherine's waist and showed everyone into the living room. "We've invited Laura. She's on her way as well," I told her.

"How's Damien?"

"Kind of hard to tell. Laura thought it was scorpion bites. He was delirious."

Charles poured a scotch and handed it to Will. "Scorpion bites? Are you serious?" he asked, after taking a sip.

"That's what I said. But she has experience with this sort of thing. She seemed pretty certain."

"Was he delirious last night, Wes? Do you think he'd already been bitten?" asked Katherine.

I gave her hand a squeeze. "I think he was just drunk, love."

"Where on earth would he have come into contact with scorpions in London?" asked Julia.

"I'm terribly sorry. I've yet to introduce you. George Grant, Julia Lawson, this is Will and Jennifer Carlton."

Will approached George, offering his hand. "Nice to meet you."

"Likewise."

Jennifer was standing over by the window, gazing outside into the darkness.

"Miss Carlton?" Charles handed her a glass of club soda. Turning toward him she said, "Hell is naked before him, and destruction hath no covering."

"I'm sorry?" asked Charles.

Jennifer shook her head and smiled weakly. "I mean, thank you. I meant to say thank you."

I dropped Katherine's hand and approached Jennifer. "But you didn't."

"I didn't?"

"No. What does it mean?"

Will joined his sister by the window and protectively draped his arm over her shoulders. "Back off a bit. She doesn't always know. It doesn't work that way."

I took a step back. "What you said just now, Damien said to me last night. As I was walking away he said hell is naked before him, and—"

"—destruction hath no covering?" Jennifer finished.

"Yes. What's it mean?"

Jennifer shook her head. "I have no idea."

"But you just said it. You finished my sentence."

"It's from the Bible," said George.

He was polishing his glasses, not a good sign.

"It's from the Bible, George?"

"It's a reference to Abaddon, I think, sometimes thought of as the Grim Reaper, also known as The Destroyer, from his role as one of the destroying angels of the apocalypse."

"Of the apocalypse?" asked Katherine. "Why would Damien be quoting some Bible verse about the apocalypse? What does this Abaddon do, exactly?"

George allowed me to refill his scotch glass. "If I remember correctly, Abaddon is a fallen angel. He opens the gates of the abyss and unleashes upon the earth swarms of demon locusts."

"Grasshoppers?" asked Katherine. "Not quite in the same category as butterflies and ladybugs, but all in all not too horribly scary."

"Not grasshoppers." George looked down into his scotch, then replaced his glasses. "He's said to have the body of a winged warhorse, the face of a human and the poisonous curved tail of a scorpion."

"Get out!" said Katherine.

"Unusual coincidence?" murmured Charles.

"Maybe it's not a coincidence," said Will.

"Of course it's a coincidence. You don't mean to suggest there's a demon flying about London on a winged horse, do you?" I asked.

"It does explain what happened to Damien," said Katherine. "I wonder if that's what Elisabeth's been trying to warn us about?"

Julia stood up and tiredly rubbed her forehead. "Who's Elisabeth?"

"A ghost that Wes and I have been seeing. Jennifer too, right?"

"Wes?" Julia was beginning to look a tad alarmed. I couldn't say I blamed her. We all sounded completely nutters. Thankfully, we were interrupted by the doorbell.

"Must be Laura. I'll get the door and show her in. Dinner will be ready in twenty minutes," said Charles.

"Sounds good. I'll get more ice." I reached for the ice bucket, then headed into the kitchen. I went straight for the freezer.

"I know it sounds fantastic, but don't just dismiss it. You promised to take care of her, of them," I heard her say. "Open your eyes, Wes."

"Julia," I began as I turned around. The bucket slipped out of my hand and fell to the floor. Water spilled out and chunks of ice skittered across the cold black and white marble.

"You know, Wes. You see his victims every day. He plays with them. Like a snake he slithers into their minds, creating doubt, showing them lies, bending reality, all for his amusement. But, Wes, he can't actually change reality. He's not that powerful," said the woman standing before me.

I slid to the floor. I couldn't take my eyes off of her. My mind was reeling. Elisabeth stood before me, fully formed, dressed in a dark green velvet dressing gown, her copper hair hanging in a long braid over one shoulder. Her feet were bare. I watched as the puddle spread, reaching out, until the cold water surrounded her delicate toes.

I closed my eyes. "You're not real. You're not real." But then I opened them again and she was still there, standing before me, as plain as day.

"Wes, you need help? I heard a crash." Katherine walked through the door into the kitchen. "Wes?"

She fell to her knees at my side. "Are you all right?"

I glanced back. Elisabeth was gone.

"Wes?"

"He can't actually change reality. He's not that powerful," I repeated.

"What happened?" asked Katherine, grabbing a towel from the counter and wiping up the spilled water.

I reached for her. "Stop it! I need to know this is real. I need to know you're real!" Desperately I ran my hands over her face and body.

Katherine looked at me, her eyes wide from fear.

"I'm real, Wes. I know we've been seeing and hearing some strange
things—"

Laughter bubbled up and spilled from my mouth. "Bloody right we have! I feel like I'm this close to snapping!"

"Wes! Look at me, baby. Maybe we should get away. We could go to California."

"I don't think running away is the answer."

"Wes, the word apocalypse? That frightens me. You, Jennifer and I? We can't all be crazy. I don't understand what's happening."

I pulled Katherine into my arms. "I think I'm beginning to."

"You are?"

I nodded. "My rational mind tells me it's impossible."

"But?" Katherine pulled back and looked me in the eye.

"Pieces are falling into place. It's starting to make sense to me. I honestly think that's the most frightening part."

"Something *is* happening."

"Yes." I nodded, reaching up to cup her cheek. "And whatever it is, we'll suss it out. I promised your mum, I promised myself that I'd protect you and I will, till the end of the world."

"End of the world? No offense, Wes, but you're just a man."

"I'm a man who loves you and love is stronger than death, it can outlast it. This isn't about destroying the world. That's not what this is about. At least, I don't think so. This is about manipulating, about controlling, about stealing."

"Stealing? Stealing what?"

"One tortured mind, one tortured soul at a time."

"We've got a fight ahead of us, you realize that?" It was Jennifer. When she'd entered, I wasn't sure.

"What kind of a fight?" I asked her.

"I don't know."

"Will we win?" asked Katherine, her hand involuntarily covering her stomach.

"Lives will be lost."

Katherine clutched at my biceps. "I want my mother out of here. I want her far away, back in California." She turned to Jennifer. "She'll be safe there?"

"I think so. This is all my fault. I messed with the natural order of things."

"I don't understand," said Katherine.

"Wesley was supposed to die on the Tube. We cheated him—Death. He's not happy." She tapped the side of her head. "There's something, I can almost see it. But not quite. Blood. A battle."

Chills ran down my spine. "Whose blood?"

"It's not clear yet."

"Are we in danger here?" asked Katherine.

Jennifer shook her head. "It doesn't end here. It ends someplace else. Someplace I've never been."

"I don't like the way you said end." I wrapped my arm

around Katherine and pulled her close to me. "Maybe you're wrong," I said, knowing in my heart that she wasn't.

Jennifer sighed. "I wish I was, but I'm not. I don't think we have long to prepare."

"Prepare?" I laughed. "For what?"

"For whatever is to come." Jennifer walked up to me and took my hands in hers. "This is why you were saved. But for tonight? For right now? We just need to get through dinner."

Get through dinner, was she joking? Spending the evening engaging in casual banter was the last thing on my mind. I reached deep down inside of myself and found the courage to ask the hardest question of all. "My surviving the crash is what started this. Will my death end it?"

Jennifer knew what I was asking. "Whatever the sacrifice, it will be of *his* choosing. Not yours. Not mine."

"There will be no sacrifice," said Katherine with determination.

Jennifer smiled. "She's scrappy. I like her."

"Me too."

"Drive safely!" I called out before closing the front door and locking it. The past couple hours had felt like torture.

"I'll go let Spike in," offered Katherine.

I reached for her hand as she turned to walk away. "I'll do it. You head upstairs. I'll be up in a jiff."

"Okay."

"Are you all right?"

"No. Are you?"

"Not by a long shot."

"But we're okay for now. Right?"

"If we believe Jennifer."

"I do." Katherine reached up and cupped the side of my face in the palm of her hand. "If I hadn't trusted her the other night, you wouldn't be here now. We wouldn't be here, together. We're going to get through this, Wesley."

I watched Katherine climb up the stairs, then proceeded through the kitchen and opened the back door. "Here, boy!" Within seconds Spike came bounding up the back steps, wagging his tail excitedly. "Hey, you knocked your water over. Let's give you a refill and let you in for the night."

Suddenly Spike spun around and growled, baring his teeth.

"What is it?"

As if in response to his question the cat belonging to the person in the neighboring house flew out of a nearby bush and shot across the yard.

"Come on, Spike. She's nothing but a tease, that one. You can do far better, mate." He turned to look at me and then without a glance back at the cat, followed me inside, and up the stairs. Katherine was in the bathroom.

I debated whether or not to intrude. The door was left partially ajar and I was craving contact. I busied myself for a moment with the mundane task of getting undressed. When I was left with only my trousers I finally gave in and eased into the doorway. Katherine was brushing her teeth. She noticed me at once.

She'd removed her skirt, but she was still wearing the tall, brown suede boots. Her silk blouse was unbuttoned and lying casually open, giving me a glorious view of her cream colored bra and knickers. The hollow of her neck, swell of her breast, curve of her waist, they beckoned to me. Despite the stress, despite the gravity of the moment, the gravity of what was to come, she had the power to move me, to excite me. That was something to hold on to.

"Do you have any idea how sexy you look?"

"No one's sexy while they're brushing their teeth," she declared before rinsing, her mouth full of foamy toothpaste.

I wrapped my arm around her waist and ground my erection into her silk-covered behind teasingly. "Is that so? I have evidence to the contrary. Look at yourself." I wanted to slip my hand inside her knickers and seek out the wet heat between her legs.

"Wes." Katherine closed her eyes and leaned her head back.

"What do you want?" I kissed up the length of the long column of her neck.

Her eyes connected with mine in the mirror. "I want to feel alive."

"I love you."

Katherine moistened her lips. "Tell me you want me, not just sexually. Tell me you *really* want me."

"This, between us, it's not just about sex. You know that, right?"

For a moment Katherine looked as if she were about to cry. She wrapped her arms around my neck and held on tight. "I know," she whispered. "I'm sorry. I'm feeling insecure, overly emotional."

"You've been through a lot. We both have."

"I signed up for the package without the moodiness, really I did."

"Shh." I lifted her into my arms and carried her to the turned-down bed. "You're tired. Sleep. Things will seem clearer in the morning."

I unbuttoned my trousers and stepped out of them. The fact that I was semi-erect was readily apparent. Katherine climbed to her knees, positioning herself in front of me, then she reached inside my boxers and freed my cock. "I want you to make love to me."

She started to stroke me up and down. It didn't take much, the slightest touch and I was hard and stiff and ready.

"Are you sure?" I climbed onto the bed and lowered her back onto the mattress. "We don't have to."

"What if this is all we have? What if tonight is all we have? I want to. I need to feel your arms around me, you inside of me." Katherine tilted her hips up in invitation. Her hands were holding on to my biceps in a way that telegraphed a sense of urgency. She wanted me, this. And she wanted it now.

I understood her desperation. Bloody hell, I *felt* her desperation. I didn't take the time to undress her any further. Instead I pushed her knickers aside and slid into her quickly, deeply. God willing, there would be time for slow, for savoring, later.

Everything else in the room disappeared. Everything else in the world disappeared. Everything but the sounds of her keening, the feel of her pussy surrounding me and the wonderful aroma of unbridled passion, of sweat and sex. The rhythm we created as we climbed together was almost dizzying. I devoured her, nibbling her ears, then pulling down the cups of her bra to nip and suck on her peaked nipples.

"God, you feel so good!"

Katherine ran her nails down the length of my back, to my ass. She grabbed it and squeezed, making me shudder. I almost let go. But I didn't. I held on and instead I arched up so that I could get a better angle. I reached for one of her legs and opened her even more so that with each thrust my cock was rubbing against her clit.

She was writhing beneath me now, her body trembling. I crushed my mouth to hers in a forceful kiss. It occurred to me that I was being greedy and inconsiderate, just taking what I wanted. At that very moment I didn't care. I should have, but I didn't. In part because the sex was so intoxicating, because she was so intoxicating, my thirst for her unquenchable. In part because she took control, showing me she could, making me realize that nothing would ever happen between us that we didn't both want to have happen.

Katherine threaded her fingers through my hair and pulled, ending our kiss. She was gasping for breath, her eyes shining with a wanton lust. She was right at the edge and I'd taken her there.

"I want to be on top."

No sooner were the words out of her mouth, we switched positions. Katherine rested her hands on my chest and closed her eyes, her body becoming completely still. It was a sharp contrast to our earlier lovemaking and slightly alarming.

"Is this all right?"

She nodded, slowly, and began to rock, gently, back and forth. "You're so deep. Never felt it this deep before."

I slid the silk blouse off her shoulders, then reached around to unhook her bra, baring her breasts.

"I've never loved a woman so deeply before," I whispered.

Katherine leaned down and kissed me, softly. We came in unison, quietly, gently. It was more of a contented sigh than a scream, more of a whisper than a roar. It was heaven.

"You keep surprising me," said Katherine before climbing out of bed. She went straight to the bathroom.

"Good." I followed her, but hesitated outside the door. "Do you want to marry me?"

I heard the toilet flush, then the water in the sink run. I was about to ask if she'd heard my question when she emerged from the bathroom.

"I can't believe that you asked me to marry you while I was sitting on the toilet."

She walked back over to the bed, slid between the covers, then rolled over.

"I take that as a no then? So, is this good-bye sex kitten, hello moody pregnant woman again? Maybe we should work out a signal of some sort."

"That wasn't a real proposal. That was just the endocrine talking."

I turned out the lights and crawled into bed, stretching out alongside of her. "The endocrine, huh?" I tried not to smile.

"Yes." Katherine turned to face me. "So, Mom, tell me the story about when Daddy proposed. Well, you see, first we had wild monkey sex, then after we shook the rafters of his house I got up to use the bathroom."

"I get it."

"Do you?"

I leaned in and kissed her on the nose. "Yes. And, just for the record, it wasn't the endocrine."

"Really?" Katherine shifted closer to me.

"I'm fairly certain. I think you mean endorphin, the neurochemical connected to the production of sex hormones. It's like an opiate, an analgesic."

"Wes?"

"Yes, kitten?"

"No one likes a smarty pants and you're not making the story any better."

"Perhaps I should just be quiet then. Throw in the towel and admit defeat for tonight."

"Probably."

"If I were to ask again sometime, really nicely, of course, do you think you might say yes?"

"Hypothetically?"

“Absolutely, hypothetically.” I spooned up against her and rubbed small circles across her tummy.

“I would get to spend the rest of my life with you?”

My hand moved up to her breast and gave it a gentle squeeze. “That would be the general idea.”

“I think I better sleep on it.”

“Ouch.” I removed my hand as if I’d been stung. “You, Miss Lawson, have a mean streak! I think I better sleep on it!”

Katherine chuckled. “I love you, Wesley Atherton.”

“Yeah? Well, I love you more, you crazy bint.”

“Promise me the world isn’t really ending?”

“Darling, for us, it’s just beginning,” I promised her. Then I kissed her on the top of her head, held her in my arms until she fell asleep and prayed that what I’d promised was the truth.

Chapter Seventeen

"Charles? I need you to come over."

"Do you realize that it's four in the morning?"

"Yes." I poured myself a cup of coffee. "I know what time it is. I've got to go into the office today and there's an errand I have to take care of first. I know you weren't going to come over until eight, but this was unexpected."

"Why don't I just run the errand on the way in?"

"No. I just need you to stay in the house for a bit. Just a half an hour, an hour tops. Then you can come back at eight, like we planned if you want. Come on, Charles, be a sport. I've just got to run down to O'Brien's. I don't want to leave Katherine alone."

"O'Brien's? The florist? Wes, they don't even open until nine."

"I called. Sheila's opening up for me." I added some sugar to my coffee and stirred.

"Do I even want to know how you managed that?"

"Are you getting dressed?"

"Yes, for heaven's sake. I'm getting dressed."

"I told her that I'd get you to ask out her eldest, Henrietta. She's looking better since she's dropped some of the weight. She still has the third nipple though, according to her mum. But really, no one need know about that. I'll never tell."

"Wes?"

"Yeah?"

"I'm on my way. You need to switch to decaf, okay?"

"Right." I poured the contents of my cup down the sink.

I quietly surveyed the room in satisfaction, then pulled open the curtains, letting the early morning sun stream inside. I'd bought every red rose that the O'Brien's had and had spent the last hour creating a path from the dining room back up the stairs to the bedroom. I paused in the door, looking back and committing the vision to memory. The velvet soft and deeply red petals were scattered across my pillow, across the bedroom floor and out the door.

Katherine began to stir. So I quickly slipped out and ducked into my office.

"Wes?"

I peered out into the hallway and watched as she tiptoed down the stairs. I waited until I thought she'd made it to the dining room before quietly following.

I'd set the table for one. It was covered in a tablecloth of roses and the only contrast was the single white plate containing a sheet of paper. Katherine pulled out the chair and sat down. Then she picked up the sheet of paper, unfolded it and read the contents aloud.

"The face of all the world is changed, I think, since first I heard the footsteps of thy soul."

"You've completely ruined me, you know."

"Wes."

I went to her then and knelt by her side. "No other woman will ever satisfy me now. You make me feel things I didn't know were even possible. I love you."

"I love you too."

"I'm not done yet, love."

"Sorry." She picked up the linen napkin and dabbed at her eyes.

"I love you with all my heart and soul and, if you'll let me, I'll spend eternity worshipping you. Marry me, Katherine."

I opened the small black velvet box and held it out to her in my outstretched palm.

"Oh!" A sob escaped her lips and she lifted the napkin up to cover her face.

"No good? I thought it was far better than the bathroom proposal."

Katherine uncovered her face and slipped the ring onto her finger, then began to fan herself. "It was really good. Really it was. Really, really."

"Those are happy tears?"

She nodded. "I don't want to cry. I'll be all puffy and that's how you'll remember this."

I pulled out the chair next to her and took her hand in mine.

"So, is that a yes?"

"Yes."

"Yes!"

Katherine looked down at her hand. "It's a beautiful ring. How on earth did you pull this off?"

"If you must know, I woke up the lady who owns the neighborhood florist at four this morning and convinced her to open up for me. The ring I had."

"Was it your mother's?"

"Nah," I said, "I bought it for myself one day when I was feeling particularly blue. I like to slip it on and dance in front of the mirror singing 'I Feel Pretty'."

"How much coffee have you had?"

"Far too much," said Charles as he walked into the dining room carrying a fresh pot for Katherine. "I cut him off hours ago. This is decaffeinated, of course." He set the pot on the table, then slipped back out.

"I'll be honest with you. The ring's only a carat and it has some flaws. I can do better. We can go and pick something out together if you want. It was my mum's. When Dad gave it to her, well, it seemed like a fortune to him at the time."

"No." Katherine shook her head. "It's perfect. I love you."

"I love you too, baby." I checked the time. "I hate to say this, but I've got to get to the office. Charles will stay with you today. I'll be home around seven. You going to be all right?"

"I've never been more all right."

I paused, not quite sure it was the right time to make my request. She caught my hesitation.

"What is it?"

"I want to do this quickly, and in the church."

"How quickly?"

"As quickly as possible. I've made an appointment to speak with the vicar tomorrow. I'm going to tell him that you're pregnant and see if he thinks the Bishop will issue us a common license. You're not a British subject so I expect it'll be approved."

"And if it isn't?"

"Then we'll have to wait a few weeks. They normally announce banns in church for three Sundays before the marriage. It's routine, but not absolutely necessary."

"I don't know what that is. What church are we talking about?"

"The Church of England, love. I was thinking St. Mary's."

"Why did you propose to me, Wes?"

"Thought we covered that."

"You don't need to do this to protect me, to protect us. That's not a good reason for two people to get married."

She sounded strong and sure.

"I know." I pulled her into my arms. "It's all a bloody ruse you know, the ghosts, all that end-of-the-world talk. I mean, when all is said and done, you and I both know exactly why I want to marry you."

"And that would be?"

"I. Love. You."

Katherine smiled. "Right. Just checking."

"Call your mum. Charles will take you shopping for a dress."

Chapter Eighteen

I arrived home shortly after seven as planned. No sooner had I entered the house and Spike was hopping up and clawing at my pants leg.

"Down, Spike."

I shed my coat and opened the closet door to retrieve a hanger. Before I had a chance to register what was happening I was pushed into the closet from behind.

As the door clicked shut and I was shrouded in darkness, my senses kicked into overload. I promptly dropped my coat and gripped the hanger tightly in my hand. Then I smelled her.

"Katherine?"

"Shh. Quiet."

"Why are we in the closet?" I whispered, dropping the hanger.

"It's private." She murmured the words into the shell of my ear, then she reached for my belt and tugged me closer. "I couldn't wait to get you to the bedroom. I've been thinking about you all day."

"Have you now?"

She worked quickly, even in the darkness. With deft hands she unfastened my belt and unzipped my trousers. I found myself holding my breath as she eagerly pushed my pants and boxers down over my hips. I was on my way to being hard; what she did next cinched it for me. She took my cock in her hand and dropped to her knees. My only regret was that it was too dark in the closet to see her.

"You're already hard for me." I could feel the pulse of her breath, followed by the smooth caress of her cheek as she lovingly ran it across the head of my cock.

I swallowed, every fiber of my being tense with anticipation.

"So soft and so hard at the same time." She swiped her tongue up my length, just one long, luxurious lick.

"Oh, Christ!"

"Shh." Katherine squeezed her hand firmly around the base and tilted me toward her mouth. I closed my eyes and leaned my head back while she bathed my cock with her tongue.

"You're going to kill me."

She took me all the way in, her lips sliding down to the root. I bit down on my lip to suppress a cry of pleasure.

I tried to stay focused, quiet, in control. But the way Katherine was bobbing up and down, increasing suction, devouring my cock, was making it impossible. I was starting to feel light-headed, dizzy. I grabbed hold of the wooden bar behind me with one hand as my knees began to weaken. At the same time I reached down with my other hand and laced my fingers through her long blonde locks.

"It feels so fucking good, baby."

"Mmm." She moaned and it made her throat rumble slightly.

"Suck it!" It came out louder than I intended. I was beginning to forget myself, forget everything, everything but the increasing pressure in her warm, wet, delicious mouth. "That's it. God, I love your mouth!"

She was using her spit to her advantage now, letting it run down my cock and into her hand. She was working hard, spreading it so that I was nice and slick. The sensations were becoming overwhelming. I was right on the verge, right on the edge.

"If you don't stop, I'm going to scream."

"Do it, I want to hear you scream." She shifted her attention from my cock to my balls, rolling first one, then the other in her mouth.

It took a few seconds for her words to penetrate through the lust-filled fog of my mind. "You want them to hear?"

"Who?"

"Whoever's out there?"

"It's just you and me, baby." Katherine swiped her tongue up along the underside one more time before swirling it about my now-weeping head. "Come for me."

"There's no one here?" It was taking me an embarrassingly long time to catch on, I know.

"Just me, Wes. Only me. And I'm all naked. Naked and naughty and wanting you to come all over me."

That's all it took. I threw open the closet door, flooding the space with light, then I came with a roar, shooting my come across her breasts again and again.

I pulled Katherine to her feet then reached down and dragged my fingers through the milky fluid, spreading it over her bare breasts and belly. As my breathing began to return to normal I stepped out of the closet and leaned against the open door.

"You are a bad, bad girl."

"And, I'm all sticky."

"Who cares?"

Before she could finish her sentence, I'd pulled her to me, crushing my mouth to hers in an urgent kiss.

"You're bloody brilliant!" I shouted out as I pulled away.

"Marry me!"

"I already said yes, silly." She looked down at her torso. "I'm thinking I could use a bath before dinner."

"Baby, you can have whatever you want. That was inspired."

"Really? I was okay?"

Her question shocked me. "Okay? Are you kidding me?"

"No." She blushed a pretty shade of pink. "I've never wanted to do that before."

"No?" I picked up the robe she'd discarded earlier and held it out so she could slip into it.

"No."

"But you wanted to tonight?"

She nodded, turning to face me. "I was thinking about you, about that kiss, about what might please you."

"You please me." I took her face in my hands and kissed her lips softly.

Confusion marred her brow. "So blowjobs don't really do it for you? I thought all guys had a thing for blowjobs."

"Don't get me wrong! Christ! As far as I'm concerned you could blow me every day and twice on Sundays!"

"Wes!" Katherine covered her face in embarrassment.

"I'm just saying that whatever we do in the bedroom, or in the closet, needs to be something we both enjoy and are comfortable with. It seemed like you were enjoying yourself, yeah?"

"Yeah. But it's new. I feel a little uncertain."

"Well, you know, I'd happily suffer through as many practice sessions as you think you need."

"Suffer through!" Katherine threw herself at me and began to tickle my side. Suddenly it occurred to me that she'd said we were alone. She wasn't supposed to be alone. Quickly sobering, I stilled her hands.

"Where's Charles?"

"Gone."

"Gone?"

Katherine gave me a peck on the cheek. "Don't go getting mad. He slipped out the back door when we saw you coming up the walk. We had fun today, by the way. Charles is teaching me how to cook. We made a Bolognese sauce."

"You don't know how to cook? But, you made dessert the other night."

"You mean the boxed brownie mix? I added some water, two eggs and stirred. That's not cooking. I want to be able to really cook. Moms are supposed to be able to do that sort of thing. I'm going to take a quick bath, then I'll throw the pasta in."

"Sounds good. Let me grab a drink. I'll keep you company." I made my way over to the bar in the living room and poured myself a scotch. "Did you find a dress?"

"No. Everything made me look fat. Why do wedding gowns have to be white? Why can't they be black? Black is slimming. Guys get to wear black."

"So, wear black if you want. I don't care what you wear."

"So, you think I'm fat?"

"I think you're beautiful, desirable and sexy. I don't care if you get as big as this soddin' house. How I see you? That's not going to change."

Spike's whimpering woke me. I bolted upright in bed, coughing. Acrid smoke had begun to fill the room. I rubbed my eyes.

"Katherine! Wake up!" I slipped from the bed onto the floor, pulling Katherine with me. She started to cough and sputter.

"What is it?"

"Fire. Stay here, stay low."

I crawled over to the bedroom door. Flames were hungrily licking up the length of the hallway, blocking our path to the stairs. I shut the door against the smoke, then grabbed my robe and stuffed it under the crack to prevent more from seeping in.

"Can we get out?"

I crawled over to the window. "Not that way." I threw open the sash and the smoke that had been hovering in the room rushed out. The sound of approaching sirens pierced the silence of the night.

"Put this on." I handed Katherine her robe.

She glanced back at the door. "How bad is it?"

"We don't have much time." I quickly slipped into a pair of jeans and grabbed my boots. "Don't be afraid. I'm going to get us out of here."

"Wes! You all right?"

I ran over to the window and looked out. Will Carlton was standing alone in the courtyard, looking up at me.

"Just peachy, Will. How are you? Out for a stroll, are you? I'd join you but *my bloody house is on fire*!"

The sound of the approaching sirens were becoming louder and louder.

"I already called the fire brigade. They're on the way."

"Katherine, there's a fire-escape ladder under the bed."

Katherine reached underneath. "Got it."

She slid it over to me.

"Get some shoes on. You're going to go down first," I told her. Thankfully, she didn't argue. She stepped into her black leather boots, putting them on over her bare feet. By then I had my own boots on and the ladder hung over the edge of the window. Katherine stumbled over to the window, gasping for breath.

"I'll be right behind you." I kissed her. It was quick, almost chaste, but it was all we had time for.

"Promise?"

"Promise."

"Spike?"

I grabbed a pillow from the bed and stripped it of its case. Then looked for the tie that I'd worn to work the day before. It was still fastened to the bedpost. "We'll both be behind you. You first," I told her as I worked to loosen the knot.

I helped Katherine climb out the window.

Spike was whimpering at my heels. I didn't have a second to waste. I scooped him up quickly and dropped him into the makeshift sack. Using the tie, I secured the pillowcase around my waist. I didn't look back. I didn't hesitate. I didn't give a single thought to what I was losing, what I was leaving behind. Instead, as I stepped onto the ladder, I was focused on preserving my future, our future.

"Steady, love. You all right?"

"I think so."

"Go slowly."

Will reached up and guided her down the last few steps. As soon as the way was clear, I jumped the remaining few feet.

"The front is completely ablaze." Will took the pillowcase from me and set Spike loose. "We can get out the back gate and circle around."

"How did you know?"

"Jennifer." Will stripped off his overcoat and held it out for Katherine. Then we headed for the gate. "She woke up coughing and hysterical. I tried to call you, but you didn't answer. So I put her in the car and we came over."

As we rounded the corner a bright red fire engine came to a halt. One of the firemen jumped off and approached Jennifer. She was standing in front of the building, dressed in a long white silk nightgown and an unbuttoned black overcoat.

"Is there anyone else in the house?"

Jennifer looked past him. She smiled broadly, seeing us for the first time. "No, they're safe."

The firefighter followed her gaze. "Any of you injured?"

"No. We're all right," I assured him.

"We'll try to keep it from spreading. I think that's the best we can do."

"There's a painting over the fireplace." Katherine pointed toward the living room window. "It's priceless."

I pulled her into my arms. "It's immaterial, it's just a thing. You and the baby are priceless. You're safe. That's all that really matters."

Even from across the street I could feel the intense heat of the blaze. Neighbors poured out of their houses, some concerned for the safety of their own homes. We watched in silence until there wasn't anything more to watch. Until the fire was out. When it finally was, nothing remained. Nothing but a pile of smoldering ash.

"I want to go talk to a couple of the guys, then we can go back to my place. You're welcome to the guest room until things are sorted," said Will.

Snow had started to fall from the sky. Neither Will nor I had coats and now that the fire had died down, I was beginning to feel the cold.

"That's awfully nice of you, but I think I'd rather head to Atherton House. I want Katherine tucked away, nice and safe.

Unfortunately, my car keys were in there." I nodded toward the remnants of my home.

Will tossed me his. "Take my car. When I'm finished here, I'll hotwire yours. I'll have a new set of keys made for you tomorrow. Call me in the afternoon."

Once Will was halfway across the street he turned back. "Jen, do you want to come with me? Maybe you'll pick up on something?"

"Yeah." Jennifer reached into her pocket and pulled out her mobile. "Here. Keep it until you replace yours." Then she took off, running across the street to catch up with Will.

"Where's Atherton House?" asked Katherine.

"Southeast of here in Kent. It's where I grew up. I should call Charles and let him know we're coming."

I quickly rang Charles; he picked up right away.

"Hello?"

"Charles? It's Wes."

"It's about time. Laura's been trying to reach you for hours. Is something the matter with your phone?"

"She's been trying to reach me?"

"Yes. She's here. Let me put her on."

The fact that Laura was with Charles and it was the middle of the night didn't escape me. Before I had time to say anything, however, Laura had taken the phone.

"Wes? Your friend, the one you brought in, he's gone."

"What do you mean, gone?" I turned around and began to scan my surroundings.

"I guess when it happened the hospital tried to call. I was in the Tube, in a tunnel. The message went to voice-mail and I didn't notice until a few hours ago. I'm off and had the setting on silence. I'm sorry, Wes."

This was too much of a coincidence.

"You were going to call me when you extubated him."

"I'm sorry. He apparently regained consciousness, extubated himself, knocked out a nurse and left."

"How long ago?"

"About four or five hours now, I'd say."

"Tell Charles that Katherine and I are on our way to Atherton House."

"But it's four in the morning!"

"There's been a bit of a mishap. We can't stay here."

Charles took the phone back. "What kind of a mishap? I'd like to have an idea as to what's in store for me tomorrow."

"I'd say you've got little to worry about, Charles. It's essentially gone—burned rubble and ashes." I looked once again at the shell of my home.

"Ashes?" repeated Charles, stunned.

"I know, you had just polished the silver."

"Sod the silver! Are you and Katherine all right?"

"We're fine, thanks to Spike. He woke the two of us up." I leaned down and gave the pup a scratch behind the ears before scooping him up. "I'm going to ring off and head out."

"I'll be here."

I pocketed the mobile, then turned to Katherine. "Come on, love." I unlocked the door and held it open for Katherine.

"Charles lives there?"

"He lives in a cottage on the grounds."

Katherine climbed into the car, pulling the coat more tightly around herself. I closed the door, ran back around to the driver's side and hopped in.

"I'll get the heater on in a minute, love." I leaned over and dropped Spike into the backseat.

"You lost the painting, and your mother's jewels, the ones you let me borrow." Katherine had turned in her seat and was looking back at the remnants of the still-smoldering house.

I leaned over and kissed her. "The pearls and peridot are safe. I gave them to Charles to have them cleaned. I only had them here in the first place because I lent them to someone not too long ago."

"Reese?"

"No. Bernie Friedman's daughter, for her engagement party." I put the car in gear. "There isn't a thing in that house that is as important as what I left with. I want you to remember that."

Katherine nodded as she choked back tears. "We could have died in there, Wes."

"But we didn't. We're here, now. And that says something."

"What if the next time we're not so lucky? I'm beginning to feel like danger is lurking around every corner. Am I paranoid?"

"No. You're not paranoid. We'll be safer at Atherton House. The security there is good, practically museum quality. At least it was when it was initially installed. In addition to my father's own works, there are others that he felt the need to protect."

"How long ago was that?"

"I honestly don't remember. I'll call Will in the morning and schedule a meeting. We'll hire him to make whatever improvements are necessary. It's what the man does."

"Wes, I'm afraid. Because of what Jennifer said, I felt safe in your house. Now it's gone. We were forced to leave. How do we know we aren't walking into certain danger? This, whatever it is, it's unrelenting and powerful."

"It has the power that is given it. No more. It uses subterfuge and obfuscation to confuse the mind, to weaken resolve. We've got to stick together and we've got to be strong."

"You think we can actually beat this? Change destiny?"

"You don't? Katherine, think. You've already done it once, love, changed destiny."

She turned to look out the window. "And we're being punished for it. Isn't that what Jennifer said? I don't know, Wes."

"This isn't new, this thing, and we're not the first to experience it. I'm sure of that. We can't give in, give up. I'm afraid if we do, it will be the end. We can't let that happen."

"What are you saying?"

"I know this sounds crazy. But, we're dealing with Death, incarnate. It seems to be seeking retribution, payback."

"You think it's after me."

"Or the baby," I added.

Katherine defiantly lifted her chin. "This thing is not taking my baby."

"Our baby." I reached for her hand and gave it a reassuring squeeze. "I know, technically, it's not. But, it feels very much to me like—"

"Our baby."

"Close your eyes, love. We'll be there in around a half an hour. I'll wake you. I know you're tired."

Time passed and I drove on. Katherine's head was resting against the window. Just when I thought perhaps she'd fallen asleep, she spoke.

"Wes?" I could hear the fear and uncertainty once again in her voice.

"Get some rest." I lifted her hand to my lips and kissed her palm. "We're a great team. We'll figure this out."

"What if we don't?" she persisted. "What if one of us, or two of us, or all three of us don't make it?"

My jaw was clenched so tightly it was painful. I wanted to be the guy who had all the answers, the guy that knew what he was doing. I wanted to be the larger-than-life action hero who, in the space of a two-hour movie, could save the girl and save the world.

But this was real. Katherine was the woman I loved, and she deserved the truth, however disquieting or unflattering. I turned into the long drive and pulled up to the tall iron gate. I parked the car, then turned to face her and laid it on the line. "Whoever is left will grieve, remember the love we had for one another and then go on living. I want you to know, here and now, that I will love you forever. Not even death will keep me from you. Do you believe that?"

"I believe in you." Katherine reached out and caressed the side of my face. I pressed my cheek into the palm of her hand, savoring the moment until the sound of Charles's voice shattered its sweetness.

"Can I help you?"

I rolled down the window. "Charles, it's me. Can you open the gate?"

"What happened to your car?"

"The car's fine. The keys didn't make it out. This one belongs to a friend." The gates slowly parted, giving us a now-unobstructed view of Atherton House.

I put the car back in gear and drove slowly up the long cobblestone paved drive. A tall wall surrounded the property. There was an expansive lawn with scattered old trees and well-manicured flowerbeds. Off to the right, in the early morning light, we could see the pathway leading down to the small pond.

Atherton House was luxuriously appointed. It was constructed of brick with stone detailing on the sills and quoins. There had always been an air of grandeur about it, yet it still managed to seem warm and inviting. Lights glowed softly in the front downstairs windows.

"Wow. This is where you grew up?"

"I'll give you the grand tour and get you settled."

"Tell me you're not going to work tomorrow?"

"I have a meeting with the vicar first thing. There are some things I have to take care of and I want to connect with Will. Charles will stay with you. I'll return home as fast as I possibly can."

"Home." Katherine looked back toward the house. "It seems so big."

I reached out and ran my fingers through her hair. "I'll remind you that you said that. In a few years, when it's teeming with children, you'll be complaining there's not enough room. Mark my words."

"Teeming? Just how many times do you think I'm going to do this pregnancy thing?"

I casually shrugged my shoulders, then turned off the engine. "It's got seven bedrooms."

Katherine's eyes narrowed. "I can't tell if you're joking."

We both stepped out of the car.

"I'm not joking. There truly are seven bedrooms."

Katherine walked up to me, pulling the coat Will had loaned her more tightly around her body. "Seriously, how many children are you thinking we're going to have?"

I let Spike out of the car and watched as he ran off, nose to the ground.

"I don't know, more than this one? I grew up here by myself, always wished I had a younger brother. You know, someone to pick on, fight with, be jealous of. 'Course, there was Charles. Come on." I held out my hand, tilted my head toward the house, then whistled for the dog. Charles opened the door as we approached.

"I've prepared the master bedroom for you. I thought you might like to retire for a bit, perhaps freshen up? There are some muffins and tea waiting there."

"Thanks, Charles. We are a bit knackered. I'm afraid we'll need replacement clothes. I have to leave to take care of some things in an hour or two. I don't want Katherine to be alone today."

"I understand, sir." He hesitated for a moment. "How bad was it?"

"Bad. Everything is gone. We were lucky. Very lucky."

"I'm very glad you weren't injured, sir, miss."

The moment felt awkward, uncomfortable. I loathed the distance that had developed between us, the barrier that had risen. I wanted to fix it, but I was exhausted and more to the point, I didn't know how. So instead, I nodded. "Thank you, Charles."

"Ring if you need anything."

Then he was gone, leaving Katherine and me alone in the grand foyer. The house had been unoccupied since my father's death, but you wouldn't know it. Charles had been taking care of it just as he had when my parents were alive.

The white polished marble floor gleamed magnificently. There was a round table in the middle of the space holding a large vase filled with fresh cut vanilla orchids.

Katherine walked over to the table and fingered one of the delicate blossoms.

I wrapped my arms around her waist and rested my chin on her shoulder. "They're probably from Mum's collection. She loved orchids. Charles takes care of them all now. How are you in the gardening department?"

"Worse than I am in the cooking department, I'm afraid."

"What is it I see in you, anyway?"

Katherine turned around and playfully batted me on the chest.

“Hey, now. There’ll be none of that!” I grabbed her and pulled her against me.

“Well, don’t tease! It’s not nice.” She pursed her lips together in a petulant pout that was irresistible.

I traced her bottom lip with the tip of my finger. “When you pout, this lip comes out ever so slightly. It begs to be nibbled.”

Katherine’s stomach growled audibly.

She glanced down. “Speaking of nibbling, I’m kind of hungry. Charles did say something about muffins?”

“Upstairs. In the master bedroom.” I took her hand in mine and led her to the large, sweeping staircase. The old mahogany wood of the banister was dark and rich and smelled slightly of orange.

As we climbed the stairs Katherine paused to look at the various swords and shields that hung on the wall.

“You know, most people hang photographs or paintings on their staircase.”

“Dad was an avid swordsman. I remember the first time I was able to best him in a bout. I had just turned sixteen. I was full of myself for weeks.”

“You and your father used to swordfight?”

“Fence. These are just some of his collection. There are more in the gym, and some in the library.”

“There’s a gym and a library? You’re going to have to leave me with a map. Ah-ha! Here are all the embarrassing family pictures,” she exclaimed when we reached the top of the stairs.

The door to the master bedroom was the first of several in the long hallway.

“You’ll have plenty of time to explore after I’m gone. You were hungry, remember?” I opened the door and waved her inside.

"I remember. Wow!" Katherine stopped. I had to give her a little nudge.

"Don't worry, you can redecorate."

"This was your parents' room?" She stepped inside and started to look around, taking in the black lacquer shutters, shantung silk covered walls and marble floor. She walked across the rich Sarouk rug, past the circa 1880 Chippendale desk, to the antique chaise that was covered in the same rich red velvet that made up the duvet on the curtained four-poster.

I scratched the back of my head self-consciously, suddenly feeling every bit the awkward adolescent.

"I'm afraid so. You see why I became a psychiatrist?"

Katherine smiled. "You know what this looks like?"

"A bordello?"

"I was going to go with vampire lair."

"Vampire lair, huh?"

She slipped off Will's overcoat, then untied the sash of her robe, letting it fall to the ground so that she stood before me in just the black leather boots. "It's making me feel kind of naughty."

"Really now?" I closed the door behind me. "How naughty?"

Katherine climbed up on top of the bed and crooked her finger, inviting me to join her. "Very naughty."

"Forget what I said about redecorating."

My arm hung off the edge of the bed, my fingers just barely touching the carpet. I looked down at the familiar pattern. The blood red background and the combination of gold and black threads were woven into intricate designs.

I closed my eyes and licked my lips to moisten them. I felt Katherine leave the bed, our bed. I rolled over and watched her walk to the bathroom through the sheer red chiffon drapes that covered the canopy and hung between the ornately carved posts.

She returned a few seconds later.

"Here's your water, sire." Katherine separated the curtains and quietly crawled back onto the bed.

"I can't move." I was bone tired. Completely sated. We'd made love as if it were the last time we'd ever make love and I had the distinct feeling that Katherine was hydrating me in hopes of one more round.

"Did I break you?"

"How can you not be tired?"

"I guess I just got my second wind!" She lifted the water glass to her lips and took in several large gulps. Then she leaned over me and placed the glass on the nightstand, the tips of her breasts grazing my back.

"You should drink some water." She paused for a second before leaning down and kissing the back of my neck. "It's good for you."

"What are you doing?"

"Nothing," she said between kisses. Then she climbed on top of me, draping her body over mine. "Don't mind me."

"Doesn't feel like nothing." I lifted my hips up slightly off the bed in automatic response to the wet heat I felt rubbing up against my lower back.

"Why do real guys have to have refractory periods? In the romance novels they never have refractory periods."

"Women shouldn't read romance novels."

"Why not?"

"It spoils them for real sex. Gives women all sorts of

unrealistic expectations."

"It does not! Romance novels are, well, romantic. They're inspirational." Katherine leaned down and nibbled on my ear.

"By inspirational do you mean sexually stimulating?"

"Uh-huh," she whispered in my ear as she continued to rub herself against my body. "So, how long is yours?"

"My dick? You may find this hard to believe, but I've never actually measured it."

"No!" laughed Katherine. She climbed off of me and stretched out, laying her head on the pillow next to mine. "Not your penis, silly, your refractory period."

I slid my hand across the bed, reached between her thighs and separated her folds. "Aren't you a greedy little girl?"

She arched her back and lifted her hips seeking out more friction. "When it comes to you, yes."

I rolled onto my side, propped myself up on one elbow and continued to give her what she wanted. I circled her clit with my thumb, then I dipped two fingers inside of her pussy. She was sopping wet, ready for me again, wanting me still.

"I wish we could do this all day," I whispered moving in and out, slowly, deliberatively, as I watched her climb. "Unfortunately, I'm gonna have to leave soon. Care to shower with me?"

"Don't stop," she gasped. "Please don't stop."

"You're so close, so beautiful."

"Wes, I—Oh, yes!" Katherine was stunning, completely unguarded, her passion for me raw and real. The orgasm washed over her. Watching it rocked me to the core.

I waited a moment while she came down then I kissed her softly on the mouth. "Was that yes in answer to my shower question?"

"Question? Were you talking?"

I playfully jabbed her in the side. "You're supposed to hang on my every word!"

"You can't expect me to track a conversation when you're doing that!"

I poked her again for good measure.

"Stop it! I have to pee!"

"You're just saying that." I caught her wrists in my hands, pinned them over her head and straddled her waist.

Katherine looked at me steadily, raising one eyebrow.

"Oh, all right! Spoil my fun!" I shifted to move off of her.

The instant I did, she pounced, knocking me over. We both slid off the bed and onto the floor. Katherine landed on top of me but she didn't maintain her position for long.

I quickly rolled over. "You little minx!"

She laughed. "Minx? Oh my God, did you really call me a minx?"

I couldn't help myself, I laughed too. "I must be delirious."

I felt light-headed, almost dizzy. We laid there, limbs tangled until the moment passed. Then I looked down into Katherine's eyes. "I love you."

I leaned over and softly kissed her on the mouth.

"I love you, too."

"I can't wait until Saturday."

"What's happening on Saturday?"

The sunlight that poured in through the slats in the window formed streaks across the floor. Katherine's hair was fanned out so that the tips dipped into the light, giving the illusion of a halo behind her, surrounding her. I sat back up and looked steadily into her deep green eyes. "Katherine Lawson, this Saturday I'm going to marry you."

Chapter Nineteen

"Charles, I'm on my way home."

"How close are you?"

"About a mile away? Sorry, I should have called sooner."

"It's not a problem. I've roasted a pork tenderloin for dinner."

"Is Katherine handy?"

"She just knocked off for the day. She's been working like a fiend."

"Working? On what?"

"I've been sworn to secrecy. She's changing now, I think. She said something about taking a swim."

"Charles, I want to ask you something."

"What is it, sir?"

"It's just me, Charles, Wes. Okay?"

There was a long pause. "Okay."

"I want you to be my best man."

For a minute I thought that I lost him.

"You there?"

"I'm here."

"We've always been best mates, Charles. I'm not exactly sure how things got so sideways between us. I want things to be the way they were."

"Are you firing me?"

"No. What I'm saying is that I miss having you as a friend."

"You're asking me to be your best man?"

"Who else would I ask?"

"Eric?"

I sighed. "Does this mean you're saying no?"

"No. I mean, I'd be delighted, Wes."

The car came to a stop and I stepped out and headed for the door.

Charles greeted me with a silver tray in his hand containing two crystal tumblers. They were both filled with scotch. He handed me one, then raised the other.

"To you and Katherine."

We both drained our glasses. Before I could set mine down, Charles slapped me on the back. "You're getting married!"

"And I'm going to be a father," I added.

He pulled on his earlobe, a sure sign that he had something to say.

"Spit it out."

"It's just so fast."

"It's just so *right*," I countered. "Let's tell Katherine. Where is she?"

"In the pool. I'm supposed to tell you that the conservatory is off limits. We'll need to go another route."

"Why is the conservatory off limits?"

The pool house jutted out from the main house. On three sides it was lined with sliding French doors so that in the summer it could be almost completely open. The roof was made of sliding panels that were easily retracted. It was connected to the house by a large bathroom and changing area that you could reach from either the conservatory, my father's studio, or a hallway that ran the length of the house. We took the hallway.

I knocked before entering the changing area. It was empty. The door leading to the pool had been left slightly ajar and we proceeded toward it, following the sensual sounds of jazz that could be heard playing inside.

The air inside the room was warm and humid. Condensation covered the tall glass windows. The lights were dim. The pool itself, softly lit from below.

Katherine was standing on the springboard. She made a confident three-step approach. Unaware of her audience, on the third step, she swung her arms forward and up over her head, lifting her right knee, leaping up from the board, and pushing off with her left leg. She sprang into the air, completely nude.

For a moment I was mesmerized. The reflection of the water below and lighting from above gave her already-glowing skin an even more profound luminescence. She looked absolutely glorious. I watched, rooted in place.

She entered the water hands first and her body followed in one smooth straight line, her toned legs extending out behind her. As the tips of her toes disappeared under the water I heard Charles whisper, "Good Lord."

I turned to find him facing the wall. "Sorry, Wes."

I watched Katherine glide through the crystal clear water. As her head broke through the surface I called to her. "Hello, cutie."

"Wes!" She quickly crossed her arms over her bare breasts.

"Charles and I have news!"

"I apologize," said Charles. "I didn't realize."

I approached the edge of the pool. "He didn't see a thing. Just a blur before you plunged into the water. I, on the other hand, have already seen your goodies. Come on out, love."

I picked up the robe that she'd left on one of the chairs and met her at the stairs

Her eyes narrowed. "What's the news?" Katherine climbed up the stairs and stepped out of the pool, water sheeting off her body.

"I'm going to be the breast man. I mean best man."

Katherine turned bright red. "Best man?"

I helped her into her robe, then leaned down to kiss her. "Yeah! I missed you today."

"Missed you too," she murmured as her lips met mine in a soft kiss.

"You can turn around, Charles."

"Dinner will be ready in an hour. Shall I serve in the dining room?" he asked.

Katherine placed her hand at the base of her lower back and winced.

"Is your back bothering you?" I asked her.

She shrugged. "Too much sitting today. I don't think it's anything to worry about."

"But I am worried. I can't help it."

Katherine frowned. "It's just a little back pain. Stop fussing." She picked up a towel and began to dry her hair.

I shoved my hands into the pockets of my slacks and resisted the urge to press the issue. The look of concern must have been plainly evident.

"Are you going to be like this through my entire pregnancy?"

"Probably."

"I'm going to go get dressed." Katherine walked away, eyes downcast. Something wasn't right.

"I thought she'd be more enthusiastic," I said to Charles as soon as we were alone. "Maybe she's just tired?"

"You'd talked about it, right?"

"What?"

"Having a best man and maid of honor?"

"No. I just figured...bollocks!"

"Katherine doesn't really know anyone here, Wes. Her friends and family are all back in the States."

"There's her mum." I suggested weakly.

Charles shook his head. "She's going back tomorrow. I didn't catch the details, but when I saw Mrs. Lawson to the door, I got the distinct impression that she thought she'd be seeing me in San Diego in a few weeks."

"In San Diego?"

We started to make our way toward the front of the house.

"Can I ask you a question?"

"Of course."

"Why are you moving so fast, Wes? Is it because you're hoping to tie this up all neat and tidy for the child's sake?"

Charles turned into the kitchen and I followed.

"That's part of it. I'd be lying if I said it wasn't."

He opened the oven door to check on the roast. "This isn't the Dark Ages, Wesley."

"I know. There are other considerations."

"What other considerations?"

I opened one of the cupboards, pulled out a bottle of scotch and poured myself another glass.

"It's complicated."

"That's what friends are for, Wes, to help you figure out the things that are complicated."

He started to pull dishes from one of the cabinets.

"I wasn't meant to survive that crash, Charles."

He turned to face me, a pained look on his face. "You think something's going to happen to you."

I nodded. "I want to make sure they're taken care of, both Katherine and the baby. I really want your support. You're the closest thing I've ever had to a brother. And, with my folks gone, you're really my only family."

The expression on his face softened. Charles extended his hand and when I accepted it he tugged me into his awkward version of a hug.

"You have my support," he said quietly. "You've always had my support."

He released me and picked up the stack of dishes. "You better go check on your future bride. I'll ring you upstairs when dinner's ready," he said before pushing through the door to the dining room.

I left the kitchen, went down the hall, then raced up the stairs. I took them two at a time and headed straight for the master bedroom. The shower was still running, but the door to the bathroom was closed so I knocked on it before opening it a crack.

"Can I come in?"

"It's your house."

Ouch. This wasn't going to be easy.

"Am I going to have to sleep with Spike tonight?"

Katherine turned off the shower and stepped out. I set my drink down and grabbed one of the fluffy, white towels from the towel warmer.

"Why would you think that?"

"'Cause I think I screwed up?"

"I'll deal."

"I don't want you to have to deal. I want to apologize. I made an assumption and I shouldn't have. Despite the rift that I'd stupidly let form between Charles and me, he's my oldest and dearest friend. He's like family."

"I understand. Really, I do. I don't know why I'm upset. Maybe it's because I'm feeling guilty. I lied to my mother, Wes. I never lie to my mother. It was the only way I could think of at the time to get her to go back to the States."

"What did you tell her?"

"That we wanted to fly out and get married as soon as Mr. Riley cleared me. She should be boarding a plane any minute. She probably has half the wedding planned already. It's going to break her heart when I tell her we're already married."

Suddenly I was studying my shoes. I had a suspicion. Why was I hedging? Why was I beating around the bush?

"This wasn't the way you imagined it, is it? Getting married."

"I love you, Wes."

"I love you, too." I reached for Katherine's hand, then led her into the bedroom and over to the chaise. I sat in silence for a moment, trying to find the words to express something that even I didn't fully understand.

"Are you feeling ashamed?"

Her question caught me completely off guard. "Ashamed? Of what?"

"Because I'm pregnant, with another man's child no less."

"No!"

"Is that why you're rushing this?"

"I think what I'm feeling is protective. I'm afraid, Katherine. I don't want to lose you."

"You're not going to lose me."

"I want to believe that."

"Something happened. There's something you aren't telling me."

She was right. It wasn't so much that I planned on keeping it from her. It was more that I'd hoped to save the discussion till later.

I leaned back on the chaise and released a ragged breath. "It's Damien."

"Oh, God." She covered her mouth. "Is he...?"

"No, he's not dead. At least I don't think so. He extubated himself last night and escaped from the hospital. Katherine, I think he's the one who started the fire."

"It could have been an accident. You said yourself, it was an old building."

I stood up, nervously ran my hand through my hair, and came clean. "I was interviewed by the fire brigade today. And someone from the police as well. The fire was started deliberately. They asked about any threats, anyone I thought might want to harm either one of us. I told them about Damien, about what's been happening."

"You told them everything?"

I shook my head. "I told them about the not-so-crazy-sounding stuff. That you broke it off with him and he's had difficulty accepting it. That he came to the house and hit you, then showed up drunk, then appeared to be downright delirious, possibly hallucinating before he was hospitalized."

"But there's more to the story, Wes. There's a lot more."

"They wouldn't believe me if I told them. And, honestly, I'm not sure it's relevant. I'm not sure it's important."

"I can't believe Damien would hurt me, hurt the baby."

"The police are looking for him. He hurt some people at the

hospital. Something's gotten to him. I think it's making him do things."

"How?"

"By twisting his reality. Making him believe things, influencing him."

"You really think he set the fire?"

"I do."

"Now I'm afraid."

I shook my head and swallowed. "That's not even the scary part."

Katherine stood up and came to me. "What's the scary part?"

"If this thing can influence Damien, it could do the same to us. It could turn us against one another."

"We'll figure it out." She said it with such confidence, such certainty.

"Oh, really? And just how do you know that?"

Katherine searched out my eyes. "I just know. You're stronger than Damien. I have faith in you, in us. We're going to get through this."

"I appreciate the vote of confidence, but Damien's a big guy. I'm in good shape, and I'm scrappy. But if it comes down to a fight between us? I'm not sure I'll win."

Katherine placed her hand over my heart. "I meant you're stronger in here, where it counts. You love me. You *really* love me."

"Till the end of the world." I sighed, then rested my forehead against hers. "I'm tired. I can't stop thinking about all of this. There's a part of me that just wants to pack a bag and take you away, far away. What if... What if I can't protect you?"

"I'll *still* love you." Tears spilled from her eyes and rolled down her face.

I wiped them away with the pads of my thumbs and choked down my own. Katherine pulled away then sat down in front of my mum's old dressing table and began to run a brush through her hair.

"Let me do that." I took the brush from her hand.

"I'm sorry, Wesley. I'm sorry this is so hard and so crazy. No matter what happens I want you to know, with complete and utter certainty, that you've kept your promise to me."

I paused, our eyes connecting in the mirror.

"I haven't regretted getting back on that train. Not for a second," she said.

I leaned down and kissed her shoulder softly. "You are a crazy bint, Miss Lawson. Think we're going to get our happily ever after, do you?"

"Yes! All we have to do is figure out how to outsmart Death, right?"

"Right. That's all."

"Simple."

"Yeah."

"So, how do we do it?"

"Haven't got a soddin' clue, love," I admitted, setting the brush down and shoving my hands into my pockets.

"Did you speak to either Will or Jennifer today?"

"We kept missing one another."

Katherine walked over to the dresser and pulled out fresh undergarments. "Maybe you should try again?" She stepped into her black lace knickers, then slid on the matching bra.

"Are we okay?" I asked her.

"More than okay."

I studied her for a moment, trying to commit every curve to memory. "Why ruin the effect with more clothes? I'm beginning to think my father was right. Clothes are terribly overrated. You should stop wearing them."

Katherine slipped on a red silk blouse and started to button it up. "Right!"

I cupped her face in the palm of my hand and ran my thumb over her cheek. "You seem to glow more each day," I said, then I bent toward her, brushing my lips across hers.

The kiss started out sweet and soulful. Just as I started to deepen it, the bedroom phone rang. I pulled back and sighed.

"Dessert will have to wait." I nodded toward the desk. "That would have been Charles signaling us to come down for dinner."

"You go on, I'll be right down."

Dinner passed quickly. As we sat down, Katherine asked me about the Medical Director appointment, and from there we went on to talk in detail about my meetings with the police, fire brigade and the vicar.

Before I knew it, we'd finished our meal and Charles had cleared the table. I looked pointedly at Katherine and patted my right knee. "Come over here."

She stood up and walked toward me. As she positioned herself in my lap, I opened up my arms and wrapped them around her. "Was I too far away?"

I nodded. "Yeah. Now that I've bored you to death with the details of my day, tell me, what did you do? Charles said you were really busy."

Katherine smiled. "Well, you know how I didn't have any luck with finding a dress the other day?"

"Yeah."

"I decided to make one myself."

"A wedding dress?"

"Yes, a wedding dress. Don't look so shocked! I came here

to do a fashion design internship, remember? I might not know how to cook, but I do know how to sew. My mother and George brought my machine over with some supplies, then we all did a bit of re-arranging in the conservatory so I could set up shop, so to speak."

"And Sara came through with just the perfect fabric," added Charles as he started to pour coffee.

"Sara?"

"I called her," he said.

I was shocked. For years he'd pined after the elusive Miss Chase. She'd broken Charles's heart more than once.

"She brought it herself, Wes, and she looked at my design. Maybe she was just being polite, but she said she liked it. She said she couldn't wait to see the finished product."

Charles set the pot on the table. "If Sara said she liked it, she did. She doesn't normally trouble herself with being polite," he said before leaving us alone.

Katherine stood up, placed her hands at the base of her spine and arched her back, gently stretching.

The soft black suede of her pants and the smooth silk of her red blouse posed an interesting contrast. The blouse was unbuttoned in front, revealing just a bit of cleavage. But that wasn't where my eyes were really drawn; they were uncontrollably drawn to her neck, where a long strip of matching red fabric was tied. I pictured myself sitting astride her, her smooth unmarred body laid out before me on the black silk sheets, her wrists tied together with that red silk scarf as I leaned forward and...

"Honey?"

"What?" My attention was pulled back to the present.

"I think I lost you for a minute."

Charles popped his head back in the dining room. "Excuse

me, I need to step out for a few minutes. Laura's on the line. It seems we've lost electricity over in the cottage."

"Why don't you take the rest of the evening off? We'll be heading upstairs shortly."

The dining room lights began to flicker.

"Power outage?" asked Katherine.

I stood up. "I don't think so."

The sound of a distant scream pierced the air and we were plunged into darkness.

"Laura? I've lost her!"

"Go!" I shouted. I needn't have bothered, Charles was already running toward the kitchen. "Come with me. I don't have time to explain." I jumped to my feet. By the time I walked the four quick strides to the wine cellar, the emergency lighting flickered on. It only dimly lit the various rooms of the house, but it was something. I unlocked the door to the wine cellar, walked to the back and gave the middle wine rack a strong pull. The back wall levered open exposing an expansive concealed room lined floor to ceiling with aging bottles. "Katherine, get inside! I want you to wait in here. Katherine?"

"Here." She was running back down the staircase. She'd pulled the late thirteenth century Wakizashi from its wall mount and was now holding it in her hands. What little light there was glinted off the polished Mino blade. "You aren't going out there alone. It's too dangerous."

She looked fierce, determined.

"Best way to protect the baby is to not go in search of trouble. You get cornered, you do whatever you have to do. I'll be fighting right alongside you. But for now? You stay right here! This could be nothing. It probably is nothing."

"You don't believe that any more than I do."

"Get inside!" I didn't have time to argue. Katherine opened

her mouth to protest, but I didn't give her the chance. She was going to be royally brassed off when I let her out, but alive and angry is better than dead any day of the week. I reached for her arm and tugged on it firmly, pulling her into the wine cellar then pushing her into the concealed room. She stumbled backward. Before she regained her footing I had the door secure.

I made my way quickly to the back of the house, following Charles out into the night. Pellets of hail stung my face as I ran across the courtyard toward the cottage.

Suddenly, I was hit from behind with something, something hard. I would have fallen to the ground if it hadn't been for the brick wall surrounding the perimeter of the property. For a moment I held onto it, blood running down the back of my head and into the collar of my shirt. Then I glimpsed a shadow behind me. I dropped and rolled just in time to avoid another blow, sweeping my attackers legs out from underneath him. But he was fast, inhumanly fast. Before I could recover, he was on his feet once again.

"Wes! Drop!" yelled Charles. I heard the unmistakable sound of a chamber being loaded. When he'd gone back to check on Laura he'd obviously grabbed his hunting rifle.

My attacker executed a powerful sidekick, propelling me back into Charles. The two of us fell to the ground. I watched, stunned, as the man, dressed in black, crouch down then sprang up onto the top of the six-foot wall before disappearing from sight.

"Did you see what I just saw?" asked Charles.

"Yeah." I gingerly touched the cut on the back of my head.

"He jumped over a six-foot wall from a standing position."

"Yup." I started to climb to my feet. I felt a little dizzy and slightly nauseous. Charles offered me a steady hand.

"But that's impossible!"

I smiled. "You saw it, Charles. I saw it. It's not impossible."

"We should call the police. All these months the house was standing empty. Someone decides to break in now?"

"It's not the police we need. Call Will Carlton. Tell him what's happened. Tell him I need him and Jennifer both out here."

"Jennifer? Carlton I understand. He's a security expert, right? Why the girl?"

"She knows things, Charles."

"What do you mean she knows things?"

"Bring Laura to the main house. The two of you should stay with me tonight. There's too much at stake."

"I don't understand! What's at stake?" Charles shouted over the now-roaring wind.

I glanced down at the blood staining my hand, then looked Charles in the eye.

"Everything."

Chapter Twenty

"Laura, you sure you don't remember what he looked like?"

"No. It happened too fast. The instant I noticed the face in the window, it seemed the lights went out."

"Maybe if you saw a photograph?"

"Maybe. I don't think so." Laura tied off the last stitch. "You're probably going to have a whopper of a headache."

"I've already got a whopper of a headache. At least the bleeding's stopped."

Katherine knelt down in front of me, concern marring her brow. "You realize that if I wasn't so worried about you, I'd be furious right now."

"Absolutely. What is it they say? Every cloud has a silver lining?"

I managed to make her smile.

She stood up and kissed me on the cheek. "Can I get you some aspirin?"

"Paracetamol and an ice pack. You'll find both in the cabinet closest to the pantry."

"Will do."

"I'll get it," offered Charles.

Katherine stood up. "Please, let me. I feel useless."

Thankfully, a knock at the door seemed to stem any further

debate.

Charles nodded. "I'll get the door then. I wager it's the Carltons."

Charles entered the room with Will, Jennifer and a man that I hadn't met before.

I stood up and extended my hand.

"Stanley Houghton. We'll need to see everything you have on the current security system."

Stanley was tall and rugged looking. The expression on his face was neutral, his gaze unnervingly penetrating, his grip firm.

"Wesley Atherton. This is Laura Stanton, a friend of mine."

Stanley nodded, then he pulled a laptop from the black bag he'd carried inside. "How many are in the house?"

"Four, not counting the three of you."

"You have the security system on?"

"Yes. When the power was cut it went down, but only for a few seconds. The generator kicks on if we aren't back on line in ten seconds."

"Is anyone armed?"

"Not at the moment. Why?"

He smiled. "Because I detest getting shot or stabbed." He turned toward Will. "Time me."

"What are you going to do?"

"I'm going to poke as many holes as I can in your security system."

"Stanley's a penetration expert," announced Jennifer.

"A what?" asked Laura.

"A penetration expert," repeated Will. "He's going to help evaluate your current vulnerabilities. While Stanley's doing that, you can bring me up to speed on what happened."

"Fine."

Katherine entered the room. She had her coat in one hand and her purse in the other. "I'm leaving," she said.

"What?"

"I can't do this, Wes. I'm in love with Damien. We're having a child together."

I closed my eyes and shook my head.

"Wes? Honey, what's wrong? Are you all right?"

When I opened my eyes, Katherine was standing before me, an icepack in one hand, a glass of water in the other.

"Are you feeling dizzy?" She set the glass of water down on a nearby table. "Maybe you should sit."

The baby will always tie them together. It'll never be yours. She'll never be yours. You know what you have to do, the voice hissed inside my head.

"I'm fine. It's nothing. Too much talk of fire and brimstone. That's all." I nervously ran my hand through my hair. "My headache's a bit worse."

"Here, take these." Katherine handed me a couple painkillers and the glass of water. I swallowed them gratefully.

You know what you have to do. The voice came from just behind me. I spun around, searching out its origin and in the process spilling some of the water.

Clock's ticking. Time's running out.

"Wes?" Laura took the glass from me. "Maybe sitting down is a good idea."

I shook my head. "I can hear him. It. Clock's ticking. Time's running out."

"Who?"

"Abaddon." I turned to Jennifer. "Can you hear him?"

"No."

Laura picked up the flashlight and shined it in my eyes. "I think we should get you to a hospital."

I pushed her hands away. "I'm not hallucinating."

She frowned.

Jennifer looked about the room. "You can hear him now?"

"Yes. Right now. Right here. You can't? He's laughing, mocking me. How do I control it?"

"Psychiatrist Goes Crazy. I can see the headlines now. Ironic, don't you think?"

The laughter was getting louder. Jennifer was saying something, only I couldn't hear what it was.

"Piss off! I'm trying to have a conversation here!" I yelled.

Then, just as suddenly as it had started, it stopped. Silence.

"The blighter's finally come out of the woodwork!" said Jennifer. "He's playing with you. Thinks he'll get you wrapped up in his mind games."

Charles reached for my arm and led me to a chair. "Wes, perhaps you're just tired. What with all that went on last night you didn't get much rest. Come to think of it, since the accident you've been under a lot of strain."

"He doesn't get it. You don't get it. But you will. There's only one way for this to end. You need to finish it. You know what you have to do. You know what you have to give me."

It came from the corner of the room, from deep in the shadows. I squinted my eyes, straining to see into the darkness.

"I'm not giving you jack."

The laughter returned. Laura knelt in front of me. She was asking me something, only I couldn't focus on what it was.

"You speak as if you have a choice. You have no choice."

"Oh! I have a choice!"

I pushed Laura aside and went after Jennifer. She was the key. "How do I control it?"

"You can't," she said, backing away from me until she reached the wall.

"Wes! You're not alone. We'll help you through this," said Will.

"Stupid boy. Don't listen to him. In the end we're all alone. You know that. Right, Wesley? You can feel it. Can't you? Can't you?"

The voice was echoing so loudly inside my head that my ears were ringing. I cupped my hands over them. "Will you stop yelling at me? I can hear you!"

"This is just the beginning. I'm going to consume you. Death. Horror. It's coming. I'm coming."

"Well, then, bring it on!"

I was plunged into complete darkness. I couldn't even see my hand in front of my face.

I could feel it, inside. Worming its way into my mind. Probing. Rifling through my memories. Searching for a way to hurt me, to shake my foundation. In the darkness my foot bumped up against something. There was a moan. It sounded like Katherine.

I dropped to my knees. "Katherine?"

"You have to help me, Wes! I'm in pain. Something's wrong."

I was momentarily blinded as a light snapped on overhead. I shielded my eyes, giving them a moment to adjust.

Katherine's stomach was swollen with child. She threw her head back and screamed, a contraction hitting hard. Blood began to pool between her legs. She was sweating profusely, writhing on the floor, pain etched clearly on her face.

"Do something!" she sobbed.

"They're both going to die."

"No. They won't."

"Yes. They will. You're going to have to make a choice, Wesley."

"Bloody right, I will."

"The time is coming. The choice is inevitable."

"Nothing is inevitable."

"Death is inevitable."

"Yeah? Well I choose not to die today, so sod off and get out of my head!"

"You think this is about you? It's not about you. It's about them. I'm taking one of them. Choose. Now."

"Piss off. This isn't real. It's not even remotely real. You have no power over me. You have no power over my friends."

"We'll see about that. You pose an interesting challenge."

"Don't you have more important things to do? Or, is it not time yet? Just when is that apocalypse due to happen?"

"So arrogant. That will change."

"Clock's ticking ever so slowly while you wait. That's it, isn't it? I suppose you've got to amuse yourself somehow. Nothing to do, and so much time."

"You think you understand me? You couldn't possibly understand me."

Katherine was reaching for me, begging for me to save her life. Pleading with me not to leave her. Imploring that I cut the child tearing up her insides out of her. I looked down at the form on the floor impassively.

"Don't be so sure," I said, my voice devoid of emotion. Then I stood up, turned my back on her and walked away into the darkness, confident that on the other side, I'd find the light.

"Oh, thank God!"

My eyes slowly came into focus. I was back in the library. Katherine was by my side, Laura next to her. I was on the floor.

"I'm all right," I assured her, sitting up.

Laura looked skeptical. "You lost consciousness."

"For how long?"

"Just a few seconds."

"He took you, didn't he?" Jennifer's voice was on the edge of hysteria. "Any one of you could be next."

"Was it Abaddon?" asked Will. "What happened?"

I nodded. "He's playing with us." I climbed to my feet. "I need a moment."

"What are you people talking about?" asked Laura.

"And the fifth angel sounded." Stanley stepped out of the shadows into the pool of light from the fireplace. When he'd entered the library, I wasn't sure.

"I saw a star fall from heaven unto the earth: and to him was given the key of the bottomless pit. And he opened the bottomless pit; and there arose a smoke out of the pit, as the smoke of a great furnace; and the sun and the air were darkened by reason of the smoke of the pit."

"That's from Revelation," said Charles.

Stanley nodded. "Chapter Nine. Abaddon is the angel of the bottomless pit. The Grim Reaper. Death itself. Face of a man, body of a horse, tail of a scorpion and wings. Huge black wings."

"The scorpion bites!" gasped Laura.

Stanley turned and glared at Will. "Why didn't you tell me this was what we were dealing with?"

"I needed independent verification."

"Fuck!" Stanley rounded on Jennifer. "What did you do?"

"I couldn't just let him die!"

"You've got to be more careful. Every time you do something like this you put yourself in danger!"

Will placed his hand on Stanley's shoulder. "It's done, Stanley. The game is in play now. We've been through stuff like this before. I've seen you—"

He shook his head. "No, we've never had to protect someone from something like this. We aren't talking about run-of-the-mill spirit possession. We're talking demon possession. We're not equipped to deal with this kind of power, William."

"What choice do we have?"

The room fell silent.

"Christ, we need a place to set up." Stanley picked up his bag and walked toward the kitchen. We all started to follow. "So, what do we think we're looking at here? A full-blown apocalypse?"

"Boredom," I said.

Stanley paused at the door. "Yeah, I can see that. Makes sense."

He set his black bag on the large kitchen table and unzipped it.

"No, it doesn't!" growled Laura. "None of this is making any sense."

"Sure it does," I said. "Think about it. Big, powerful demon with nothing to do but sit around and wait for the signal? And wait...and wait...and wait. So much time, so many lower beings, so many evil, fiendish plots to hatch."

"Wes!" Laura stepped close to me, grabbing hold of my shirt. "Demons? You of all people have to realize how this sounds."

"Crazy?"

She nodded. "Yes, Wes. It sounds crazy."

I smiled. "I know it does. Rest assured, I haven't completely gone 'round the bend." I pulled out one of the kitchen chairs and sat down. "This is real. You yourself said they were scorpion bites."

"Maybe I was wrong."

"You weren't wrong."

"Maybe we should try to explain from the beginning?" suggested Katherine.

Laura took the seat across from me and leaned forward intently. "I'm all ears."

Katherine walked over to me and sat down in my lap. "Shall I start?"

With comfortable ease I wrapped my arm around her waist and nodded.

"Wes and I were out on our first date. We'd taken the Tube to the theatre. When I got off at my stop there was this woman."

"That would be me," interjected Jennifer. "I'd been hearing him for days. Telling me I was wrong, all wrong. Laughing. Taunting me. Saying that he was going to take Wes. Saying that I had nothing to live for. Sometimes it was just its voice, but sometimes he appeared as..."

"Go on," I encouraged.

"Most times it was Will, sometimes Stanley, sometimes even you." Silent tears formed a path down her cheeks. "I knew none of you would ever want me to take my life."

Will reached out for his sister's hand and gave it a reassuring squeeze.

Katherine continued. "Because Jennifer interceded, I got back on the Tube and some things changed."

Jennifer nodded. "Wesley lived."

"Tell Laura about the ghosts," prompted Katherine.

"The ghosts of some of his former victims, they've been trying to make contact, to help us. He infected their minds," said Jennifer.

"He stole their lives," I added. "And now he's targeting Katherine's ex-fiancé, Damien. I'm sure of it. Damien was here tonight. He was the one that attacked us."

"Not just here, tonight," added Charles. "He hit Katherine the other night, also the personnel at the hospital. Do you think he could have had anything to do with the fire?"

"It's just so unlike him," said Katherine, shaking her head in disbelief.

Jennifer leaned back against the refrigerator and folded her arms protectively across her chest. "He's lost touch with what's real."

"That's the trick, isn't it?" I asked her. "Holding onto what's real, knowing what that is?"

"Do you have any pictures of this Damien?" Stanley asked Katherine.

"I don't have any with me," she replied. "But there are some in my online photo album. Is the Internet connection working in the house?"

"I'll get my equipment out of the van. I've got satellite." Stanley stood up and walked toward the door. "It seems like this Damien guy is the one Abaddon is focusing on triggering. I'll concentrate on him first."

"Stanley!" He paused and turned back to face me. "I don't think that's true."

"You don't?"

I shook my head. "What happened to me is just the beginning. Sure, there's Damien. But, frankly, I'm more worried about us."

"Us?" asked Charles.

"Yes, Charles. Us. What we might do to ourselves, to one another. That's our biggest threat."

"But you and Jennifer have both successfully resisted him."

Jennifer began laughing. "Successful? I was committed. I may not have killed myself but I wouldn't call getting myself locked up a rollicking success."

Suddenly it felt as if I carried the weight of the world on my shoulders. I took a deep breath, then let it out and said what needed to be said. I said it as plainly as I could, with as much conviction as I could muster.

"As unbelievable as this may sound, we have to face facts. This thing is real. It knows us. It knows what we can do, and it isn't impressed. It's laughing. You want to know how we're going to beat it? We're going to prepare. Get ready to face your fears. Be prepared to dismiss what you see and hear and taste and feel."

"And?" asked Charles.

I clutched my hand to my heart. "And rely on what you *know*."

"Or what?"

"Or we're just a bunch of silly mortals, waiting to be picked off, driven mad and buried. That's it, isn't it?" asked Katherine.

I gathered her into my arms. "I'm afraid so."

Katherine leaned back. "That's not how this is going to end."

"No?"

She looked so confident. "No."

"I'm not sure I can sleep." Katherine was staring at the closed door of the bedroom.

"You're exhausted. You have to sleep." I turned down the bed.

The hand-held radio crackled, then I heard Will's voice. "Test. Test."

I picked it up and pushed the button. "I hear you."

"You're locked in. Call if you need anything."

"Thanks, mate. How much am I paying you to lock me up in my own bloody house?"

"You don't want to know, man. It sounds like Stanley has finished emptying the van. We've got work to do. Out."

Katherine walked around to the far side of the bed and began to remove the various throw pillows, tossing them onto the floor. I moved to the other side of the bed and as our eyes connected we pulled down the covers slowly.

"Penny for your thoughts," whispered Katherine.

"I was just wondering how many times my parents must have done this simple task together, turning down the bed. It feels odd, us sleeping in their room. Yet, it's strangely comforting at the same time."

I sat down on the edge of the bed and removed my boots and socks. By the time I'd stood back up and turned around, Katherine was dressed only in her bra, knickers and the unbuttoned red silk blouse. She was struggling to untie the knot in the scarf around her neck.

"Here. Let me help." I walked across the room, unbuckling my belt and pulling my shirt free. "Your hands, they're shaking." I stilled them, clasping them between my own.

"Hold me?"

I wrapped my arms around her protectively and sighed. "I love your scent."

"I'm not wearing any perfume."

I buried my nose in her neck and inhaled deeply. "You

mean this is just you? I wonder if you taste as good as you smell." I nibbled at her neck.

"What's the verdict?" she asked as her head lolled to the side, giving me even better access.

I pulled back and silently went to work on the scarf. After loosening the knot I untied it and gently slid the silk from around her neck. Then I dipped my head and kissed the hollow of her throat.

"Wesley?"

"Yes, love?"

"I just had the strangest thought." Katherine's eyes became slightly unfocused. "What if none of this, you, what if it's not real?"

"Close your eyes." I slipped the blouse off of her shoulders. The luxurious red silk fluttered to the floor and pooled at her feet. Then I gently guided her toward the bed. "You're tired, love. It's all real, you know it is, you—"

Katherine gasped, her eyes widening in surprised panic.

"What is it?"

She opened her mouth, but nothing came out. I reached for her waist and pulled her toward me. "Katherine? Katherine!"

Her knees folded beneath her, every muscle in her body became limp and she crumpled like a rag doll.

"Oh, Christ! Stay here with me baby." I lifted her up and placed her on top of the bed. "Focus on my voice, sweetheart."

She was unconscious. Her pulse was strong, her respirations slow and steady. I chastised myself for not asking more questions about my own presentation when I'd gone under. Was that what this was? Just as I reached for the radio to call for help Katherine bolted upright gasping for air, her eyes darting around the room, frantic and desperate.

I ran back to her side. Katherine wrapped her arms around

my neck and held on, melting into my arms.

"This is real. You're real. Tell me you're real."

"Of course I'm real."

She began to sob. It twisted my guts and wrenched my heart. I held on tight, holding her close, wishing that I could absorb her pain.

"It's all right," I assured her, running my hands over her body. "You're here. You're safe. It's all right."

"How long?" Her voice was hesitant, unsteady and laced with emotion.

"Just a few seconds, not even a minute. I didn't even have time to call for help." I leaned back so that I could see her face. "How long was it for you?" I asked her, using the pads of my thumbs to wipe away her tears.

"Longer. Much, much longer."

"Tell me."

She took a deep breath, then released it. I picked up the carafe of water by the bedside and poured her a glass. "Drink this. Take a moment to gather your thoughts. Do you remember?"

Katherine accepted the water and drank half of it down.

"Yes."

She was shivering now, her hands shaking.

"Let's get you under the covers."

I quickly stripped off my clothes, then slid into bed alongside of her, gathering her against me. "Let me warm you. Talk to me, love."

"I was in a hospital. You were my doctor. You kept telling me that I was in San Diego. That I was hospitalized after I tried to..."

"To what?"

"Kill myself. You were kind, but cold, aloof. You said I'd lost Damien in a plane crash, then our baby a month after. You kept telling me that I needed to talk, grieve, accept the loss, accept the fact that my husband and child were dead."

I swallowed as I watched Katherine place her hand protectively over her stomach.

"Only I knew my baby wasn't dead. I knew it was alive and growing inside of me."

"And that's when you came back?"

She shook her head. "It went on for months. In my room, I kept a calendar."

"Months?"

"We had sessions daily. They were almost always the same. I would beg you to let me go. You would lecture me about transference. You would tell me that I needed to accept the truth, that you weren't my lover, that there was no other life. Day after day we would go through the same thing. I knew in my heart it wasn't you, that it was really him, it."

"How did you end it?"

"You came to me, it came to me, in the middle of the night. The approach, it was different."

"Different how?"

"More like you. So much like you." Katherine was tracing invisible patterns across my chest. "And I so much wanted it to be you, to be over. I missed you and this time, under the cover of darkness, by the light of the moon coming in through the window, you confessed that you missed me, that you loved me, and you made me an offer, a very tempting offer."

My heart was pounding in anticipation.

"An offer to take away all the hurt, all the pain. It was getting harder and harder every day you said. Seeing me and not being able to touch me, hold me, kiss me."

I closed my eyes and held my breath.

"You said we could have a life together outside of the hospital. You told me about a beautiful house, right on the beach. You wanted to take me there, have children with me there, grow old with me there. It was everything I could imagine wanting."

"Only it wasn't real."

Katherine leaned up and searched out my eyes. "Only it wasn't real and for what was probably the thousandth time, I said so."

"What was different about that time?" I asked her, hoping to discover the key, some common denominator.

She shook her head. "I'm not sure."

The bedroom door splintered. "You bastard!"

The radio crackled. "We've got a breach."

"No shit." I jumped out of the bed, positioning myself between Katherine and Stanley. "Bathroom! Now! Lock it!"

Katherine scrambled out of bed and flew across the room.

"What the fuck is going on?"

"You get her to tell you all of her secrets, you get her to trust you, then you do this? I'm not going to let you hurt her!"

"Who?"

Stanley stepped back, turned his body sideways and threw a right hook in my direction. I bobbed underneath his arm getting in a punch to his unprotected midsection. Stanley doubled over and stumbled back a few steps, but he quickly recovered.

"Don't hurt him!" Jennifer cried out frantically from the door. "He's hallucinating. He doesn't know what he's doing!"

The next sound I heard was a round being fired, then another. Stanley stood stock still when the first dart hit. When the second one pierced the skin of his shoulder his eyes rolled up and he unceremoniously slid to the ground.

"What did you do?" shouted Jennifer.

"Tranquillizers," said Will. "He'll be out for a couple hours, give or take."

Jennifer knelt down alongside of him and lifted his head into her lap. "I guess we should find him someplace to sleep it off?"

"Well, he's not sleeping here! That's for damn sure." I walked toward the chaise to retrieve my robe. Before I could reach it, however, I found myself with an armful of towel-clad Katherine.

"Are you all right?"

"I'm fine, love."

Laura and Charles both ran into the room.

"What happened?"

"Stanley was hallucinating," explained Jennifer. "Abaddon got to him. He thought… I'm not sure what he thought."

"It's not about what he thought, it's about what he feared. His nightmare. I got the impression he thought he was protecting you," I said.

"Protecting Jennifer?" Will glanced down at the two of them.

Jennifer was running her fingers tenderly through Stanley's hair. "He's in love with me, Will. He just doesn't know it yet."

"Really? Stanley?"

Jennifer nodded. Then she looked at me as if noticing me for the first time. "Wes, you don't have any clothes on."

I quickly slipped the robe on. "Give us a few minutes to get dressed and I'll help you get Stanley tucked in bed."

"Charles and I can handle it," said Will, grabbing the throw from the chaise. He laid it on the floor and started to roll

Stanley onto it. "You two need to get some rest. Katherine looks tired."

"Abaddon took her. It was just for a minute, right before Stanley burst through the door," I said.

Will looked at Katherine. "Are you up to telling us what happened? The more we know, the more we can learn, the better prepared we'll be."

"Yes," said Katherine.

Will smiled. "Good. We'll get Stanley settled first," he said, then he reached down, grabbed the edge of the throw and dragged Stanley from the room.

Chapter Twenty-one

"Does anyone want some coffee?" Charles asked.

Both Will and I raised our hands.

"Laura, can you let Spike out? He's been stuck inside all night. It looks like the sun's coming up."

"Sure thing. Katherine's still sleeping?"

I nodded. "Yeah, much to my relief. Reliving everything she experienced again last night exhausted her."

Charles placed two steaming mugs of coffee on the table then sat down to study the detailed map that Will had drawn during the night delineating each and every potential exposure. "I had always thought that the security here was excellent. I didn't realize we were so vulnerable."

"Your goal is different now. Previously you were worried about theft. People who want to steal art don't want it damaged. They have to get inside, then get themselves and the merchandise out unscathed."

Will picked up one of the cups and took a sip.

"Are we really this vulnerable?" I asked.

"In a word, yes. I'm not sure we can protect you here. Not with the resources available. Not with what we're up against. The best we can do is to know when it's coming and try to stage a defense."

Charles pointed to a notation on the map. "What do you

mean by airspace?"

"Damien's a pilot. An air attack is a possibility. That's why I'm monitoring the air traffic." Will pointed to one of the many monitors set up in the kitchen.

"Good Lord," said Charles.

"Quite honestly? I'm convinced we need to move you. I've started making arrangements. We'll be leaving in a few hours."

"I'll go wake Katherine and take a quick shower," I said. Then I grabbed a second cup of coffee and headed upstairs.

"Hey, sleepyhead." I leaned down and kissed Katherine tenderly on the lips. "Time to wake up."

Her eyes fluttered open. "How's Stanley?"

"He's still out like a light. Let's shower up. Will says he's made arrangements to move us someplace safer. He wants us ready to leave in a few hours."

Katherine followed me toward the bathroom. I set both cups of coffee on the bathroom counter. "Brought you some coffee." I shed my robe, relieved myself, flushed the toilet, then moved to turn on the shower. Katherine was standing in the doorway, an amused smile on her face.

"What?"

"You're so open."

"Open?" I adjusted the temperature of the water and stepped inside the shower stall.

"Damien always shut the door." She followed me inside and slid the door closed. "I don't think I ever really saw him. I didn't even realize that until now. I didn't even realize how wrong that was."

"Switch," I said placing my hands on Katherine's shoulders and exchanging places with her so that she could get her hair wet. "It's not the fact that he never took a piss in front of you, love, that he shut the door. That's just a metaphor."

"Are you analyzing me?"

I reached past her for the shampoo and squeezed a dollop into the palm of my hand. "What? No! Certainly not." I replaced the bottle and began to lather up my hair. "Switch."

Katherine shifted to the back of the shower and continued to glare at me while I rinsed. "Well?"

"Well, what?"

"Don't keep me in suspense. What do you think?"

"Turn around." I picked up the shampoo, pouring out a generous amount and began working it into her long, golden tresses.

Katherine tilted her head back and sighed. "Are you trying to distract me with your magic fingers?"

"It's not about magic." One soapy hand slid under her arm and found her breast. "It's about intimacy."

She gasped.

I released her and moved her back into the water so that she could rinse her hair. Then I leaned back against the cold tile and watched as the lather coursed down her body, running over her neck, breasts, stomach and between her thighs.

"That's what was missing with you and Damien. It was missing in my relationship with Reese. Well, that and a lot of other things. In order to have that, you need more than love, you need trust."

"Do you trust me?"

"Yes. Do you trust me?"

"With my life."

"Let's get a move on and get dressed, love. They're waiting for us."

“Wes, have you seen Laura?” asked Charles. He looked frantic, downright panicked.

“No.” I’d just reached the bottom of the stairs. “Want me to check upstairs?”

“Yeah, she was going to let Spike out and then make more coffee. That was twenty minutes ago. She’s not in the kitchen and the dog’s not answering when I call him. The back door was left wide open.”

“I’ll check upstairs. Lock the bloody door, Charles.”

“We’ve got trouble, mates. It looks like something just breached the front gate. It’s heading toward the shed where the generator is.” Will tossed Charles a weapon. “Take this. I want you to cover me. The hedge along the front should shield you.”

“I’ve never fired something like this. What the hell is it?”

“That would be an MP5. And the safety is off. You don’t want to be waving it around.”

“Good God! I’ve never used an automatic weapon. A hunting rifle, yes, but never something like this.”

“Who is the better shot? You or Wes? I’m guessing you.”

“You’re right,” replied Charles. “And we don’t have time to argue.”

“These are wireless. They’ll allow us to hear one another.” Will handed Charles and I each a small device. I watched him insert his into his ear and did the same.

“I’ll look for Laura,” I said.

“No, you find her,” Charles insisted, his expression grave.

Will pulled his pistol out of the shoulder holster he was wearing and ran to the door. “We’re going to go out the living room window. It’s behind the hedge that runs along the side of the house. We’ll stay low and follow the hedge until we’re across from the shed. No talking. Move fast. Got it?”

“Yes. Yes, I’ve got it.” Charles followed him into the living room.

I ran immediately into the kitchen and secured the open door. Then I stood back, behind the shutters and examined the backyard. Nothing. Remembering Charles's original idea I ran up the stairs, taking them two at a time.

"It's the bloody dog," I heard Charles say.

I paused in the hallway just outside the upstairs bathroom. The door was closed. I knocked, then twisted the knob. The door was locked.

"Laura? You in there?"

The door opened a crack. "I just need to get dressed. I took a quick shower. Hope you don't mind."

I shook my head. "Not at all. I've got Laura. She's fine."

"It's wired," said Will.

"It's what?" asked Charles.

"Wired," said Will. "It looks like someone's strapped explosives to him. Cover me. We've got to get to the dog before it gets to the shed."

"Jesus!" I gasped. "Are you sure?"

"I'll make a run for the shed where the generator is stored," said Will.

"Let me get into position over by the wood pile first. From there I can get a better look at Spike and cover you," said Charles. "Ready?"

"On three," replied Will. "One. Two. Three. Go!"

I held my breath.

"I'm in position," said Charles.

"Wait." It was Will. "Are you seeing what I'm seeing? It looks like a decoy. That means—"

"Fuck," whispered Charles.

The bathroom door opened again and this time Laura

stepped out. “I hope you weren’t worried. I probably should have said—”

The rest of her sentence was cut off by the sound of an explosion. Then I heard Stanley yell from down the hall.

Katherine rushed into the hallway. “What the hell was that?”

“Don’t know.”

The door to the room where we’d put Stanley opened and he stumbled out. “Where are the others?”

I gestured to the room next to his. “Jennifer’s in there, Will and Charles—”

The remainder of my sentence was lost to him. As soon as he heard Jennifer’s name headed straight for her door. I pushed Katherine back inside the room and shoved Laura in after her. “Don’t come out until I tell you to. Lock the door.”

“But—”

“Don’t fight me on this. We don’t have time.”

“I love you,” said Katherine.

“I love you, too.”

“Something’s blocking the door. She isn’t answering. Help me!” Stanley called out. He was at Jennifer’s door, covered in scrapes and trying to push it open. He’d been in the room next to hers, the explosion must have woken him.

I ran down the hall

I braced my shoulder against it and the two of us pushed. We managed to get the door open about six inches. A bookcase had toppled over and was wedged between the door and the bed.

“Jennifer?” I shouted out. “Are you all right?”

I could see her upper body. She was on the floor, surrounded by debris. The outside wall had crashed in; brick, plaster and glass were scattered about.

"Christ!" gasped Stanley doubling his efforts to open the door. It moved another inch. "Jennifer!"

She lifted her head and coughed. "I'm all right! I'm all right! Hurry, go, before it's too late!"

Stanley and I looked at one another.

"Charles," I whispered.

"Will!"

We raced down the stairs and into the library. Stanley quickly unlocked one of the many cases that he'd brought and started to assemble a weapon.

I didn't wait for him to finish. I grabbed the only weapon other than my fists that I knew with confidence I could use, the set of Hibben throwing knives that my father had bought me for my thirteenth birthday. I ran back through the entry and down the hall, Stanley trailing not too far behind.

"Wes, wait!" he called out.

Only I didn't wait. I ran through the kitchen and out the back door. It was stupid, I know. But they were out there because of me. It was all happening because of me.

As I rounded the corner of the house I caught sight of Charles. He was lying on the ground, on his back, seizing. Will was by his side, shirtless. His leg was obviously broken. Bone was visibly sticking out through the torn fabric of his dark trousers. He was drenched in blood, some of it his own.

"Charles! Shit!"

"I'm sorry, Wesley," he choked out, blood bubbling out of his mouth. "I'm not going to make it."

"You're going to make it!" said Will.

I pulled my shirt off and placed it on top of Will's soaked one. Charles was bleeding out, fast. I took over applying pressure.

"There's nothing you can do for me. Go!"

"I'm not leaving you," I told him. Tears burned my eyes.

"They're vulnerable. Go."

I looked down at his now-saturated shirt, my hands covered in blood. "Stanley?" I called, for the first time realizing that he hadn't followed me out into the yard.

"Go," whispered Charles.

"I'll stay with him," offered Will. "You've got to protect the girls."

Of course I did.

Without another moment's hesitation I sprinted back toward the house, retracing my steps. I flew through the door. As soon as I crossed the threshold into the kitchen I heard their voices.

"Damien, you don't have to do this. Just let me go! You don't want to do this. You wanted children, Damien. Remember?"

"Surely you can see that this is for the best. I love you. Trust me, it's the only way."

I slammed my shoulder against the door that led from the kitchen to the hallway. It wouldn't budge. Something was blocking it.

"You don't love me. You're not even Damien, not anymore, you're something else. You've given up, given in!"

"You think I haven't tried not to?"

I heard it then, the unmistakable sound of flesh striking against flesh. "Try harder," said Katherine. "Why are you doing this?"

I kicked at the door. Once.

"Because you ruined my fun!"

Twice.

"Because you had the unmitigated gall to get in my way!"

Three times.

"Because you have to pay."

It was no use.

"There has to be a sacrifice. An eye for an eye, Katherine. You took him from me. Now I'm going to take something from you."

"No!" I shouted. I had no choice. I had to approach from the front of the house. I took off. My surroundings became a blur, the only thing that was important was that next step, and the one after that. Time stood still as the familiar landscape of my childhood sped by me.

The front door to the house was open. I could see them through the window as I ran toward it. Damien was dressed in black, his face, neck and hands painted in camouflage. He had Katherine pinned against the wall toward the top of the stairs.

"Get away from me!" Katherine screamed. She was trying to fend him off. As she reached back to hit him one final time, Damien stepped out of the way. The momentum of the abandoned punch sent her spiraling forward.

Katherine tumbled down the stairs, rolling, sliding. For a moment I lost sight of her. When I flew through the door she was on the floor, Damien standing over her. I came to a full stop just inside the entry.

"You can feel it, can't you? Death is close now, for both you and the little one. Is it like you thought it was going to be? It can be easier. Stop fighting the inevitable."

I took a deep breath, let it out, and adjusted my stance so that my weight rested on the ball of my back foot.

"This isn't over," spat Katherine.

I swung my knife hand back behind my head, judging the distance, knowing that the release would have to be flawlessly timed and balanced. There would be no second chance. There was only this. Now.

Damien laughed. "Look at you, you can hardly breathe. You've got nothing Katherine! It's over."

"You're wrong. She's got me!"

I swung my arm forward, my weight shifting to rest on my front foot. My focus narrowed until all I saw was the target. When the tip of the blade was exactly in line I let go, releasing the knife with practiced ease.

I'd expertly judged the distance. My selection of grip and stance combined with the force and control of the follow through had the knife spinning through the air, blade over hilt. The rotation and forward motion were perfectly timed.

At the sound of my voice, Damien turned and the tip of the knife embedded into the soft tissue of his neck, nicking his jugular. Clumsily, Damien grasped at the knife, pulling it out. Blood rushed out, suddenly it seemed everywhere.

I had to resist the urge to run to his aid, to help him. Was it even him? I didn't know. Damien took one unsteady step toward me, then his legs buckled beneath him. He stumbled, slipping in a pool of his own blood, tripping over Katherine's legs and then finally, finally falling unconscious onto the floor.

I ran to Katherine, gathering her up into my arms. "It's going to be okay, love."

"No, it's not." Her voice was barely a whisper. She was so pale, the pallor of her skin turning a dusky grey. She was having trouble breathing. One of her lungs had obviously collapsed. I spied Laura, on the ground at the top of the stairs.

"Laura! Help me!"

I watched in horror as Katherine closed her eyes.

"No! This is *not* happening!" I jumped to my feet and looked wildly about the room. "Get back here you bloody coward. You want someone? Take me! Take me!"

"Wesley." It was the barest of whispers. Katherine was tugging on the bottom of my trousers.

I dropped to the floor, lifting her head and cradling it in my lap. "Hold on, love. You hear that?" There were sirens in the distance. "That's help on the way. It's going to be all right." Tears clouded my vision as I brushed the hair from her ashen face. "Don't leave me. Please, Katherine. Don't leave me. You and the baby, you mean everything to me."

A sudden noise drew my attention. It was Jennifer helping Laura down the stairs. Laura was bleeding from a head wound and unsteady on her feet.

"It's too late," said Jennifer.

"It's not too late!"

She stopped, lowering Laura to the ground.

"It's over."

I followed her gaze. There was a rapidly growing stain of blood pooling around Katherine. She was hemorrhaging. "No. This can't be real. Please don't let this be real."

The sirens were closer now. Then there was the sound of doors slamming, voices shouting, and approaching footsteps.

"Wes, you've got to give them room to work. There's not much time," said Jennifer. She laid her hand on my shoulder and coaxed me back. "It's what needs to happen. Trust me."

And I did. I did trust her. I scooted back until I hit the wall. I felt a strange sense of detachment as I saw the paramedics rush in. Voices started to blend together. Suddenly I was aware that Spike had crawled, whimpering, into my lap, seeking comfort that for the moment I was too numb to provide.

"Collapsed lung. Get her some oxygen. We're going to have to insert a chest drain. We're losing her," I heard someone say.

"Blessed be the man that provideth for the sick and needy: the Lord shall deliver him in the time of trouble."

"What are you saying?" I asked Jennifer. "What am I supposed to do?"

She knelt down beside me and took my hand. "Pray."

"I'm not sure I can believe in God anymore," I admitted.

"That's okay," she said. "He believes in you."

"Katherine?"

Katherine's eyes fluttered open. "Wes?"

"Yes, love. I'm right here. How do you feel?"

"Tired," said Katherine. "And thirsty."

"Here you go." I reached for a cup of water, placed a straw in it and offered it to her. "You have some broken ribs. One punctured a lung. I was so afraid that I was going to lose both of you. You're going to be fine. It's over."

"The baby?"

I sat down on the edge of the bed, leaned down and touched my forehead to hers. "I'm so bloody sorry, love. We lost the baby."

Katherine started to cry. I wanted to cry too, to cry again. But I couldn't, I wouldn't. Not until I admitted my failure.

"I'm sorry, Katherine. So sorry that I couldn't, that I didn't... I should never have left you alone in that house."

"No. Don't do that. Don't blame yourself. This isn't your fault. Damien?"

"He's gone."

"Gone? Dead?"

I nodded.

"He hit Laura on the back of the head."

"And Stanley. They're both fine. Just mild concussions. Will had surgery yesterday. He had a fractured tibia. Jennifer took him home last night."

"What about Charles?"

Charles, the boy I'd grown up with, the brother I never had, the man I'd left to die alone, drowning in his own blood. The lump in my throat was impossible to swallow.

"Wes?"

I started to cry. I'd failed so miserably.

"Is Charles...dead?"

I nodded. "You wouldn't have made it either if the neighbors hadn't called 999 when they heard the explosion."

"I'm so sorry, Wes."

We held on to one another, providing comfort, taking solace, realizing it was the only thing we could do, the only thing left to do. Hours passed. Night came. Katherine and I both drifted in and out of sleep, murmuring words to one another in the darkness that were meant to chase away the pain. Only when the sun rose again, the pain was still there. I had a feeling it always would be, a persistent reminder.

Finally, after what seemed like an eternity, Katherine opened her eyes.

"Morning," I said, trying for a smile.

"Morning. Do you think they'll let me go home?"

Home. The place I'd most recently called home was burnt to the ground. The one I'd grown up in was now splattered with dust, debris, blood and haunting memories.

"I'm not sure I can go back to Atherton House just yet," I admitted. "It's a shambles and..."

"I was thinking of my home," she said.

My stomach lurched and my heart clenched.

"You want to go back to California?"

"Not alone. With you. I want us to go to California. There's a wedding being planned there, remember?"

"I remember," I said. "I'll go anywhere you want to go, love."

"Anywhere?"

I nodded. "Anywhere. Wherever you are? That's home."

Epilogue

Seven months later

Even before the taxi rounded the fountain at the end of the historic Laurel Street Bridge and pulled in front of the San Diego Museum of Art, I could see that the parking lot was surprisingly empty. "I thought more people would be here for opening night."

"This is our opening night. It opens to the public tomorrow."

"Sunday?" I quickly paid the driver, then stepped out of the car, offering Katherine my hand.

"Father's Day. Mom wanted you to be the first to see it. I have to tell you, she's never been so nervous about an exhibit before."

Katherine and I walked hand in hand up the stairs to the tall doors of the grand museum. As we approached the doors they opened, and a security guard greeted us. "Dr. and Mrs. Atherton, take your time."

I paused just inside the entryway in front of the sweeping staircase by the water fountain. The area was replete with orchids of every variety, reminding me immediately of my mother and the hours she would joyfully spend in the conservatory tending to them. I paused for a moment, suddenly awash in memories. Then I noticed Katherine waiting for me.

She was standing in the entry to the room on the left. The iridescent silver and gold threads of her simple gown enhanced her already glowing skin and honey blonde hair. She tilted her head in invitation toward the inside of the room and disappeared within.

I was powerless to do anything but follow her. I rounded the corner to find her standing in front of a large wall. It was covered in black shantung silk, like the walls in my parents' bedroom. On it hung a huge gilt frame. Painted within the frame, on a blood red background, was an excerpt from a journal Julia had found in my father's studio, something that he'd written during the last few days of his life:

"Since the moment I laid eyes on Margo she captivated me completely: the curve of her breast, the angle of her nose, the color of her eyes, the depth of her soul. I would have given her anything she wanted. I would have been her willing slave. I would have played the hero. She was everything to me, my inspiration, my reason, my life, my wife."

The words before me blurred. The flood of emotion was unexpected and slightly embarrassing. Although they'd been gone for some time, I still missed them, and their love, deeply. I stepped back and brushed the tears from my face.

"Are you all right?" Katherine reached for my hand.

"I don't know. It's so personal."

"It's beautiful. It's inspiring."

"Inspiring?"

"You don't have any idea? Do you?"

"What?"

Katherine walked around the corner and I followed, walking into the center of a large room. This one contained the red velvet chaise, encased under glass in the middle, with paintings of my mother lying upon it on the surrounding walls.

"Do you have any idea how many real love stories there are these days? Do you have any idea what little it all has come to mean for most people? How many people have just forgotten the point of it all?"

"Katherine, what my parents found in each other, it was rare."

"No. That's what you don't get." She walked over to a small table I hadn't noticed in the corner of the room. A table containing an ice bucket with a bottle of champagne. Katherine picked up the bottle and poured out two glasses.

"It wasn't that they found one another in the first place that's so special. It's that they continued to find things in one another. That's what people need to know is possible, be reminded of. That love can be lasting. That's what this exhibit celebrates."

I crouched down in front of the encased chaise, untied my bowtie and unbuttoned the top two buttons of my shirt. Then I read the plaque displayed inside the case, explaining the history of the piece.

"You're being uncharacteristically quiet. What do you think?"

Katherine handed me a glass of champagne.

I took a sip, then resisted the urge to spit it back into the glass.

"No good?"

"Have you tried it? It's bloody awful!" I walked over to the table and pulled the bottle out of the ice to examine it. "I hope they don't intend to serve this tomorrow."

The instant I recognized the label I froze. It was the same one that Charles had served to us the night of the Black and White Ball.

"I know it's a day early."

I spun around. "We're going to have a baby?"

Katherine nodded. "Happy Father's Day."

I took her glass of champagne from her, set it next to mine on the table, then said it again. "We're going to have a baby."

"I thought we covered that," she said, stepping back, a smile lighting up her face.

I walked toward her. "A baby. You're pregnant."

Katherine walked backward until the wall pressed up against her. "Are you okay?"

"Okay? Are you kidding? I'm probably the happiest man alive!" I laced my fingers through hers and lifted both hands above her head. "No, scratch that. Definitely the happiest man alive!" I crushed my mouth to hers, then began to inch up her gown.

"What are you doing?" Katherine panted.

I lavished kisses on her neck and throat as my hands caressed one thigh, fingering the top of her stocking.

"Groping you. Pay no attention." I started to nibble on her earlobe.

"Wes, stop, I think they have surveillance cameras in here."

"Oh, really?" I gave her ass a firm squeeze and at the same time nudged her legs even farther apart.

"Yes!" Katherine began to stiffen.

"I won't leave here without the tapes. Promise."

"You're impossible."

"Just think, if we ever get hard up for money we can get a web site, charge people to watch the videos, then act all surprised and indignant in front of the press."

"But, your mother, it feels like she's watching!"

That made me smile. "Are you kidding? My parents would so appreciate this."

She pushed me away. “We could get arrested!”

“Nah! They’ll just deport me.”

Katherine started laughing.

“How did I get to be so lucky?”

She sobered quickly. “Are you just trying to soften me up so you can have museum sex?”

“What? No! Of course not.”

Katherine raised an eyebrow.

“Am I that transparent?”

“Take me home?”

“I’ll take you home, Mrs. Atherton. I’ll take you any number of ways. Let’s get out of here.” I pulled out my mobile from my jacket pocket. “What’s the number for the taxi service?”

“I’ll ask one of the security guys to call for us.” Katherine kissed me on the cheek then used her thumb to wipe off the remnants of her lipstick.

As she turned to leave I reached for her hand and held her back.

“Thank you.”

“For what?”

I’d said it on impulse, not because of anything specific, but because my heart was close to bursting with gratitude. Suddenly I felt choked up, tongue-tied.

Katherine was looking expectantly at me.

I thought about all that she’d given me thus far, all that I had to look forward to. We all experience those turning points in life. That one seemingly mundane moment that we later look back on and with certainty realize has defined the rest.

“For taking the Tube,” I finally said, recognizing that from the moment I looked into her bright green eyes that day in the Tube, my life had been utterly transformed, irrevocably changed.

"You're thanking me for using public transportation?"

I nodded.

"You're a little weird sometimes, Dr. Atherton."

I wrapped my arm around her waist and pulled her close so that her body was flush with mine. "But you're in love with me anyways."

She nodded. "Yes. I am."

"Forever and always?"

"Till the end of the world."

About the Author

Samantha Sommersby lives in San Diego with her husband and teenaged son. She is the author of multiple novels and novellas including the critically acclaimed *Forbidden* series. In 2007 Samantha left what she used to call her "real life" day job as a psychotherapist to pursue writing full-time. She now happily spends her days immersed in the world of the *Forbidden*, a world where vampires, werewolves and demons are real, where magic is possible, and where love still conquers all.

To learn more about Samantha Sommersby, to follow her on Myspace, Facebook, Twitter, or Yahoo, or to sign up for her monthly newsletter, visit www.samanthasommersby.com. You may contact the author through her website or by sending an email to samantha@samanthasommersby.com.

The road to hell is paved with good intentions.
Or is that wicked seductions?

Devil Take Me

© 2008 Anna J. Evans

Annie Theophilus is used to life not going her way, but now the future is looking bright. She's engaged and finally getting her happily-ever-after—until she catches her fiancé cheating. The garage seems to be the safest place for a well-deserved crying jag. Instead, it proves to be a portal from hell, out of which a sexy denizen of the underworld has just emerged.

Namtar, one-time death-bringer to mortals, has come through an Earth portal for one thing—power. If he can convince a human to willingly sacrifice mortality for eternity in the Underworld, he will gain the power he needs to get the queen off her throne and secure a future for his people.

But Annie's seduction doesn't go as smoothly as planned. Somehow she steals a piece of his heart, and he finds himself struggling with a depth of feeling he's never known. Now, thanks to his own hesitation, they're on the run from a murderous ex-fiancé and a few enraged demons.

How can he ask her to give him her soul—when all he can offer her is pain?

Warning: This book contains sex in a garage, sex on the run, and shades of BDSM experimentation between willing partners as well as graphic depictions of an insane demon queen punishing her male and female lovers with stuff that put the ick in icky...I mean kinky.

In the beginning there is always darkness...

Divinity in Chains

© 2008 Danielle Devon

Aramon's blood runs hot for the ravishingly beautiful Eliyn, the mysterious young woman who seemed to appear like magic out of the woods, lost and alone. But as Garde Lumia of the kingdom of Kinra, he is bound by duty to his country and the divine family he has sworn to protect. Aramon must marry according to his high station, the laws of the kingdom have no care for the desires of his heart.

Eliyn lost the only family she has ever known to the barbaric Viscans, and is grateful to the royal family for taking in. She knows Aramon would willingly defy his king to bond with her if she would only say the word, but she is mindful of her low-born status. All she can ever have of him are nights of forbidden passion.

Then a dark ship appears on the horizon, a ship bearing Araqael, the Night Lord cast from the heavens by the goddess herself. The centerpiece of his plot for revenge is his intended bride—Eliyn. The world would be hers to command if only she would take her place at his side. She must choose between the demon who could offer her everything and the man who could offer her nothing but his heart.

But Divinity has other plans...

My Bookstore & More
www.mybookstoreandmore.com
Green for the planet.
Great for your wallet.

LaVergne, TN USA
15 March 2011
220133LV00003B/39/P

9 781605 047713